KIMBERLY DERTING is the author of the Body Finder series, which are as much coming-of-age romance as they are paranormal thrillers, as well as the dystopic-fantasy, *The Pledge*. She lives in the Pacific Northwest where the gloomy weather is ideal for writing anything dark and creepy. Her three beautiful (and often mouthy) children serve as an endless source of inspiration, and often find the things they say buried in the pages of their mother's books.

www.kimberlyderting.com

a&b

The
PLEDGE

KIMBERLY DERTING

First published in Great Britain in 2012 by
Allison & Busby Limited
13 Charlotte Mews
London W1T 4EJ
www.allisonandbusby.com

A CIP catalogue record for this book is available from
the British Library.

10 9 8 7 6 5 4 3 2 1

ISBN 978-0-7490-1185-7

Typeset in 10.5/16 pt Sabon by
Allison & Busby Ltd.

The paper used for this Allison & Busby publication
has been produced from trees that have been legally sourced
from well-managed and credibly certified forests.

Printed and bound by
CPI Group (UK) Ltd, Croydon, CR0 4YY

To Abby, Connor, and Amanda.
You know why.

PART I

PROLOGUE

142 YEARS AFTER THE REVOLUTION OF SOVEREIGNS

The air crackled like a gathering thunderstorm the moment the girl entered the chamber. She was just a child, but her presence changed everything.

With effort, the queen turned her head on her pillow as she watched the little girl pad into the chamber on slippered feet. The child kept her chin tucked tightly against her chest as her fingers clutched the sides of her nightgown, clenching and unclenching nervously.

Maybe the queen's guards weren't even aware of the charge in the air, but she was suddenly conscious of the blood coursing through her veins, the quickening of her pulse, and the sound of each breath that she took – no longer ragged and wheezing.

She turned her attention to the men who'd escorted the child. 'Leave us,' she declared in a voice that had once been filled with authority but now came out hoarse and papery.

They had no reason to question the command; certainly the girl would be safe with her own mother.

The child jumped at the sound of the door closing behind her, her eyes widening, but she still refused to meet her mother's stare.

'Princess Sabara,' the queen said softly, in her quietest voice, trying to gain the young girl's trust. In her daughter's six short years, the queen had spent little time with her, leaving her in the care of governesses, nurses, and tutors. 'Come closer, my darling.'

The girl's feet shuffled forward, but her eyes remained fastened on the floor – a trait reserved for the lower classes, her mother noted bitterly. Six was young, maybe too young, but she'd delayed for as long as she could. The queen was young too; her body should have had many good years remaining, but now she lay sick and dying, and she could no longer afford to wait. Besides, she'd been grooming the girl for this day.

When the girl reached her bedside, the queen held out her hand, tipping the child's small chin upward and forcing the young princess to meet her eyes. 'You're the eldest girl child born to me,' she explained – a story she'd told the child dozens of times already, reminding her of just how special she was. How important. 'But we've talked about this, haven't we? You're not afraid, are you?'

The little girl shook her head, her eyes brimming with tears as they darted nervously one way and then the other.

'I need you to be brave, Sabara. Can you be brave for me? Are you ready?'

And then the girl's shoulders stiffened as she steadied herself, finding her queen's eyes at last. 'Yes, Mamma, I'm ready.'

The queen smiled. The girl was ready; young but ready.

She will be a beauty in her time, the queen thought, studying the girl's smooth porcelain skin and her soft, shining eyes. *She will be strong and powerful and feared, a force to be reckoned with. Men will fall at her feet . . .*

. . . and she will crush them.

She will be a great queen.

She took a shaky breath. It was time.

She reached for the girl, clutching the child's tiny fingers in hers, the smile evaporating from her lips as she concentrated on the task at hand.

She ushered forth her soul, that part deep inside of her that made her who she was. Her Essence. She could feel it coiling tightly inside of her, still full of life in ways that her body no longer was.

'I need you to say the words, Sabara.' It was nearly a plea, and she hoped the girl didn't realize how badly she needed her, how desperate she was for this to work.

The little girl's gaze remained fastened to the queen, and her chin inched up a notch as she spoke the words they'd rehearsed. 'Take me, Mamma. Take me instead.'

The queen inhaled sharply, the muscles of her hand seizing around the girl's as she closed her eyes. It wasn't pain she felt. In fact, it was closer to pleasure as her Essence unfurled, misting and swirling like a dense fog as it spread through her, breaking free from its constraints at last.

She heard the child gasp, and then felt her struggle, trying to free her fingers from her mother's grip. But it didn't matter now; it was too late. She'd already said the words.

The overwhelming sense of ecstasy nearly shattered her, and then dulled, fading again as her Essence settled into a new space, curling into itself once more. Finding peace at long last.

She kept her eyes squeezed tight, not ready yet to open them, not ready to know whether the transfer had worked or not. And then she heard the faintest of sounds, a soft gurgling. Followed by nothing.

A deafening silence.

Slowly – so very slowly – she opened her eyes to see what it was . . .

. . . and found herself standing at the side of the bed, staring into the empty eyes of the dead queen. Eyes that had once belonged to her.

I

81 YEARS LATER

223 YEARS AFTER THE REVOLUTION OF SOVEREIGNS

I gritted my teeth as Mr Grayson's voice grew louder and louder, until there was no mistaking that he meant for the people in the congested street to hear him, despite the fact that he knew full well they couldn't understand a single word he spoke.

It was the same thing every day. I was forced to listen to his shameless bigotry simply because his shop stood across the crowded marketplace from my parents' restaurant. He didn't bother disguising his contempt for the refugees that flooded our city, bringing with them their 'poverty and disease'.

And he did it right in front of them, smiling falsely to their faces while they filed past his shop, displaying wares he hoped to sell them. Of course, they had no real way of knowing – other than his scornful tone – that the shopkeeper mocked and ridiculed them since he spoke in Parshon, and they were obviously *not* vendors. They were the impoverished, sharing the downcast gazes of the Serving class. Yet even as the merchant called them names they couldn't understand, they never glanced up. It wasn't permitted.

Only when he finally addressed them in the universal language of Englaise did their eyes lift to meet his. 'I have many fine fabrics,' he boasted in an effort to draw their attention, and hopefully their wallets. 'Silks and wools of the finest quality.' And beneath his breath, but still loud enough to be heard, 'And remnants and dirty scrap pieces as well.'

I glanced across the swell of tired faces crowding the market at this hour and saw Aron looking back at me. I narrowed my eyes to a glare, a wicked smile touching the corners of my lips. *Your father's an ass*, I mouthed.

Even though he couldn't hear what I said, he understood my meaning and grinned back at me, shocks of sand-colored hair standing up all over his head. *I know*, he mouthed back, a deep dimple digging its way through his left cheek. His warm golden eyes sparkled.

My mother poked her elbow into my ribs. 'I saw that, young lady. Watch your language.'

I sighed, turning away from Aron. 'Don't worry, I always watch my language.'

'You know what I mean. I don't want to hear that kind of talk from you, especially in front of your sister. You're better than that.'

I stalked inside, taking shelter from the glare of the morning sun. My little sister sat at one of the empty tables, her legs swinging back and forth as she bobbed her head and pretended to feed the threadbare doll perched on the table in front of her.

'First of all, she didn't hear it,' I protested. 'No one did. And, apparently, I'm not better than that.' I raised my eyebrows as my mom went back to wiping down the tables. 'Besides, he *is* an ass.'

'*Charlaina Hart!*' My mom's voice – and her words – shifted to the throaty mutterings of Parshon, just as they always did when she lost her patience with me. She reached out and snapped me on the leg with her towel. '*She's four; she's not hard of hearing!*' She threw a glance toward my sister, whose silver-blond hair gleamed in the sunlight pouring in through the windows.

My little sister never even looked up; she was accustomed to my mouth.

'*Maybe when Angelina's old enough for school, she'll learn better manners than you have.*'

I bristled against my mother's words. I hated when she said things like that; we both knew Angelina wouldn't be going to school. Unless she found her voice soon, she wouldn't be permitted to attend.

But instead of arguing, I shrugged stiffly. 'Like you said, she's only four,' I answered in Englaise.

'*Just get out of here before you're late. And don't forget: we need you to work after school, so don't go home.*' She said this as if it were unusual. I worked every day after school. '*Oh, and make sure Aron walks with you; there are a lot of new people in the city, and I'd feel better if the two of you stayed together.*'

I stuffed my schoolbooks into my worn satchel before dropping down in front of Angelina as she silently played with her dolly. I kissed her on her cheek, secretly slipping a piece of candy into her already sticky palm. 'Don't tell Mommy,' I whispered close to her ear, wisps of her hair tickling my nose, 'or I won't be able to sneak you any more. Okay?'

My sister nodded at me, her blue eyes clear and wide and trusting, but she didn't say anything. She never said anything.

My mother stopped me before I could go. '*Charlaina, you have your Passport, don't you?*' It was an unnecessary question, but one she asked daily, every time I left her sight.

I tugged at the leather strap around my neck, revealing the ID card tucked within my shirt. The plastic coating was as warm and familiar to me as my own skin.

Then I winked at Angelina, reminding her one last time that we had a secret to keep, before I hurried out the door and into the congested streets.

I raised my hand above my head, waving to Aron as I passed his father's shop, signaling that he should meet me in our usual spot: the plaza on the other side of the marketplace.

I pressed my way through the bodies, remembering a time – before the threat of a new revolution – when the streets were not so crowded, when the marketplace was simply a place for commerce, filled with the smells of smoked meats and leather and soaps and oils. Those smells were still here, but now they were mingled with the scent of unwashed bodies and desperation, as the market became a refuge for the country's unwanted, those poor souls of the Serving class who'd been forced from their homes when trade lines had been cut off by the rebel forces. When those they served could no longer afford to keep them.

They flocked to our city for the promise of food and water and medical care.

Yet we could scarcely house them.

The monotone voice coming from the loudspeakers above our heads was so familiar I might not have noticed it if the timing weren't so uncanny: 'ALL UNREGISTERED IMMIGRANTS MUST REPORT TO CAPITOL HALL.'

I clutched the strap of my bag and kept my head low as I pushed ahead.

When I finally emerged from the stream of bodies, I saw Aron already standing in front of the fountain in the plaza, waiting for me. For him it was always a race.

'Whatever,' I muttered, unable to keep the grin from my lips as I handed him my book bag. 'I refuse to say it.'

He took my heavy load without complaint, beaming back at me. 'Fine, Charlie, I'll say it: I win.' Then he reached into his own bag, which was slung across his shoulder. Behind us, the water from the fountain trickled musically. 'Here,' he said, handing me a fold of soft black fabric. 'I brought you something. It's silk.'

As my fingers closed around the smooth material, I gasped. It was like nothing I'd ever felt before. *Silk*, I repeated in my head. I knew the word but had never actually touched the fabric before. I squeezed it in my hand, rubbing it with my fingertips, admiring the way it was almost sheer and the way the sun reflected back from it. Then I turned to Aron, my voice barely a whisper. 'It's too much.' I tried to give it back to him.

He shoved my hand away, scoffing, 'Please. My dad was going to throw it in the scrap bin. You're small enough; you can use the pieces to make a new dress or something.'

I glanced down at my scuffed black boots and the dull gray cotton dress I wore, plain and loose-fitting like a sack. I tried to imagine what this fabric would feel like pressed against my skin: like water, I thought, cool and slippery.

When Brooklynn arrived, she dropped her bag at Aron's feet. As usual, she didn't say 'Good morning' or 'Would you please?' but Aron reached for her bag anyway.

Unlike his father, there wasn't an unkind bone in Aron's body. Or maybe 'stupid' was the word I sought to describe the elder Grayson. Or rude. Or lazy. It didn't matter; any of those unflattering traits that his father possessed had apparently bypassed his son.

'What? You didn't bring me anything?' She jutted her full lower lip in a pout, and her dark eyes flashed enviously as she eyed the silk in my hands.

'Sorry, Brook, my dad would notice if I snagged too much at once. Maybe next time.'

'Yeah, right, Midget. You say that now, but next time it'll be for Charlie too.'

I smiled at Brook's nickname for Aron. He was taller than Brooklynn now, taller than both of us, yet she still insisted on calling him Midget.

I slipped the delicate fabric into my bag with great care, wondering what, exactly, I would make from it, already anxious to put needle and thread to it.

Brook led the way as we moved around the perimeter of the plaza, where the crowds were already gathering. As always, we took the long way, avoiding the central square. I'd like to think that it was Brook's or even Aron's idea – or that either of them was as disturbed by the things that happened in the square as I was – but I doubted that was true. I knew it bothered me more.

From somewhere overhead, another message crackled: 'ALL SUSPICIOUS ACTIVITY MUST BE REPORTED TO YOUR NEAREST PATROL STATION.'

'Passports,' Aron announced solemnly as we approached a new checkpoint at the base of the giant archway that led to the city streets. He reached beneath his shirt, just as Brook and I did, pulling out our IDs.

There were more and more of the checkpoints lately, with new ones appearing overnight. This one was no different from most: four armed soldiers, two for each line – one for the men and one for the women and children. After the photo on each Passport was visually matched to the person wearing it, the identification card was scanned through a portable electronic device.

The checkpoints didn't matter, really; they weren't meant for us. We weren't the revolutionaries they sought to keep from moving freely about the city. To Brook and Aron and me, they were simply another security measure, one of the consequences of the war brewing within the borders of our own country.

And if you asked Brooklynn, the checkpoints were a bonus, new opportunities to practice her flirting techniques.

Brook and I stood in our line, remaining silent as we awaited our turn. While our Passports were being scanned into the system and we waited to be cleared, I stood back and watched as Brook batted her thick black lashes at the young soldier holding her card.

He glanced down at the scanner, and then back to her again, and the corner of his mouth rose subtly, almost unnoticeably. Brook stepped closer than she needed to when the light on the portable computer flashed green, clearing her.

'Thank you,' she purred as she held his gaze, her voice low and husky. She slipped the Passport down the front of her shirt, making sure he watched it fall.

The IDs weren't anything new to us. They'd been issued for as far back as anyone could remember. But it was only in the last few years that we'd been forced to start wearing them in order to be 'tracked', so that the queen and her officials knew where we were at all times. Just another reminder that the revolutionaries were tightening their stranglehold on the crown.

I'd once seen someone taken into custody at one of the checkpoints, a woman who had tried to slip through using another person's Passport. She'd passed the visual inspection, but when the card was scanned, the little light on the machine flashed red instead of green. The Passport had been reported stolen.

The queen had no tolerance for crime. Theft was

treated just as severely as treason or murder would be: All were punishable by death.

'Charlie!' Aron's voice dragged me out of my own thoughts. I hurried after them, not wanting to be late for school, as I tucked my Passport back inside the front of my dress and ran to catch up. As I reached them, a loud cheer went up behind us – coming from the crowded square we'd just left behind.

None of us flinched or even faltered in our steps. Not one of us so much as blinked to acknowledge that we'd even heard the sound, not when we were so near the guards at the checkpoint who were always watching.

I thought briefly of the woman I'd seen that day, the one with the stolen Passport, and I wondered what it had been like for her, standing on the gallows in the square surrounded by a crowd of onlookers. People who jeered at her for the crime she'd committed. I wondered if her family had come to watch, if they'd seen the trapdoor drop open beneath her feet. If they'd closed their eyes when the rope had snapped her neck, if they'd wept while her feet swayed lifelessly beneath her.

Then the voice from the loudspeaker reminded us: 'A DILIGENT CITIZEN IS A HAPPY CITIZEN.'

Inside, my heart ached.

'Did you hear that the villages along the southern borders are all under siege?' Brooklynn asked once we were past the soldiers at the checkpoint and on the less-crowded city streets, away from the marketplace.

I rolled my eyes at Aron. We already knew that towns along the border were under attack; they'd been under attack for months. Everyone knew. That was part of the reason our city was suddenly so overpopulated by refugees. Almost everyone had taken in stray family members and their servants.

As far as I knew, mine was one of the few families unaffected by the migration, but only because we didn't have any relatives in the outlying areas of the country.

'I wonder how long until the violence reaches the Capitol,' Brook continued dramatically.

'Queen Sabara will never let them reach us. She'll send her own army before they get too close,' I argued.

It was laughable calling our city 'the Capitol', since its concrete walls housed no one who held any real sway. The term implied authority and influence, when in reality we were simply the closest city to the palace. The queen was still the only person who held any true power.

But at least our city had a name.

Most of the cities of Ludania had long ago been stripped of that privilege, having been renamed simply by the quadrant of the country in which they were located and then ranked by size. 1West, 4South, 2East.

Children were often named in remembrance of the old cities. Once, it had been a form of rebellion to name a new baby Carlton or Lewis or Lincoln, a way of expressing dissatisfaction with the crown's decision to reclassify cities into statistics. But now it was merely tradition, and babies were named after cities from countries across the globe.

People often assumed that my real name was Charlotte, after a faraway, long-ago city. But my parents claimed that they refused to partake in anything that would be considered rebellious, even a long-accepted custom like naming.

They preferred *not* to draw attention.

Brooklynn, on the other hand, liked to brag about her name's roots. A great borough, in an even greater city that no longer existed.

She leaned in, her eyes feverishly bright. 'Well, *I* heard . . .' She let those three words hang in the air, assuring us that she had information we didn't. '. . . that the queen's army is gathering in the east. Rumor has it that Queen Elena plans to join forces with the rebels.'

'Who told you that? One of your soldiers?' I whispered, so close now that my forehead practically touched hers as I searched her eyes probingly. I didn't actually doubt her. Brook's intelligence was rarely wrong. 'How do you know they're telling you the truth?'

Brook grinned, a slow, shameless grin. 'Look at me, Charlie. Why would they lie to me?' And then she added, more seriously, 'They say the queen's getting tired. That she'll be too old to fight back much longer.'

'That's a bunch of crap, Brook. Old or not, Queen Sabara will never give up her country.' It was one thing to share real news from the front; it was another entirely to spread lies about our queen.

'What choice does she have?' Brook shrugged, continuing. 'There's no princess to take her place, and she certainly won't allow a male heir to inherit the throne. It hasn't been done in almost four hundred years; she's not about to let it happen now. She'll renounce the royal line before she allows the country to have a reigning king again.'

As we approached the Academy, I could feel my stomach tightening into angry knots. 'That's true, I suppose,' I said distractedly, no longer interested in a political debate. 'She probably won't allow herself to die until she finds a suitable female heir.'

I wished I could remain calm in the presence of the imposing school, impervious and unaffected. Above all, I desperately didn't want the Counsel kids to see my discomfort.

Everything about the upscale school, including the students' immaculately matched uniforms, screamed, *We're better than you*. Even the white marble steps that led to the grand entrance of the Academy were polished to a high shine, making them look as if they'd be treacherous to maneuver.

I hated myself for wishing I knew the sound my shoes would make walking up them.

I tried not to look in the direction of the Academy students who loitered near the top of those steps. For some reason these particular girls bothered me most of all; these two who watched us more closely than the others, who enjoyed taunting us when we walked by.

Today was no different. The skirts of their identical uniforms were creased, and their snowy white shirts were starched and pristine. These girls most definitely knew the feeling of silk.

I tried not to notice as one of the girls moved purposefully down the last steps, her eyes targeting us. She flipped her golden-blond hair over her shoulder; her cheeks were flushed and rosy; her eyes glittered with malice.

She stopped on the sidewalk in front of us, holding up her hand, signaling that we should stay where we were. '*Where are you three off to in such a hurry?*' she intentionally asked in Termani, aware that we weren't permitted to understand her.

Her words made the air vibrate around me, making it hard for me to breathe. I knew what I was supposed to do. Everyone knew. Beside me, Aron's gaze shot to his feet, and Brooklynn's did the same. A part of me wanted to ignore logic – to ignore the law – and my jaw clenched in response to her caustic words. But I knew that I wouldn't. It wasn't just my fate that I tempted if I broke the law – Brook and Aron might be held responsible as well.

I dropped my head and tried to ignore the prickling on my arms as I felt the girl's eyes drilling into me.

Her friend stood beside her now, the two of them forming a wall in front of us. '*I don't know why they even let vendors go to school at all, do you, Sydney?*'

And, again, the air shivered in hot waves.

'*Don't be ridiculous, Veronica, they have to go to school. How else are they going to learn to count our change when they work for us? I mean, just look at their hands. They're already working somewhere, and they probably have no idea how to count or read or even how to write.*'

I hated them both for thinking we were ignorant, and my teeth ached from biting back my retorts. But my cheeks burned as I stole a quick glance at Sydney's perfectly manicured hands. She was right about that part; my nails were short and my skin raw from washing dishes in my parents' restaurant. I wanted desperately to hide them behind my back, but I couldn't risk letting her know I'd understood her insults.

Keeping my gaze averted, I tried to sidestep her, but she matched my stride, moving with me and keeping herself in my path. Blood pulsed in my ears.

'*Don't go yet,*' she cooed. '*We're just starting to have*

fun. Aren't you having fun, Veronica?'

There was a wooden pause, and then her friend answered, her voice apathetic. '*Not really, Syd. I'm going back inside. They're not really worth it.*'

Sydney waited only a few seconds longer, still blocking our way, before she finally grew bored and left us standing there so she could follow her friend back up the polished marble steps. I didn't lift my head until I heard the doors of the Academy close behind them.

And then I exhaled loudly.

'Why do they do that?' Brook asked, once we were away from the gleaming school. Her cheeks were red, and her eyes glistened with unshed tears. She reached over, her fingers closing around my hand. 'What did we ever do to them?'

Aron seemed just as shaken. 'I wonder what it is that they're saying about us, when they do that.' His voice was ragged, and he shook his head wearily.

I just shrugged. It was all I could do. I could never tell them the truth of what Sydney and her friend had said.

We reached our school, which was far less grand and polished than the Academy. The building was old brick, not the eye-catching kind of brick found on historical buildings with charm, but rather the crumbling kind that looked like it might cave in on itself at any moment. We didn't have fancy uniforms or even a name, like the Academy; we were merely known as School 33.

But it was hard to complain. It was a school, and we were allowed to attend. And it was still open, despite the fighting going on within our country. These were all things to be grateful for. There were worse things in life than attending a Vendor's school.

Like attending no school at all.

The morning bell sounded, and everyone in the classroom stood, as did every other student at every other school throughout the country. In unison, we raised our right hands, our elbows bent, our fists raised skyward, and for the only time during school hours, we spoke in Englaise.

It was the Queen's Pledge:

My breath is my pledge to worship my queen above all others.
My breath is my pledge to obey the laws of my country.
My breath is my pledge to respect my superiors.
My breath is my pledge to contribute to the progress of my class.
My breath is my pledge to report all who would do harm to my queen and country.
As I breathe, I pledge.

I didn't often listen to the words of the Pledge. I just

spoke them, letting them fall negligently from my lips. After years of repetition, they'd become second nature, almost exactly like breathing.

But today, maybe for the first time ever, I heard them. I noted the words we emphasized: worship, obey, respect, contribute, report. I listed the order of importance in my head: queen, then country, then class. The Pledge was a command as much as it was a promise, yet another way that the queen demanded that we protect her and our way of life.

I looked at the kids around me, my classmates. I saw clothing in shades of grays, blues, browns, and blacks. Working-class colors. Practical colors. The fabrics and textures were sensible – cottons, wools, even canvas – durable and hard to soil. I didn't even have to look to know that every student in the classroom stood erect, chins high. That was something our parents and teachers instilled in us each and every day, to be proud of who we were.

I wondered why we had been born of the Vendor class. Why we were better than some, yet not as good as others. But I knew the answer: It had nothing to do with us. It was simple fate.

Had we been born to parents of the Serving class, we would not be attending classes today. And had our parents been Counsel folk, we would have climbed the gleaming steps to the Academy.

The instructor cleared his throat and I jumped, realizing that the Pledge was over, and that my fist – and mine alone – was still raised.

My face burned hot beneath the stares of the forty-five merchant-born children who shared this hour with me as I dropped my fist to my side, clenching it tightly as I took my seat. Beside me, I saw Brooklynn grinning.

I glared at her, but she knew it wasn't a real glare, and it only made her smile grow.

'You heard, didn't you?' Aron spoke in a low whisper when I joined him in the courtyard for the lunch hour. Other than during the Pledge, Parshon was the only language we were permitted to speak in *our* school.

Aron didn't need to elaborate. Of course I'd already heard the latest gossip. I dropped my voice too, as I scooted closer to him on the stone bench. *'Do you know if they got her whole family? Did they take her parents and her brothers and sisters?'*

Brook joined us then and immediately recognized the hushed tone and the way our eyes darted nervously, watching everyone and trusting no one. *'Cheyenne?'* she asked in a half whisper.

I reached into my book bag and handed Brook the lunch my mother had prepared for her, just as she had every day since Brook's own mother had died.

She sat down on the other side of Aron, our three heads ducking close.

Aron nodded, his eyes meeting first mine and then hers. '*I heard they came in during the night and took only her. She's being held at the palace for questioning, but it doesn't look good. Word is, there was real evidence this time.*'

We stopped speaking, sitting straighter as the young boy made his way across the grass, gathering garbage along the way. He didn't talk to anyone, just moved slowly, methodically, minding his step. As a member of the Serving class he had only one language, Englaise. So within the walls of our school – except during the Pledge – he wasn't permitted to speak. He simply stared downward as he gathered refuse.

He was scarcely older than Angelina – six, maybe seven – with unruly black hair and calluses on his dirty bare feet. With his head down, I couldn't see the color of his eyes.

He paused beside us, waiting to see if we had any trash he could collect. Instead, I reached into my own lunch and palmed a cookie my mother had baked. I held it out to him, making certain that no one else could see it in my hand. I raised my eyes, hoping he might lift his, but he never did.

When he was within reach, I slipped him the cookie, in the same way I would have given him garbage from my lunch. Anyone watching would've thought nothing of it.

The boy took the cookie, just as he did every day, and while I'd hoped to see eagerness or gratitude from him, I got neither. His expression remained blank, his eyes averted. He was careful . . . and smart. Smarter than me, it seemed.

As he padded away, I saw him slip the cookie into his pocket, and I smiled to myself.

Brooklynn's voice drew my attention. '*What kind of evidence did they find?*' she asked Aron, her voice tight. News of Cheyenne's imprisonment was making everyone edgy.

Unfortunately, however, Cheyenne wasn't alone. Whispers of disloyalty to the crown had begun to take root, starting like a virus and spreading like a plague. It infected and corrupted ordinary citizens, as rewards were being offered to those willing to report anyone they suspected of subversion. People turned against one another, seeking information against friends, neighbors, even family members, in order to gain favor with the queen. Trust had become a commodity that few could afford.

And *real* evidence – the kind that could be substantiated beyond petty gossip – was deadly.

'*They found maps in her possession. Maps belonging to the resistance.*'

Brook's lips tightened, and her head dropped. '*Damn.*'

But I wasn't convinced. '*How can they be certain they're rebel maps? Who told you this?*'

He looked up, and his sorrowful gold-flecked eyes stared back at me. '*Her brother told me. It was her father who turned her in.*'

I spent the rest of the day thinking about Cheyenne Goodwin.

What did it mean when father turned on daughter? When parent turned on child?

I wasn't worried for me, of course. My parents were as solid as they came, as trustworthy and loyal as any parents could be.

I knew because they'd been keeping my secret for my entire life.

But what of everyone else? What if the rebellion continued to gain momentum, if the queen continued to feel threatened?

How many more families would cannibalize their young?

THE QUEEN

Queen Sabara drew the wool throw over her lap and smoothed it with her crooked fingers. She was too old for the chill, her skin too thin now – nearly paperlike – and her lean flesh clung to her tired bones.

Two servant girls entered the room, crouching low and speaking quietly to each other so as not to startle her where she sat.

It was ridiculous, she thought. She was aged, not skittish.

One of them – the newer of the two – foolishly reached for the switch on the wall that would turn on the electric lights overhead. The other girl stopped her just in time, clamping her fingers around the girl's wrist before she could make that mistake. Clearly, she hadn't been there long enough to know that her queen detested the glare of an electric bulb, that she much preferred candlelight.

Sabara watched the pair cautiously – her eyes sharp as ever – as they added more wood to the hearth and stoked the flames. After a moment, she turned to gaze through the wall of windows overlooking the verdant lawns of her estate.

She had much to think about and her heart was heavy, bearing the burden of a country in turmoil . . . *her* country. She couldn't help wondering what would become of her throne if the rebel forces were not soon stopped. Already they were doing too much damage, and her body ached in sympathy from the injuries they'd done to her lands, and to her subjects.

She wondered how much more an old woman could bear.

But she once again reminded herself that she had no choice. If there had been another to take her place, she would gladly have stepped aside. The bitter truth was, there was no one.

This body had failed her, and she cursed it for providing her with just one heir, and a son at that. One lowly male child.

Then she silently cursed her only son, whose seed was more plentiful than her own, yet not one of them female.

Fools, all of them. Weak and lacking the skills required

to rule a country . . . unable to provide her with what she needed.

If only the whispers from the past could be proved true. If only she could find *the One*, a survivor to the old throne, the lost heir who could succeed her. But even if such a girl did exist, the queen would have to find her first. Before her enemies could get to her.

Until then, or until another suitable child was born, she must remain in power. She must stay alive.

She scrutinized the servants as they went about their work, never casting a single glance in their queen's direction. They understood their place in this world. When her chief adviser crashed through the doors, he barely drew their attention.

Sabara watched as he rushed forward and bowed low before her, waiting impatiently until she gave him permission to rise again.

She stared at the top of his head, drawing out the time longer than was necessary, knowing that it made him uncomfortable, knowing that age made his back ache.

Finally she cleared her throat. 'What is it, Baxter?' she intoned, giving him the signal to stand upright at last.

He cast a suspicious glance toward the servants in the room, and two pairs of eyes stared back at him. But the moment his words slipped into the cadence of the Royal language, both sets of eyes shot downward, anchoring to the floor beneath their feet.

'*General Arnoff has gathered his troops along the eastern border. If Queen Elena insists on siding with the rebels, then she'll have a fight on her hands. And blood on her conscience.*' He paused, just long enough to take a steadying breath, before continuing. '*But I fear we have a bigger problem.*'

Anger simmered below the queen's cool exterior. She shouldn't be dealing with such matters. She shouldn't be listening to war reports, or deciding which troops to sacrifice next, or wondering how long until the rebel factions would have her palace under siege. These should be the problems of a new ruler, not a decrepit old woman.

She watched the girl servant – the new one – and she willed the girl to raise her eyes, daring her to break not only etiquette, but law, by casting her gaze upward in the presence of a language above her own.

The girl had been in the queen's service for only a couple of weeks, but that was long enough to be noticed, and long enough to understand that her queen was not a forgiving one. She knew better than to look up at this moment, and she kept her eyes focused on her feet.

'*Well, what is it? Say what you've come to say,*' Sabara insisted, knowing he wouldn't have disturbed her if he didn't have news. Her eyes remained trained on the girl.

'*Your Majesty,*' Baxter groveled, bobbing his head respectfully. He was unaware that he did not have his queen's full attention. '*The rebellion grows stronger. We believe their numbers have doubled, possibly tripled. Last night they took out the train tracks between 3South and 5North. It was the last remaining trade line between the north and south, which means that even more villagers will be moving into the cities seeking food and supplies. It'll take weeks to—'*

Before Baxter could finish his sentence, Sabara was on her feet atop the dais, staring down at him. *'These rebels are simple outcasts! Peasants! Are you telling me that an army of soldiers is incapable of shutting them down?'*

And it was at that moment that the servant girl made her fatal error. Her head moved, only millimeters. The shift was barely perceptible, but her eyes . . .

. . . her eyes glanced upward in the presence of the queen's words. Words she was unable to comprehend, and forbidden to acknowledge.

And the queen had been watching her.

Sabara's lips tightened into a hard line, her breath becoming erratic. She quivered with excitement that she could barely contain. She'd been waiting for it.

Baxter must have realized something was happening, for he remained where he was, frozen in time as he watched his queen lift her hand slowly, regally, into the air, signaling for the guards who stood beside the door.

The girl appeared too stunned to do anything but

stare, like an animal caught in the sights of a hunter. Sabara had her cornered.

She thought about dealing with the girl herself, and her fingertips tingled in anticipation as her hand began to curl into its telltale fist. Were she a younger woman – stronger – it would have been effortless, a simple clenching of her fingers. The girl would be dead in seconds.

But as it was, she knew she couldn't afford the energy it would cost her, so instead she uncurled her hand and made a quick, flicking gesture toward the condemned serving girl instead. 'Send her to the gallows,' she commanded, switching to Englaise so that everyone in the room could understand. Her shoulders were stiff, her head high.

The guards strode toward the girl, who didn't bother to fight them, or even to beg for mercy. She understood her breach. She knew the penalty.

The queen watched as the men escorted the girl from the room. It was the most alive she'd felt in ages.

She'd just discovered a new sport.

II

I bent to retrieve the fork, which made a tinny racket as it clattered onto the floor, and smiled sheepishly at the man sitting alone at the table. 'I'll be right back with a clean one,' I said, plucking it up for him.

His answering grin reached all the way to his eyes, which was surprising. Sincerity was a rarity when dealing with someone of the Counsel class.

I was glad, I supposed. At least I wouldn't have to lick his fork, I thought, smirking at Brooklynn as I passed her on my way to the serving station.

Brook carried a basket filled with freshly baked bread out of the kitchen. 'Did you see the guys at table six?' She winked at me. 'Hopefully I'll make some decent money tonight.'

Brooklynn told everyone that the reason she worked for my parents at our restaurant, rather than at her father's butcher shop, was for the tips, but I knew better. Since her mother's death, she'd used every excuse she could to stay away from her home – and from the family business – whenever possible. Working for the extra money was just a convenient way to avoid painful memories and a father who no longer acknowledged her existence.

Whatever her reasons, I liked having her around.

I glanced over my shoulder to the three men crowded into the corner booth. Two of them – looking far too large for the table they sat at – watched Brooklynn with hungry eyes. It was the way most men looked at her.

I raised my eyebrows. 'I don't think getting tips from them is going to be a problem for you, Brook.'

She frowned back at me. 'Except I can't seem to get the cutest one to notice me.' I saw who she meant. The third man, younger than the others and only somewhat smaller, appeared to be bored by his companions, and by his surroundings in general. Brook didn't like to be ignored, but she also didn't give up easily. Her eyes sparkled mischievously. 'I guess I'll have to turn up the charm.'

I shook my head, grabbing a new fork for the man at my own table. I had no doubt that Brooklynn's pockets would be full by the end of her shift.

When I returned with the utensil, I felt my heart beating a little faster, and my cheeks flushing hotly.

The Counsel man wasn't dining alone after all, and in my absence, his family had joined him.

I immediately recognized the girl sitting with him – his daughter, I assumed. A girl I passed nearly every morning at the Academy. The one girl who took perverse pleasure in mocking me and my friends as we walked by: Sydney. And here she was, still in her uniform, reminding me that hers was a life of privilege, and not about rushing to her parents' restaurant after school so she could work the rest of the evening.

Suddenly I wished that I had spit on *all* the forks. I had an overwhelming urge to turn around and excuse myself from work for the night, to tell my father that I was ill so I could go home.

Instead I forced my best false smile – one that most certainly did *not* reach my eyes – and concentrated on not tripping over my own two feet as I walked the rest of the way to their table.

I replaced the fork and glanced around at the perfect Counsel family before me: the mother, looking poised and professional; the doting father; and the overindulged daughter. I tried not to pause for too long on any one of them. I wouldn't give Sydney the satisfaction of knowing that I'd recognized her, even though I was certain she recognized me. 'Can I bring you anything to drink?' I asked, relieved that the quiver I felt didn't make it to my voice. It was a good sign.

I didn't want to be nervous. Just the opposite, in fact. I'd passed those arrogant Counsel kids – *her* among them – every day for the past twelve years, and I was tired of pretending that I couldn't hear the contempt in their voices. Or the words behind it.

Sydney didn't bother answering me directly, which made my skin itch all the way down to my bones, in places I would never be able to scratch.

She looked to her mother, dressed in an impeccable white suit – a color rarely found among the Vendor class. It was too impractical, it stained too easily. She was a doctor probably, or an attorney, or possibly even a politician. And the moment Sydney opened her mouth to relay her words through her mother, the world around me vibrated, a familiar warning that I should no longer be capable of understanding them. '*Tell her I'll just have the water.*' I could feel Sydney's glare fall upon me. '*Wait! First ask if they serve clean water.*' The smooth dialect of her foreign tongue slithered from her mouth and felt greasy to my ears.

I forced my eyes downward while they spoke among themselves.

'Thank you,' the woman answered, her voice absent of the oily feel as she slipped back into Englaise for my benefit. 'We'll just have some water.'

When I heard the universal language once more, I tipped my head back up. 'I'll give you a few minutes to look at the menu,' I answered as blandly as I could, trying to mimic the mother's diplomatic tone. *Politician, for sure,* I thought. 'I'll be back with your drinks.'

I hid for as long as I could behind the wall of the serving station, slowly pouring water into three glasses. As much as I wanted to do unsavory things to their drinks, I knew my father's heart would stop beating in his chest if he caught me, and I didn't want to be responsible for widowing my mother or leaving my little sister fatherless. I considered it a sign of monumental willpower that I was able to resist, and I was more than a little proud of myself.

I took several breaths as I looked around the restaurant. I thought about asking Brooklynn if she'd be willing to trade tables with me, just this once, but I knew that would be considered offensive – an insult to the Counsel family at my table. And Brook was happy with her table – men she could flirt with and flatter, trying to pad her tips. Besides, she hated the Counsel kids almost as much as I did.

She would hate them more if she could hear what I heard.

When I realized I had no other option, I gathered the glasses and went back into the crowded dining room.

'Have you decided what you'd like yet?' I asked in smooth Englaise.

Again, Sydney didn't bother disguising her toxic tone, and I felt my resolve slipping. *'I'd like to eat somewhere else. I don't know why we can't eat somewhere less . . .'* She looked up at me before I had the chance to drop my gaze, and our eyes locked momentarily. *'Shabby.'*

My cheeks burned, and I tried to tell myself to look away from her, but I couldn't. It was the right thing to do. It was respectful. And it was the law. She wasn't speaking to me; I wasn't even supposed to understand what she was saying.

But I did.

My hands were shaking as I set the glasses on the table. Water sloshed over the sides, splashing the candle's flame and making it sizzle and then sputter out.

Sydney squealed theatrically and jumped up from her chair as if I'd just thrown the entire glass of water in her face. She glared at me, her mouth gaping in disbelief, and when I glanced down, I could see tiny water droplets on her snowy white blouse.

'Idiot!' she shrieked, and this time I understood perfectly. Everyone did. 'She looked at me,' she accused, making her statement not *to* me but *about* me in a voice so loud that the entire restaurant could hear her now. 'Did you see that? She was looking right at me when I was speaking Termani!'

Her father – the man with the smiling eyes – tried to

calm her, slipping into the Counsel tongue of Termani to soothe his daughter. '*Sydney, calm down*—'

'*Don't tell me to calm down, that moron practically assaulted me! Something needs to be done. She broke the law. I can't believe you're not outraged. I can't believe you're not already calling for a hanging.*' She dabbed frantically at the nearly invisible splash marks with her napkin. '*Mother, do something! Tell them that this – this imbecile should be turned in!*'

This time I *did* gaze downward while I pretended not to listen to things she was saying about me, most of which should never have been spoken aloud in any language.

Panic paralyzed me, and my throat squeezed shut. I dared a quick look around me, with only my eyes. Brooklynn stood frozen, staring back at me, and behind her, all three of the men sitting at her table were watching me. For a moment, my gaze locked with that of the third man – the one Brooklynn had been intent on making notice her. His eyes were dark and intense, focused solely on me as he leaned forward now, no longer disinterested.

I grimaced as I heard my father rushing out through the kitchen doors to see what all the commotion was about. I turned my eyes his way, and recoiled as I met his stare, knowing that I'd made a mistake.

A deadly one.

'I'm sorry,' I said aloud, to no one in particular.

* * *

'What happened out there?' Brook asked, rushing to my side and squeezing my hand so tightly that the blood was cut off from my fingers. 'What was she talking about? You didn't look, did you?'

I stared at her, unable to speak, or even to breathe. Still.

Out in the restaurant, I could hear the girl's mother, her voice calm and even – very diplomatic. My father had fallen silent, and all other sound in the restaurant had ceased. I wanted to hear what she was saying, but the closed doors – and the blood rushing past my ears – made it impossible.

Brook clutched my hand even tighter as she looked at me, her eyes widening, searching my face for answers.

Suddenly the woman stopped speaking, and we both turned toward the doors to wait.

There was a long pause, and I thought my heart might explode. Each beat was painful as I told myself that this wasn't happening, that I hadn't just made such a grievous misstep. Surely I couldn't have forgotten. My parents had worked so hard to teach me, to instill the importance of never, *ever* mistaking one language for another. And to never, *ever* break the rules.

And yet, here I was. Waiting to see if I would die.

Brook's fingers laced through mine as the door swished open, and my father's solemn face regarded us as we stood there, his eyes falling to our intertwined hands.

My mother had taken Angelina outside until a resolution could be reached, one way or the other. She didn't want my sister to hear what was being discussed.

'Well.' Brook exhaled, her voice pinched. 'What did she say? What did they decide to do?' Her nails cut into my palm.

My father stared at me, and I could practically hear his disapproving thoughts and sense his disappointment. But it definitely wasn't a look you gave someone on her way to the gallows, and I felt my breath loosening from the knot in my chest.

'They're not turning you in,' he stated flatly, and I wondered if he even realized he was still speaking in Englaise. 'They think the girl might have been mistaken, that she was upset because you spilled water—'

'But I didn't—'

His hard glare stopped me from trying to defend myself. *Don't you dare lie to me*, he told me with that look. And he was right. I fell silent, waiting once more.

'You were lucky, Charlaina. This time no one realized—' Now it was his turn to stop short as he glanced at Brooklynn. Brooklynn, who knew nothing of what I could do. At last he sighed, and when he spoke again, this time in Parshon, his voice was softer. '*You need to be careful, girls.*' And even though he addressed both of us, I knew his words were directed solely at me. '*Always be careful.*'

* * *

50

'Come on, it's the first club we've heard about in weeks. I don't think we should miss our chance to go.'

I'd just finished clearing the last of the tables and I was exhausted, but I knew better than to complain. I worked hard, but my parents worked harder – from sunup to sundown – never giving voice to their weariness, even though I could see it etched in the new lines on my mother's face and in the worried expression my father wore each and every day.

'I don't know, Brook, a club is the last place I feel like going tonight. Besides, where'd you even hear about this place?'

'Those guys. The ones from table six. They gave me the address and said I should bring you with me.' She wiggled her eyebrows. 'They were asking about you, or at least one of them was. I think he kind of likes you.'

'Or maybe he just felt sorry for me after I nearly got myself hanged.' When Brook stiffened, I realized it might be too soon to be glib about the incident. Clearly, she wasn't amused.

'I think it's better if I just go home,' I said, trying to change the subject. 'My dad's really mad at me.'

But Brooklynn was determined. 'It's early, and you can stay at my house tonight. That way he doesn't have to know you're going out. Besides, it'll give him a chance to cool off.' She turned her wide eyes on me, the way I'd seen her do to hundreds of different men. 'Just go for a while, and if you don't want to stay, then we'll both leave.'

I stopped what I was doing and put my hands on my hips, practically daring her to look me in the eyes and lie like that. 'No, we won't.'

'We will. I swear it.'

I pursed my lips, but felt myself relenting even as I asked, 'What about Aron? Is he going?' I already knew the answer, of course. Brooklynn never asked Aron to come with us.

Brook rolled her eyes as if my question was unreasonable. 'You know they're not exactly looking for more boys at the clubs, Charlie. Besides, Midget gets all twitchy and overprotective.'

The door between the kitchen and the dining room had been propped open while we cleaned up for the night. My father passed the doorway, and I caught a glimpse of his hard stare. I felt him pinning me to the ground, reminding me with that single glance that I'd messed up.

When he was gone again, disappeared into the depths of the kitchen, I looked back at Brooklynn. 'All right,' I muttered, deciding that maybe Brooklynn was right, maybe my father did need some time to cool down. 'I'll go.'

III

Brooklynn must have known that I was having second – and even third – thoughts.

I glanced around. Something didn't seem right. Most of the clubs were downtown, tucked away in the industrial districts, but somehow this was darker – and dirtier – than any of the places we'd ever been before.

From the streets behind us, I heard the faint crackle of the loudspeaker. The message was so muffled and tinny that if I hadn't already memorized the words, I wouldn't have been able to make them out: 'PASSPORTS MUST BE CARRIED AT ALL TIMES.'

It felt as if even the queen had abandoned this part of town.

'Seriously, stop worrying, Charlie. We're in the right place.'

The brick buildings were defaced with layers of fading graffiti. The windows that weren't broken or boarded over were coated with grime. Cigarette butts littered the ground amid the rotting garbage. The stench of decomposing food was bad enough, but the mingling odor of human waste made it hard not to gag.

And yet conspicuously absent were the new homeless of the Serving class who had infiltrated the city, sleeping on the streets and sidewalks, seeking refuge in doorways and alleys, scavenging for food scraps and spare change.

But as we walked, I heard – and felt – the distant stirrings of music trying to break free from one of the warehouses ahead of us.

Brooklynn stopped, pointing at a flash of red paint near the end of the alleyway. 'I told you! That's it.'

I knew she was right, because it was the only door that was freshly painted. Probably in years. Possibly decades.

Brooklynn hurried down the alleyway and bounced up the two steps in heels that seemed recklessly high, heels that had once belonged to her mother. I glanced down at my plain sandals, the brown leather straps laced around my bare ankles.

She reached out to knock on the solid door, rapping her knuckles against the red steel. The sound was swallowed by the bass resonating from within.

She tried again, pounding with the side of her curled hand, striking the door as hard as she could.

Still, nothing.

I pushed her aside. 'I think we just go in.' I gripped the iron handle and pulled as hard as I could. When the door opened, the noise beyond reached inside me, rattling my bones. It beckoned me.

Brooklynn hopped up and down, clapping her hands before rushing past me in a blur.

I hurried after her, not wanting to be left outside alone.

The large man inside the door stopped us, holding up an arm that was the girth of my entire body as he reached for Brook's Passport. I was certain his silence was meant to be intimidating, and he wasn't half-bad – with all of his brawn and his menacing scowl – but he was just like any other bouncer at every other club we'd been to.

It wasn't until his gaze fell on Brook – not her Passport – that my throat tightened. I hated this part.

He knew we were underage, and we knew that he knew it, so he would be doing us a favor by letting us in. He would admit us, of course, but not before getting something out of it in return.

He inspected *her*, his eyes devouring her, appraising her from head to toe.

Brooklynn didn't mind. She grinned, trying her best to look alluring, and I had to admit, she was convincing.

Better than convincing. It was no wonder she'd attracted the attention of so many military men throughout the city.

My stomach turned as he dissected her through half-lidded eyes. His gaze paused over the bare spots of her skin: her neck, her shoulders, her arms.

When he was finished, the burly man gave a quick nod of his head to the almost undetectable girl who stood beside him, lost in the shadows of his bulk. Her inky-black hair was swept up into a cascading ponytail, with tiny black wisps skimming her pale face, making her look young. Too young to be in a club.

Just like Brook and me.

The girl skipped forward, reaching for Brook's hand and marking it with a stamp, the ink indiscernible in this light.

And then it was my turn.

I pressed my Passport into his enormous hand, hoping to avoid his scrutiny, but he stared anyway.

It was impossible not to feel violated. I did my best to block out his gaze from my mind, but goose bumps broke out over my skin wherever his eyes roamed.

When I felt him studying my face, I looked up again, locking eyes with his. My shoulders stiffened, and I refused to look away.

He grinned at my show of defiance, pleased, his teeth flashing scarlet beneath the glow of the red lights overhead, his lips thinning around them. This was a man who didn't belong to any class in particular – at least not any longer. Of that I was certain. Everything about him spoke of something else entirely. I wondered which class it was that had cast him aside, or whether he'd simply been born to Outcast parents, condemned through no fault of his own to a life in which he was never permitted to speak in public . . . not even in Englaise.

I tried not to be the first to blink, but he was better at this game than I was, and too soon I turned my head away, training my eyes toward the floor.

His laughter boomed above the music, and from the corner of my eye I saw him nod again. The slight girl with the ponytail hopped forward, grabbing my hand in hers and marking it before she disappeared behind the bouncer once more. As always, the skin beneath the hand stamp tingled, a little something they added to the ink to loosen up the patrons. Particularly the female patrons. Especially the underage ones.

We considered it the price of admission.

He ignored the fact that neither of us was legal as he scanned both of our Passports before handing them back to us. I had no idea where the scanned information went, but I knew that it wasn't the military tracking us here, since the clubs weren't exactly legitimate.

They weren't necessarily illegal, either, but only

because no club ever stayed open for more than a few days. A week at most.

Brooklynn took my arm and dragged me away from the entrance, pulling me toward the hypnotic music coming from within.

I could feel the steady rhythm of the bass thrumming through my veins, and my heart beat in time with the flashing lights that were mounted in the rafters overhead. And, for the moment at least, I forgot to be irritated by the flesh examination I'd just been subjected to.

It had been far too long since I'd been out, too long since I'd listened to real music, the kind that came from an electric sound system. It slithered beneath my skin, finding a warm, safe place there.

'This place is amazing, isn't it? Are you out of your mind? Do you love it here?' Brooklynn's manic speech patterns would have been impossible for anyone else to keep up with, but I'd known Brook since we were children. I could eat her rapid-fire sentences for breakfast.

I followed her eyes around the club. She was right. It *was* amazing.

It had all the right things. The mood was dark and sensual, amplified by throbbing red, blue, and purple lights that pulsed to the music. A glass-and-steel bar had been built into an entire wall of the massive interior.

Impressive, considering it probably hadn't existed yesterday and could be gone as early as tomorrow.

The large dance floor was crowded as bodies rubbed together, sliding, grinding, and swaying to the seductive beat. Just watching made me want to join them, as they moved in and around one another.

The beat continued to thread its fingers around me.

'What did you say they were calling this club?'

'Prey,' Brook answered, and I grinned.

Of course it was Prey. It was always something dark and dangerous. Something carnal.

Brooklynn dragged me toward the bar, reaching into her purse to pull out some loose bills. 'Can we get two Valkas?' The tremor in her voice was barely noticeable.

The bartender was a sinewy woman with lean, bare arms. She was strong and looked like she could be a bouncer in her own right. Her short, spiky hair was a deep shade of blue, and her tongue shot out to touch the piercing in her lower lip. She was beautiful in a strangely androgynous way, and her comfort in her own skin was evident in the way she moved as she reached for a bottle. She narrowed her black eyes at the jumpy girl in front of her bar.

Brooklynn squared her shoulders and met the direct gaze as unwaveringly as she could.

Finally the bartender set two glasses on the countertop and filled them with a shimmering blue liquid. 'Twelve,' she stated in a raspy voice that was both hard and sensual at the same time. As she slid the drinks toward us, I was instantly very aware of just how underage we really were.

Brooklynn dropped a single bill on the bar, and the woman pocketed it. There was no discussion of change or tips.

I picked up one of the drinks and took a sip. The sweet taste barely masked the caustic burn of the liquor, which sizzled all the way from my throat down to my stomach. Brooklynn was in more of a hurry and guzzled hers, downing half her glass in three long swallows.

I rolled the chilled glass over the sting on the back of my hand, where the girl at the door had stamped it. I glanced down and could see the angry red outline of welted skin in the shape of a crescent moon.

I didn't need a black light to see it now. No one would.

I felt off, out of sorts. I knew that whatever was bothering me was probably just the drug from the hand stamp finding its way into my system. Paranoia was always a potential side effect.

Brooklynn pointed across the room. 'Look, they've got the good stuff here,' she said in a voice that was thick like honey.

Above the dance floor, on the opposite side from us, a man with a daring grin stood at the railing overlooking the tangle of bodies below.

He had captured Brook's interest.

It was nothing new. Men of all types enthralled

Brooklynn. She'd been boy crazy since we were little girls; she'd only had to wait for her body to catch up. And now that it had, there was nothing to stop her.

'Here,' she said, draining the rest of her drink. 'Hold this, I'll be right back.' And over her shoulder she added, 'We need an appetizer.'

Typical Brooklynn, I thought as I searched for a place to set her empty glass. I tried not to look too abandoned as I eased myself toward the railing to watch the dancers while I prepared to wait, getting comfortable.

I rested my elbow against the steel balustrade and again tried to figure out what was wrong with me. I should be having fun; we'd made it past the bouncer at the door. And, more importantly, the bartender.

I was sure it had more to do with what had happened earlier at the restaurant than the drug-laced stamp on my hand.

Around me, I listened to conversations spoken in every tongue, and was never forced to look away, or even to pretend I couldn't understand what was being said. None of these people would ever realize I actually knew what they were saying.

Because here there were no rules.

I was born into the Vendor class, to a family of merchants. Other than Englaise, the universal language of all people, Parshon was the only language I was permitted to know. It was the only other language I should have been capable of comprehending.

But I wasn't like the others.

I was like no one.

For me, that was part of the appeal of these underground clubs, places where class didn't matter, where the social boundaries were blurred. In places like these, the military sat beside the wanted, the degenerate, and the cast-aside, and they all pretended, at least for a short while, to be friends. To be equals. And a vendor's daughter could forget her lot in life.

It was everything I'd ever dreamed of.

But I was pragmatic. I didn't spend my days dreaming of a different life, of ways to escape the limitations of my class, mostly because there were none. I was what I was, and nothing could change that. A place like Prey was only make-believe; the reprieve was only for the night.

I moved away from the railing and drifted into the sea of bodies, noticing the colors. I always noticed the colors. Here, clothing didn't have to be utilitarian – dull shades of browns, blacks, grays. In a place where class division didn't exist, colors materialized. Brilliant hues of emerald and scarlet and plum blazed in the form of clothing, temporary hair dyes, tints for lips, and polishes for nails. Somehow even the indigos and blacks were deeper and more intense within these walls.

Brooklynn fit right in, wearing a shimmering gold dress that revealed a generous expanse of her toned legs and glittered beneath the flashing lights. I, on the other hand, wore my usual drab linen tunic that fell just below my knees.

I glanced at the people around me. Mostly, they were like us – the underage crowd. Youthful and energetic, with not enough outlet in their real lives. They – *we*, I corrected myself, even though my dress was dull and boring – created a bizarre human rainbow.

I worked my way toward the stages, positioned high above the dance floor, where scantily dressed girls danced for the crowds below. Their bodies, and the way they moved, were utterly hypnotic. They provided entertainment for the evening.

One particular girl caught my attention as her hips rocked in perfect rhythm to the song pulsating through the air. A blue spotlight shone down upon her, making her skin glow an unnatural shade of sapphire. The beads she wore were strung from a slender collar clasped around her neck and draped to a belt that was slung loosely around her hips. When she swayed, the beads clattered together, moving, shifting, parting. Just like every other girl up on the stages, the beads covered almost nothing, but I was certain that was the point.

Her long legs were willowy and graceful, as if

she'd been trained to perform in this manner. And she probably had been. The outcasts lived a different lifestyle from everyone else, doing jobs that were considered objectionable to those living within the class system.

Dancing would definitely fall into that category. Especially the kind of dancing that this girl did.

I watched her for several long moments, admiring the freedom she had up there, on that stage. A vendor's daughter would never be permitted to perform for a living.

'I'm glad you decided to come.' The deep voice rumbled from behind me, interrupting my musings.

I spun around, my eyes wide, embarrassed to be caught staring at the dancers.

'Do I know you?' I asked, but I realized immediately that I did. I'd seen him before. 'From the restaurant,' I amended. 'You were there tonight.'

Strong black brows drew together as he watched me, his expression unreadable. I felt like I was being inspected, but in an entirely different way from the bouncer at the front door. Something dark and unrecognizable tangled in the pit of my stomach, something uncertain.

He was larger than I'd remembered, entirely too large for the crowded space in which we stood, making me feel childlike and small. He took up far too much room, breathed far too much air.

The skin at the nape of my neck tightened, my head clearing instantly as the drug that had been bleeding through my system evaporated in a blink. In fact, all of my senses were heightened as my eyes remained fastened on his.

'I wasn't sure you'd be here tonight.' His voice was low – almost hushed – despite the loud music pounding around us.

'Yeah, me either. I wasn't sure I'd be *anywhere* tonight,' I shot back.

He raised one brow uncertainly. 'Is this a bad time? If you'd rather be alone, I'll go.'

I could feel the restless crowd around us. If I'd really wanted to be alone, Prey would be the last place I'd be. But I suddenly felt trapped by his cool, flint-colored eyes. They were disquieting in a way I didn't understand. My breath lodged in my throat, and I had the strangest feeling that I should look away from him. Yet I was captivated.

'It's – it's okay,' I finally managed, and that tangle knotted deeper, taut threads of hesitant emotions. The feeling that he was to be avoided deepened.

He frowned, but his lips quirked. 'Good, because it was an empty offer. I had every intention of staying. I'm Max.' His smile grew, and I could tell, too, that he was teasing me. I wished in that moment that I could be more like Brook. I wished that I was more confident around boys. He held his hand out to me.

When I didn't take it, he drew it back and rubbed it along his jaw, a nothing of a gesture, yet I couldn't help noting that he was almost too graceful when he moved.

There was a long silence as the music changed. I knew I should tell him my name, but instead I turned my gaze away from him, feigning interest in the dancers on the stage above us. The truth was, though, all I really noticed was him, stealing surreptitious glances whenever I could. His clothing was finer than anything I'd ever seen before – even the silk Aron had given me – and without meaning to, my fingers inched up, straining to stroke the rich fabric of his jacket. Just once.

I caught myself in time, dropping my hand back to my side and jerking my chin up a notch, thankful that I'd stopped myself before actually touching him, before making a fool of myself. It was then that I saw him smiling at me, *for me*, and my heart stopped.

I turned to look at him. The hard planes of his face softened, and suddenly he was dangerously boyish. And beautiful. Far too beautiful. And, like the fabric of his coat, my fingers itched to touch him . . . to rake through his short, dark hair, to feel his smooth-shaven jaw, to trace my thumb across his full lower lip.

I jolted. What was I thinking? Maybe I was *too much* like Brooklynn!

'I – I changed my mind. I think I should go.' I fumbled over my words as I stepped backward . . . first one awkward step, and then another.

Max frowned, reaching out to stop me. 'Wait. Don't leave.' I could feel the warmth – and the strength – of his fingertips seeping through the simple dress I wore, and I suddenly wished that I'd let Brooklynn talk me into borrowing one of hers. They weren't any newer, but the fabrics were richer. And infinitely more revealing. I wondered what his touch would feel like against my bare skin.

I lifted my eyes to his, marveling at his thick fringe of dark lashes, and once more was unnerved by the sensation that I shouldn't do that, that I was meant to look away. I reminded myself that here – in the club – class bore no distinction. Even if it was only an illusion.

But that thought emboldened me, and I let a half smile find my lips as I tipped my head to the side. 'Why would you care if I go?'

I was rewarded by a grin even as he released my arm. It was a fair exchange. 'I was hoping you might at least tell me your name. It's the least you could do, since I came here to see you.' His eyebrow lifted, and my pulse quickened.

I shook my head, certain he was still teasing me. Surely it was Brooklynn he'd meant to meet up with. But

I decided to play along. 'So what's the deal, do you have a thing for the underdog best friend? Or was it the fact that I nearly got myself sent to the gallows that attracted you?'

A troubled look crossed Max's face, and I realized that, like Brooklynn, he wasn't amused by the predicament I'd gotten myself into with the Counsel girl. But his next words had nothing to do with what he'd overheard at the restaurant. 'Do you not realize how beautiful you are?' he asked, leaning closer.

My face grew warm, and then hot.

I heard Brooklynn then, her voice rising above all else, even the music. Her laughter was musical and throaty, and just the thing to break the spell I was under. I turned to find her, searching the crowd, and spotting her glossy black curls easily.

'I'm sorry, I have to go,' I explained, but only as an afterthought, and only over my shoulder. I pushed my way forward, moving through hands and arms as I eased my way through the supple, shifting crowd to get to Brook.

And away from the unfamiliar feelings that besieged me.

When I finally saw Brooklynn, standing atop one of the raised platforms that overlooked the dance floor, she was crushed between the other two men from the restaurant, the ones who'd told her about Prey in the first place. They were even taller than their friend Max, and beside Brook's petite frame, they made her appear miniature. A lovely, fragile doll.

I hesitated for just a moment. I wasn't easily intimidated, but there was something about these two, something that gave me pause.

Brook's head was tilted back, her face lit up with laughter as she gazed adoringly at the dark-skinned man by her side. She was allure and promise in one seductive bundle. But it was the other man who drew my attention, the one with lighter skin, a shaved head, and sharp green eyes. He was just as tall as his friend, and equally muscular; the silver buttons of his black shirt strained across his broad chest. He leaned down, closer to Brooklynn, while her attention was diverted, lifting one of her dark curls to his face. And then he inhaled, breathing it in.

Smelling her.

'Charlie!' Brooklynn called when she saw me, waving eagerly and signaling me to join them. 'You remember my friends, from the restaurant?' It was her way of introducing me to the men on either side of her.

Goose bumps prickled my arms: a visceral warning.

I reached for her hand. 'We have to go,' I urged, trying to draw her away.

But Brooklynn pulled her hand from mine, clutching

it to her chest as if I'd just burned her. 'Stop, Charlie. I'm not ready to go yet.'

I recognized her tone, I'd heard it countless times before. She had no intention of leaving.

Frustrated, and unsure how to convince her, I struggled to come up with an excuse, but Brooklynn demanded my attention.

'Come on, Charlie. Check it out, these two have the best accents ever. Listen!' She turned to the man who had, just seconds earlier, *smelled* her. 'Show her. Say something,' she commanded sweetly.

Before I could tell him that I wasn't interested, the man accommodated Brooklynn's request. But he didn't speak in Englaise. His language was thick and gravelly.

In all my life, I'd never heard anything like it.

The world shivered around me in protest.

His language was strange, and the inflection of his voice was heavy and rough-edged, but the meaning of his words was crystal clear.

I heard what Brooklynn never would:

'This childish beauty smells delicious.'

The two men smiled knowingly at each other and my apprehension deepened, but not because of what he'd said.

This time, when I grabbed Brooklynn's wrist, I didn't let go. I felt better just having my hands on her.

I shot a nervous glance in the direction of the man

who had made my skin itch, but it wasn't what he'd said, it was *how* he'd said it. I spoke quietly to Brook, tugging on her arm. 'We have to go. I'm not feeling well.' It wasn't entirely a lie; my hands wouldn't stop shaking.

'Nooo!' Her voice was loud and petulant. 'Let's stay. I want to dance with . . .' She stopped, perplexed. 'What was your name again?'

'Claude.' His deep voice distorted the word, so that even though he pronounced it in Englaise, it came out sounding like he'd said *Cloud*.

Brooklynn giggled. 'Cloud. I want to dance with *Cloud*.'

Claude watched her with sharp eyes that didn't miss a thing.

'Brook,' I insisted, looking only at her. 'You promised.'

Brooklynn chewed on her red lip, her black brows pulled together in a delicate frown. 'But we just got here. What if I don't see him again?' She pouted for Claude's benefit when she said this.

His lips parted, a patient smile, his green eyes practically glowing. His smile would have been fine, maybe even nice, at any other time, on any other person. But when he spoke again, the air around me trembled in sweltering waves.

Again, his words were like nothing I'd ever heard, yet I understood them perfectly:

'*I'll be watching for you, my lovely.*'

The second man's dark brown eyes crinkled at Claude's statement, and he added, '*She'd be hard to miss.*'

I blinked, afraid my face would betray me after hearing those strange words. Words I knew I was never meant to understand.

I jerked Brooklynn's arm. 'No!' I shouted, no longer caring that I was drawing the attention of others in the club. And then I grabbed her arm and pulled her close. 'We *have* to leave, Brook. You promised,' I begged through gritted teeth.

Brooklynn frowned at me, but her shoulders slumped, accepting her fate.

'I'm sorry,' she sulked as she turned to Claude. 'Will you save me a dance? For next time?'

A meaningful smile played across his lips. He leaned down and whispered something in Brooklynn's ear.

While Claude held her attention, I realized that Max had followed me onto the platform. I had no idea how long he'd been listening.

He stood just a few feet away, *too close*, watching me intently and wearing a new expression now: *curiosity*.

It wasn't a look I cared to attract.

I told myself that I'd only imagined it. That there was no way he could know, or even suspect, that I'd recognized the meaning behind his friend's strange words.

I glanced back to Brooklynn as she tucked a silken black tendril of her hair behind her ear. She nodded at Claude and grinned wickedly. No doubt she'd understood 'Cloud' *perfectly* that time.

But already I was pulling her, dragging her away from the enormous men and their mysterious language. And away from the suffocating dread that bore down on me.

MAX

The barracks were never fully silent, even in the dead of night. Around him, Max could hear the rustle of bedding, the bark of an unrelenting cough, and the hushed voices of a faraway conversation.

He lay in his bunk, as still as he could, pretending to be asleep despite the fact that he was nowhere near it. He didn't try to keep the girl from his thoughts, but he didn't want to share those thoughts with the others. Better to feign sleep. Better to avoid questions from those around him, those who kept him under constant watch.

It would be easier if he were alone. If he were ever truly alone.

But this was the life he'd chosen, and alone was

no longer an option, so he'd have to settle for stolen moments in the blackest part of the night, hiding in plain sight.

Clear blue eyes stared back from inside his own memories, eyes he wished he'd never seen in the first place. Yet eyes he hoped to glimpse again. Soon.

She would be trouble, this one; the fact that he was lying awake now was proof of that. Just a few words exchanged, a smile, scant minutes spent together at the club, and already he was tortured and restless.

He replayed those last moments, after he'd followed her in the club, when he'd watched as she'd listened to her friend's flirtatious banter. He recognized the moment immediately, it would have been impossible not to notice it; her eyes going wide, her voice trembling, her conviction shattered.

She wasn't as strong as she wanted to be.

He worried for her, even though she was safe for now – probably at home, probably with her family, asleep in her own bed.

Unaware of the torment she'd already unleashed in him.

IV

Brooklynn had refused to speak to or even look at me on the walk home, no matter how many times I'd tried to apologize. If I could have explained why I'd insisted on leaving, she might have forgiven me, but I couldn't. No one, not even my best friend in the world, was allowed to know what I could do . . . that I could understand everything I heard.

By the time we were nearing our neighborhood on the west side of the city – the vendors' part of town – I'd decided it would be better if I just stayed at my house. My parents would know that I'd been out instead of at Brook's, but with her silent glare aimed directly at the street ahead of her, she'd made it more than clear that she wasn't going to forgive me. Not that night anyway.

But I wasn't sorry for making her leave. Even the next morning, in the light of a new day, I was certain I'd done the right thing.

I'd heard Claude when he spoke last night, and there was something wrong with it . . .

Why had I never heard his language before? How was that possible? With the threat of the revolution drawing interest from outside countries – countries hoping to prey on the fact that our defenses were weak, hoping to take advantage of a queen in peril – Ludania's borders had been closed off, and all foreign visitors had been forced to leave. No more tourist Passports were being issued.

Yet I had heard all the regional variations of Termani, Parshon, and Englaise; I knew all their intonations, their cadences, their rhythms. Or so I'd believed. Until now.

Now I'd heard something new.

But why was I so certain that I was never meant to hear this language in the first place?

I couldn't help wondering who Claude and his friend were. Spies? Revolutionaries speaking in code? Something worse?

Those questions, and the strange sounds of this new language, had haunted me far into the night, chasing me into sleep and making me restless.

Other things had kept me awake too, and occupied

my thoughts, things I had no business thinking about. Dark gray eyes, soft lips, a brash smile.

I tried to tell myself it was foolish to entertain such notions, but every time I forced him out, he found his way back in again.

The next morning I was relieved when I saw Brooklynn waiting in our usual spot in the plaza before school. I nearly smiled, until I realized that she was pretending not to notice me. Aron wasn't there yet; it was only the two of us. I approached warily, uncertain how to deal with last night.

'Hi,' I offered apprehensively, wishing I had something better to start off with.

Brook kept her arms crossed over her chest, her book bag lying crookedly at her feet. Yet even with her defiant stance, I knew she must be wavering. Why else would she have come?

She turned her cheek, still refusing to acknowledge my presence.

'Fine,' I said with a sigh, realizing I would have to make the first move and hating the bitter taste of apology on my tongue. 'Brooklynn, I'm sorry. I know you liked that – that *Claude* guy.' I purposely said his name like 'Cloud', hoping to crack her cast-iron shell. But I got nothing as she continued to glare skyward. 'I can't explain it, I just can't,' I tried. 'There was something . . . strange about them. Something I didn't trust.' It was as clear as

I could be, but at least her foot was tapping now. She was listening to me, and that was a start. 'You know I wouldn't have asked you to leave if I wasn't worried . . .' I paused, trying to think what more I could possibly say.

Brooklynn turned to me then, a concerned frown taking the place of her unrelenting glower. She thought for a moment, and when she finally spoke, I wished we could go back in time. The silent treatment was easier than the truth. 'It wasn't about the guy, Charlie. It was about you. Something happened last night, and not just at the club, at the restaurant, too. You're the one who's acting *strange* . . .' Her voice dropped to a discreet whisper as she closed the gap between us, standing so close now that no one could possibly overhear. 'You're the one who's going around breaking the law. And don't fool yourself, I saw what you did at school yesterday, when you gave that boy a cookie. It's dangerous. The deadly sort of dangerous.' Her mouth became a firm line as she nearly pressed her cheek to mine then, her voice almost inaudible. 'I'm your friend, Charlie. If there's something you want to tell me, I'll listen. I'll keep your secrets. But you need to be more careful. For the sake of everyone around you.'

My eyes were wide and my mouth had gone dry as I jumped back, startled by her words and her tone. Brook was seldom serious. Worrying to this degree was practically unheard of. I stared back at her, unblinking.

She was right, of course, I was the one who'd been causing trouble. Not her. Not Claude.

I nearly jumped when the loudspeaker blared above us: 'ALL SUSPICIOUS ACTIVITY MUST BE REPORTED TO YOUR NEAREST PATROL STATION.'

I was so tempted to tell her everything.

But it was Aron that I heard above all else, shattering the moment. 'No fair cheating, you know? I never even saw you leave. This doesn't count.' He grinned, all crooked and goofy. But his brows creased when he looked at the two of us, standing as still as the statues of the queen that filled the city. 'Everything okay . . . ?'

I sucked in an unsteady breath as I shot a questioning look at Brooklynn. *Are we okay?* I asked with that look.

Brook, her eyes still on mine, bumped me with her shoulder, a playful nudge. 'We're fine,' she said, more to me than to Aron. And as she started walking, she glanced over her shoulder to him. 'Get my bag, will ya, Midget?'

I grinned when I saw Aron standing at the bottom of the steps after school, waiting for me. Aron, who was always reassuring and safe, and the moment I saw him I felt myself relaxing.

I couldn't recall a time when it hadn't been that way. Aron was bright and steady and clear, like finding a beacon in the darkness.

At times it was still difficult reconciling the man's

body that had grown around the boy I'd once known, but there were subtle remnants of my childhood friend – the way his hair was permanently mussed, and the small patch of freckles on his nose that was vanishing a little more with each passing year. Automatically, he reached for my bag.

'Brooklynn wanted me to tell you she had to leave early. Her dad needs her at home today.'

I frowned despite Aron's uncomplicated smile and tried to recall just when his voice had deepened. Was it possible that it had happened without my notice?

'She could have walked with us,' I responded, but there was no real conviction in my words. Even though she was no longer upset with me, Brooklynn never wanted company on the days when her father called her home.

Her father rarely paid her any attention, but when he did it was because the house required cleaning or the kitchen was in need of restocking. I knew she felt unimportant to be noticed so infrequently, and for strictly utilitarian purposes.

I'd begun to hate him because she didn't seem capable of it.

'Hey, Aron, your dad talks a lot . . .' It wasn't a question. Mr Grayson was the kind of man who craved gossip in the way others needed air. He would be dangerous if he weren't such a fool, but his mind was as frivolous as his tongue was loose.

Aron just nodded. He didn't take offense at the insinuation . . . he knew, of course. Then he cast a curious grin in my direction. 'What are you after?'

I shrugged, worrying that I was overstepping. I proceeded cautiously. 'What does he say about Brooklynn? About her father?'

The grin disappeared. 'What do you mean?'

My shoulders lifted again. 'You know what I mean. Does your father ever talk about them? Does he say if they're doing okay? Is Mr Maier working enough? Can he support the two of them? Is Brook . . .' I had a difficult time asking this last part, even though I'd wondered it a thousand times. 'Is there any danger that she'll be taken away from him?' Brooklynn was nearly seventeen, only a few weeks younger than me, and in just over a year would be of age to make her own decisions. But until then she was at risk of being claimed as a ward of the queen. Which meant being sent to a work camp, something Brooklynn would rather die than face, as it meant losing her Vendor's status and slipping down in standing. All orphans became members of the Serving class.

Aron stopped walking, his face serious now, his eyes uncommonly sad. 'I've heard things,' he said regretfully. 'The customers in my father's shop talk about Brook sometimes, but it's not about her well-being. They say she's too wild, that her father has given up on her, that he gives her too much freedom. Some say he should keep her under lock and key, others just talk about how sad it is that her mother isn't there to keep her under control.' He shook his head. 'I haven't heard anyone say that her father can't support her, but I worry when her name comes up. I'm afraid that someday I'll hear their complaints become something worse' – he looked up at me, capturing my eyes with his – 'something dangerous.'

We both knew what he was talking about, and my breath lodged in my throat as I reached for his arm. I wanted to tell him that it was impossible, that no one could possibly suspect Brooklynn of being a traitor, that no one would dare accuse her of collaborating with the rebels. But I knew I was wrong.

Not because I thought Brooklynn was a revolutionary, but because I knew it was entirely possible that someone might voice their opinions out loud. Sometimes – more often than I cared to admit – the rewards of turning in a neighbor were enough to shift loyalties. And someone like Brook, a girl with no mother, and no father to speak of, made for an easy target.

'You'll warn me if you hear that kind of talk?' I asked, not sure exactly what I'd do with the information but knowing that I couldn't just let her be taken away. Not the way Cheyenne Goodwin had been.

'You know I will,' Aron assured me, and I knew he meant it. He slipped his hand around mine as we walked, reminding me that he was still my friend. That I could still count on him.

I leaned my head against his shoulder, once again comforted by his presence.

'How many times do I have to tell you? It was an accident. I didn't realize she'd switched to Termani.' I was tired of explaining myself, but it didn't matter how many times I'd repeated those words, my father still wasn't satisfied.

He was too worried.

He paced the room, and even though he'd had an entire day to calm down since the incident at the restaurant the night before, his shoulders were still heavy with the burden of what I'd done. Of what I'd let slip.

'*Charlaina, please, those aren't the kinds of mistakes you can afford. All I'm saying is that you must be careful. Always careful.*' His skin was flushed as he pressed his calloused palm against my cheek. Stress creased his forehead and wrinkled his brow. '*I worry about you. I worry about all of us.*'

'I know,' I answered, stubbornly refusing to indulge my parents' love of Parshon. I much preferred to speak Englaise. All the time, Englaise. That way there was no room for misunderstandings, no room for errors. I wished that everyone felt as I did.

He sat down on the sofa in the small central living space of our house. It was cozy, and filled with years of memories. I knew every nook, every stone, every plank of wood, and every darkened crevice by heart.

This was the house I was born in, the house in which I'd been raised, and yet suddenly I felt unworthy of its refuge for betraying my father's trust. I understood – maybe more than anyone – just what he'd sacrificed to keep us safe.

I still remembered that night, when I was only Angelina's age. The night the man had banged on our door, demanding to speak to my father and refusing to go away without answers.

My father had pushed me into my bedroom, warning me to wait there until he told me it was safe. Or until my mother came home. And I'd tried to obey, tried to remain hidden beneath the bed – just as he'd insisted – but I'd been so afraid.

That night was still so vivid in my memory: the cold stone floor beneath my bare feet as I'd crept out from my hiding place, the doll I'd clutched against my chest, the words exploding from the other side of the heavy door.

'*I heard what she did, Joseph. That man spoke to her in Termani, and she answered him. She understood what he said. She's an abomination!*' It wasn't my father's voice I'd heard raised in alarm and traced with outrage.

'*You heard nothing. She's a child. She was only playing.*'

'She wasn't, and you put us all at risk by keeping her here!'

I'd held my breath, leaning my forehead against the rough-hewn wood, the only barrier that separated me from my father.

And then my father's voice, angry and firm. 'You need to leave my home. You've no business here.'

The silence that followed was too long, and so heavy with meaning that even then I knew enough to be terrified of the hollow space. I'd stepped back, shivering in the still black air.

Then I remembered the other man speaking again, quietly, almost whisper-soft. 'What she's done is illegal. Either you turn her in, or I will.'

There was no pause when my father answered. 'I can't let you do that.'

I'd gripped my doll so tight as I stole backward, taking slow and steady steps without watching where I was going.

I slid as soundlessly as I could beneath the bed again, just like my daddy had instructed, curling myself tightly into a ball as tears slipped down my cheeks. I covered my ears as I tried to block out first the sounds, and then the crackling silence, that came from just outside my bedroom as I closed my eyes.

I cowered there in the darkness, terrified that the sounds that rattled the closed door would somehow find their way over to my side. But they never did, and the hush that followed stretched endlessly. When I grew weary, I lay my head down on the cold floor and waited.

Finally I heard the door's creak, and my heart seized within the cavity of my chest. I was fully awake in the space of a breath. My eyes went wide, trying to absorb enough light from the darkness around me to see whose feet were shuffling toward my bed. The scraping sound of heavy boots against stone made my skin shiver.

I leaned up on my elbows, staring out. My throat felt choked by the thick lump that had formed there.

And then the weight of the mattress above me shifted heavily, and I heard a heavy sigh.

'*You can come out now.*'

At the sound of my father's voice, I scurried forward, scooting along on my stomach as quickly as I could. Before I was even out from beneath the bed, he was reaching for me, drawing me up. I crawled onto his warm lap, curling my knees and feet underneath me as I wrapped my scrawny arms around his waist. I breathed in the smell of him.

He held me for a long time before speaking again, probably because there were so many things we shouldn't be saying, so many things that should remain unstated. But finally his voice rumbled up from his chest against my ear.

He spoke in Englaise now, the softer syllables of

the language making his words seem less harsh than before, when he'd been speaking to the man in the other room. 'You can't do that anymore. You must be cautious.' Then he switched back to the more guttural tone of our native tongue as he lifted me from his lap and dropped me onto my soft pillows. *Now get some rest, lamb. I need to clean up before your mother gets home.*

He tucked the blankets around me and leaned down, gently pressing his lips against my forehead. My heavy eyelids closed, and I remember feeling safe and secure, knowing that my father had protected me, just as he would always protect me . . .

. . . as I tried to forget about the blood that covered his shirt.

I sighed as I looked at my father now, knowing that all he'd ever wanted was to keep us safe, me and Angelina. So why was it so difficult for me to admit that I'd made a mistake? 'You're right, Daddy,' I finally said. 'I'll be more careful. I promise.'

He smiled up at me. It was a puny attempt, but I appreciated the effort. *'I know you will, lamb.'* He reached out and took my hand, squeezing my fingers in a fierce grip.

The front door burst open then, and Angelina came bounding inside, small and energetic, her blond hair tangled and wild, making her look like a tiny whirlwind. My mother trailed in behind her.

'Are you ready for bed?' I asked my sister, swinging her into my arms and using her as an excuse to escape the lingering feeling that I'd disappointed my father.

Angelina nodded, looking anything but sleepy.

I shrugged at my parents over my shoulder as I carried the wiggly little girl into the bedroom we shared and settled her down on the only bed. I left her to undress as I went to fetch a wet rag so I could wipe away some of the filth she'd managed to accumulate throughout the course of the day.

'You're a mess,' I accused as I scrubbed away the grime from her alabaster skin. She flashed me a toothy, four-year-old grin. 'Muffin's a mess too,' I complained, looking at the grubby doll she carried everywhere she went, the worn-out, hand-me-down rabbit I'd given her.

The years hadn't been good to Muffin. His fur was worn so thin it was transparent in spots, making him look mangy. Stains made his original soft white appear brown and blotchy, sickly even.

Angelina clutched the tattered bunny, refusing to even allow the washrag near him.

By the time I finished cleaning my little sister and changing her into her nightgown, Angelina was leaning heavily against my side, barely able to hold up her own head.

'Come on, sleepy girl,' I whispered, slipping her small body beneath the blankets and nestling the dirty little rabbit beside her on the pillow. Angelina never slept without Muffin.

I climbed into bed beside her, leaving on the bedside lamp and pulling out the fabric Aron had given me. I'd already cut it into pieces, fashioning a pattern of my own creation, and pinned them all together. I plucked a sewing needle from the spool of thread I'd left sitting on my bedside table and set to work, noting, once more, the feel of the silken fabric between my fingers, and wondering what it would feel like to wear something so scandalously fine.

Angelina's feet moved over to my side of the bed, across the cool sheets, and found their way beneath my legs as she sought my warmth.

It was Angelina's way of saying good night.

It was the only way she could.

V

It hadn't been difficult to talk Brooklynn into going to the club again, and I really hadn't expected it to be. Brook was predictable if nothing else.

'So? Who is he?' she'd asked in a conspiratorial whisper, leaning close and hooking her arm through mine. She winked at Angelina, who was sitting cross-legged on the bed, watching Brook with rapt admiration. 'I didn't see you with anyone the other night, but you've never wanted to go to the clubs twice in one week.'

She wasn't wrong; I hadn't stopped thinking about those stormy gray eyes since that night at Prey. And that was two days ago, longer than any boy had ever occupied my thoughts.

I wasn't sure what it was about Max. He frightened me almost as much as he intrigued me. Still, as much as I worried about the possibility of running into his friends, I was desperate to see him again.

'It isn't like that,' I'd tried to explain, but Brooklynn refused to listen.

'Really, Charlie? I don't believe you for a second, especially if you're planning to wear that.' She narrowed her eyes suspiciously as she appraised me.

I almost smiled. Even though I'd designed the dress myself, it felt like too much. Or not enough, really. I wasn't like Brooklynn. I wasn't accustomed to feeling so exposed; one shoulder was bare, and the other was covered only by a thin strip of the dark silk. The fabric felt sheer as it hugged my body in ways that my loose cotton dresses never would.

'Whatever. If you don't want to tell me . . .' Her words trailed off in a pout that I imagined worked on every boy she'd ever used it on. 'Has she told you anything?' she asked my little sister.

Angelina shook her head, setting her chin on her hands as she leaned forward expectantly, her blue eyes wide.

'Seriously, Brook, it's nothing. He's just someone . . . *unusual*. I only want to talk to him again. It's not what you think.'

But in the end, my motivations hadn't mattered;

Brooklynn would've gone regardless of my reasons. So later that night, when I found myself back at the red steel door, I was relieved to find that Prey was still open, that it was still a club. Yet I was even less comfortable than I had been the first time we'd gone.

But some things never changed: different bouncer, same routine.

Brooklynn, as usual, seemed to enjoy the skin inspection, while I felt defiled and revolted by it. More so, because so much of my skin was bared.

As always, the man at the door let us pass in exchange for dosing us with a hallucinogen-laced hand stamp. Even before we could tuck our Passports away, my skin smoldered where the ink was working its way beneath my flesh. I barely glanced at the mark; I was too busy searching, scanning the club for something – *someone* – else, but I knew there would soon be a welt.

With the same ease that we'd gotten by the bouncer, we made it past the blue-haired bartender, too, and this time she even gave Brook change, although not before claiming a hefty tip for herself.

The club itself was busier tonight, and I glanced up to the stages where, instead of beads, the dancing girls were adorned only in bright feathery plumes. They were stunning to watch, like exotic birds of purple and blue and green.

I was aware of Brook pulling me through the crowds,

her attention captured by the lures of the music, the men, and the drug seeping its way in through her hand.

My eyes darted about, searching . . . searching.

Max was nowhere to be seen, not on this night. I looked for the others, too – his friends who'd spoken in a strange, throaty language – although not for the same reason. Them, I would avoid if possible.

I could hear Brooklynn telling me she wanted to dance, and I let her go. I was too busy hoping Max might still appear. I watched as she slipped easily through the mass of bodies, finding her place on the dance floor.

My head felt heavy, but I knew it was only the drug bleeding into my system. I spared a quick glance downward at my hand, at the inflamed mark made by the hand stamp. A six-pointed star.

I closed my eyes, waiting for the discomfort to pass, but it was suddenly too warm in here, too crowded, too loud. I needed air.

I glanced toward the entrance – to where the bouncer was raking his licentious gaze over the skin of yet another underage girl – and my stomach lurched. Surely there had to be another way outside, a back door.

I eased away from the handrail, mindful of my surroundings, searching for an exit. I wasn't certain exactly where I was going, but in the opposite direction of the bouncer seemed a good place to start. It was as logical as I could be at the moment.

'Excuse me,' I mumbled, pushing my way through the dance floor, finding myself surrounded by the writhing bodies. I looked for Brooklynn, but I couldn't see her; she seemed to be lost in the sea of faces that surrounded me.

I couldn't help thinking that I should just find a place to sit and wait it out, this delirium. But the nausea gripping me demanded that I get away from the chaos.

When I reached the other side of the dance floor, I climbed the steps to one of the platforms, trying to find a doorway that might lead outside. But I saw none.

I hesitated for a moment, watching two men and a woman who were wrapped in a passionate embrace, stroking and kissing one another. The girl's hair was the color of polished ebony, and it seemed to change color whenever the lights overhead fell upon it. One of the men had dyed his spiky hair a brilliant shade of red, while the other's was golden, curled and soft.

The threesome's actions felt synchronized as they moved, like those of the dancers on the stages overhead. The giant mirrored wall behind them reflected their arms and legs as they tangled and twisted together, until each person became merely an extension of the next.

But it was beyond them, just off to the side of the mirrored wall, that I spied a heavy black curtain, fringed at the bottom with thick gold braids. It was just the right size to conceal a doorway. I was spurred forward by a sudden need to find out what was behind that curtain. The music pulsed rhythmically, a heavy beating bass.

I worried that one of the threesome might notice what I was doing, that they might try to stop me, as if they were somehow the sentinels of this spot. But none of them even seemed aware of my presence, and I slipped easily past them without notice.

As I reached the curtain, I fingered the edge of the thick fabric, easing it back and trying to peer beyond.

Behind it was a black hallway, and with only the dim flashes of light coming from the club through the sliver of an opening I'd created, it was impossible to see where it went. Still, I needed to get outside, to take a breath of fresh air.

I eased through, letting the curtain fall closed behind me and holding my breath as I stood there, waiting to see if anyone had noticed me. My heart raced and my skin tightened. I wondered what was back here, and whether or not I should even be here. Surely the curtain was there for a reason.

The flashing lights of the club couldn't find their way beyond the solid black drapery, and my eyes were slow to adjust, but eventually I could make out the floor and the walls and the faint outline of two closed doors. When I was certain I hadn't been discovered, I inched forward, against my better judgment, taking one cautious step at a time.

I stopped at the first door and pressed my palm flat against its wooden surface. Fear rose up, choking me. I reached down, trying the knob, but it was locked.

I exhaled, my shoulders falling heavily.

Sweat prickled across my upper lip as I moved to the other door, the one at the end of the black corridor. This time, I spread my hand over a cool metal surface.

This was it, I knew. The door I'd been searching for.

My fingers fumbled for the knob. I tested it, and it turned easily, the latch releasing with a click that I felt rather than heard from above the music behind me.

Just as I was about to lean into it, a hand gripped my shoulder, squeezing tightly. My heart slammed in my chest, hammering a reckless rhythm.

I whirled, crashing into a solid wall of muscles, and immediately thought of the bouncer from the door. My dulled mind raced as I willed it to clear, to think faster.

'May I help you?' A man's voice asked. I knew immediately that it wasn't the bouncer – I'd have recognized his sleazy tone. But for once, I couldn't read the intention in it. Curiosity? Disbelief? Something worse . . . threat?

'I-I—' I struggled to find the right explanation for what I was doing. 'I-I just got lost,' I finally stammered.

I saw him reach for the wall beside him. Then there was a soft click. I was bathed in the glow of a bare red bulb that was mounted on the ceiling above us, and I found myself staring, wide-eyed, at a man with a suspicious scowl. His dark hair fell loosely around his shoulders, and his scruffy jaw hadn't seen a razor in days, maybe weeks. But it was his eyes – catlike and predatory – that held me as they reflected the red light back at me.

'You shouldn't be back here,' he stated flatly. 'It's not safe.'

Unconsciously, I rubbed at the back of my hand, the skin itchy, stinging. 'I needed some air,' I gasped. My heart beat faster, and I swayed slightly.

His hand snaked out to grab my wrist, steadying me, as he asked, 'Do you need to sit?'

I nodded, blinking. 'Yes,' I rasped, scratching at the hand stamp. 'Sitting would be good.' The world felt as if it were tilting beneath my feet, and the blood drained from my face.

He slipped his arm around my waist, surely afraid I would topple right there in the corridor, as he led me not back into the club, but to the first door in the hallway – the locked door. He pulled a key from his pocket and opened it before I could find the words to object.

And within seconds I found myself collapsing onto a green velvet sofa that smelled of smoke, from both drugs that were legal and those that were not, as I leaned my head back and closed my eyes.

I had never seen a private club room before. In some clubs, they were said to be luxurious box suites perched high above the bars and dance floors, where the elite – those who paid a steep price to the club's proprietors – were treated like royalty for the night. Others were said to be dens of iniquity, where one's every wicked desire could be fulfilled . . . for a price.

This appeared to be something else altogether, something both less sinister and less opulent.

I glanced at the man in the chair across from me. He leaned forward, his elbows balanced on his knees as he surveyed me closely. I wasn't sure I should be here, in this room with him. I wondered where he'd been coming from when he'd run into me.

'Is this your club?' I asked, my voice hoarse.

His eyebrows drew together in a deep scowl and I saw the scar there, running from just above his brow all the way down to the edge of his angular jaw. It was pale and faded – an old wound – but when he frowned like that, the silvery edges puckered. 'No, it's not my club. But the people who run it let me do business here.'

Something about the way he said the word 'business' made it sound illicit.

The constant strobe of lights pulsed from the club, finding their way into the room through a huge window that made up an entire wall. They flickered over his face, casting it in an ever-changing rainbow of hues. On the other side of the window, I could see the threesome, the two men and the black-haired woman, still kissing and caressing one another, and I remembered the mirror they'd been standing in front of.

I got up from the sofa, weaving around the mismatched furnishings to stand before the glass wall. With my fingertip, I traced the outline of their single form, seemingly fused together. 'They can't see us?' I was awed. I'd never heard of such a thing.

He was beside me then, an enigmatic presence. 'No. The other side is mirrored; it only works one way.'

'Strange,' I whispered.

I was still dizzy, and having a difficult time concentrating. Everything moved in slow motion, my throat felt dry and tight, and my eyelids were weighted. I couldn't stop scratching my hand.

He followed my gaze as I peered down at the welt.

'May I?' he asked, his hand reaching for mine. White scars zigzagged across his knuckles.

I stared at him, at the scar barely concealed by his long hair, at his strange silver-flecked eyes. I stared for too long as I tried to make up my mind. Beneath his whiskered jaw, his skin was weathered and his face was hard, but his expression was earnest as he waited for me, so patiently, that I wondered what possible harm it could do to let him take a look.

I allowed him to take my hand in his.

His skin was cool and dry as one of his calloused fingertips followed the swollen ridge of the star. And then he reached into his pocket, pulling out a small black container. Inside there was a salve that smelled like an odd combination of pungent earth and crisp citrus, yet wasn't entirely unpleasant.

He didn't ask this time, he just smoothed it over the burning skin, massaging it with his thumb.

I wasn't sure what to make of that. A part of me insisted that this was a bad idea, that I was allowing a man I didn't know – a man I wasn't even sure I trusted – to rub some kind of ointment onto my skin. Who knew what it contained?

But there was that other part of me, the part that just watched silently, curious at myself, at how easily I'd succumbed to his intense gaze.

'There,' he said, closing the container and pressing it

into my palm. 'You'll feel better soon.'

He was wrong, though. It was already happening. The skin on the back of my hand had already stopped tingling, and my head had stopped spinning. Already my thoughts were clearer.

'Who are you?' I finally asked.

He cocked his head, smiling. 'My name is Xander. And you' – he raised his eyebrows – 'are Charlie.'

I jerked forward, suddenly wary. How did he know my name?

He chuckled, explaining, 'I've seen you around the clubs. You and your pretty friend.'

Of course he meant Brooklynn. Everyone noticed Brooklynn.

It was hard to imagine that I'd never noticed him before. He was hard to miss.

'I'm sorry. It was nice meeting you, Xander, but I really need to find my friend now.' And it was true. With my head clear, I realized the position I was in: that no one knew where I was, or who I was with.

For a moment I thought he might argue, or try to convince me to stay. He was standing between me and the exit, and there was a long, tense pause. I held my breath, trying to calm my heart.

But then the moment passed, and he stepped out of my way. Again I was struck by that sense that there was something predatory about him, in the grace with which he moved and the way his silver eyes remained trained – focused – on me. But I squeezed the container of salve in my palm, reminding myself that he'd done nothing wrong.

'Right this way.'

He led me back into the darkened hallway, and to the club beyond. He stayed with me, keeping his hand on my elbow, whether to steady me or to keep me within arm's reach, I didn't know.

We stood there for a moment, silently surveying the crowd. 'There she is.' His voice was so low and deep that it very nearly blended into the bass of the music.

There was a sudden burst of activity near the entrance, and everyone seemed to turn at once, straining to see what was happening. Xander's fingers tightened on my arm. I was certain it was unintentional. I doubted he even realized he'd done it. Beside me, he'd gone completely rigid, anxious and alert within the span of a breath.

As we watched, bodies shifted and the crowds parted. Even without seeing who'd just arrived, their appearance charged the air like static electricity.

And then three men emerged from the mass of people crowding the entryway, and as they came closer, I recognized him – Max – immediately. My breath caught in the back of my throat.

That was when I noticed it, the same thing I had when I'd first met him: Max didn't belong here.

Not in the way someone like Xander did. Not like I did.

I was scarcely aware of his companions, watching only him as his assessing gaze moved around the club. I couldn't help wondering if – even hoping that – it was me he searched for.

I remained still as his eyes paused on Xander, flashing darkly. But his hesitation was so slight, so fleeting, that I could have easily convinced myself I'd only imagined it.

Then that same self-assured gaze stopped on me, staking me to the ground as I stared back at him, unblinking, unwavering. I held my breath as I waited for something to happen, as I hoped to see some glimmer of recognition from him. And I thought there *was* something, an almost imperceptible narrowing of his eyes and the slight lift at the corners of his mouth. But it was over so quickly I could barely process it, and his long stride never faltered.

Disappointment surged through me as Max and his companions continued through the crowds. I felt foolish for coming here to see him, for stitching this dress while dreaming of him, for hoping he might notice me.

'Who are they?' I finally managed to ask Xander,

meaning more than just their names.

But when I turned my head, Xander was gone.

I glanced down at the back of my hand, just to make certain I hadn't been dreaming . . . that Xander really had been there in the first place.

My skin no longer burned, and the mark – the six-pointed star – had all but disappeared. I opened my fist and touched the container of salve I still held.

Xander was real, all right.

And suddenly I was sure he had the answers I wanted.

XANDER

'So, X? Was it her?'

Eden moved like a living, breathing hurricane, energy brewing just beneath her skin at all times. She sat in the chair across from him, leaning her elbows on his desk, meeting his gaze head-on.

Irritated to be interrupted, Xander shoved the crumbling photograph beneath the papers in front of him, and then traced his thumb along the ragged line of his scar, an old habit. But Eden was one of the few people who could get away with disturbing him. 'I don't know yet. I think she might be.' Then he amended his words. 'I'm almost certain of it.'

Overhead, music from the club still pounded a vicious

rhythm, hammering the ceiling above them. It would continue like that until dawn.

Eden pondered his statements, running her hand through her spiky hair. Then she asked the other questions, the ones he'd been considering all night. 'What about the guards, did they see her? Do *they* know who she is?'

He didn't have a good answer for her, so he shrugged. 'I don't know. They definitely saw her, and I think they knew she was with me, even if they didn't know why. But I have no idea if they've guessed who she is.' He waited, wondering if he should even ask his next question. He trusted Eden – with his life – but he could see she was already anxious, and he didn't want to add to her troubles.

She stood and paced the dark space below the club, one of their latest installations. But they wouldn't be able to stay there any longer. He didn't know if he'd been followed, and he couldn't take the chance. The clubs were a good place to hide, a good place to move information, but they could never get too comfortable in one place for long. If they did, they could be raided, and their secrets would be discovered, their plans exposed.

They would have to be out of there by daybreak.

Eden checked the small arms cache they kept on hand, using the key that only she and Xander had access to.

Finally he asked, 'Did you see who was with them tonight?'

Her gaze shot back to him, and at first he thought she wasn't going to answer. Her black eyes were filled with worry, fear, alarm. She picked up a handheld grenade launcher, cradling it like a baby.

'It was Max, wasn't it?'

MAX

He approached his queen in the same manner he always did, with suspicion and great care.

The room was warm, overly so, as it always was now that the queen had grown old and her body was increasingly frail. But it wasn't her body he worried about. Her mind was still sharp, her moods turbulent.

She was not a woman to underestimate.

'*Your Majesty*,' he purred, speaking in the language of the royals and hearing his two companions repeat his words as they all three bowed to the ground before her.

They waited milliseconds before she snapped at them, her intolerance apparent. '*Get up! I don't have time for your nonsense. Just get to it.*' She leveled her gaze on the dark-skinned man in front of her. '*What's your report?*'

Since she wasn't addressing him, Max stepped aside, clasping his hands behind his back, waiting until he was spoken to directly.

'*We believe we've found their latest command center, Your Majesty. Another club in the city. We're checking intel now, and once we have confirmation, we'll go in.*'

The queen mulled the information over before speaking again, staring at the giant before her. A lesser man would have cowered beneath her withering gaze, but Zafir could hold his own against his regent. All the royal guards were handpicked for their fearlessness.

'*Anything else to add?*' She looked to the other guard, the second monster-sized man before her.

'*No, Your Majesty.*' Claude's answer was brief, to the point.

At last she turned her stare to Max, the third uniformed man in the room, addressing him for the first time. '*What about the girl? Any news of the girl?*'

He looked at his queen, studying her shriveled gray skin and her ghostlike eyes, wondering how she could even see through the haze that coated them. He knew, however, that nothing escaped her. Except, perhaps, this: '*No, Your Majesty. We know nothing of the girl.*'

The lie felt easy rolling from his tongue, and he wondered if that was how his head would feel when the guillotine separated it from his body were she to discover the truth.

He wondered, also, why he hadn't told her, why he'd decided to keep the information to himself. She was his queen, it was his duty to divulge any and all information she demanded of him.

He pictured the pale girl with the silvery blond hair whom he'd seen twice now at the club, and he justified to himself that he wasn't actually lying. He didn't know who she was. He had no way of knowing if this was the girl for whom they'd been searching.

The queen scrutinized him, her milky gaze raking him from head to toe, and – he knew from the antipathy on her face – finding him lacking. But not, he realized, discerning the inaccuracy of his statement.

'*Leave*,' she commanded, releasing them, at last, from the cruel heat.

VI

I stayed awake well into the night, replaying the moment that Max had walked into the club – and then deliberately ignored me – over and over again in my mind. When I awoke, I was frustrated to find that I'd overslept and my parents had gone ahead without me. Since there was no school today, I thought about pulling the covers over my head and just staying there, avoiding the real world and pretending that last night had never happened at all. Unfortunately, my parents still needed me, and I couldn't let them down.

I dressed quickly, binding my hair away from my face and rushing out the door, into streets that were already crowded and sun-scorched.

Morning in the marketplace had always been one of my favorite times. I'd loved the bustle of activity, the rush of the Serving class as they attended to the needs of their assigned households. It was when the first loaves of bread were being pulled from the ovens and fresh tea leaves were being brewed. When Englaise was the only language spoken, as shopkeepers were forced to trade in the universal language.

But now the streets were choked, and the new refugees suffocated me as I was propelled forward by the swell of bodies.

I stopped once, as did nearly everyone around me, to notice that the flags in the plaza had been changed overnight. The white flags of Ludania no longer flew – spotless and crisp – above the square. In their place, the queen's flags had been raised, a golden profile of the queen herself set atop a bloodred field.

Yet another reminder that queen came before country, and I could feel her grip tightening like a noose as I wondered where this would end.

I was glad to be swallowed again by the claustrophobic mass.

When I reached my parents' restaurant and saw who awaited me, I suddenly wished that I *had* stayed home in bed, and I hesitated midstep, nearly stumbling as the urge to run away overwhelmed me.

There was Max, sitting at one of the small sidewalk

tables out front, his long legs stretched casually before him. I quelled the sudden rush of embarrassment I felt as I remembered how easily he'd disregarded me the night before, without hesitation. And no matter how hard I tried to push it down, the memory stayed with me, just as it had throughout the night.

I could still leave, I realized. He had yet to notice my approach.

But then he glanced up, his gaze capturing mine. I was unable to move. Or even to breathe. I became a clog in the constantly shifting foot traffic, as people bumped and crowded me.

In broad daylight, away from the darkened shadows of the club, he appeared even younger than he had in my memories. I doubted he was much older than I was: eighteen, perhaps nineteen. His eyes were intense, and I again had the feeling that I shouldn't be meeting them directly, that I ought to look away. Yet they were as deep and mesmerizing as they were alarming. And I was spellbound.

I tried to find those feelings again, the ones from that first night, the trepidation and imminent danger that had forced me to flee from the club when I'd heard his friends speaking. But somehow, standing here in the bright sunlight of the marketplace, I was unable to recall them. And the longer I stayed there, my eyes locked with his, the harder it was to imagine that I'd ever felt them at all.

I *was* afraid of him, and my heart beat entirely too fast inside my chest, but not for the same reasons that I'd been frightened that night.

He stood from the table as I approached hesitantly, and I tried to read his expression, but just like the night before, it was impossible to interpret.

I frowned. 'What are you doing here?' I asked when I finally reached him.

His eyebrows raised just the barest degree, making me feel things I had no business feeling as a rush of heat surged through me. But I refused to let him see how he affected me.

'I came to see you,' he answered far too easily.

'I guessed that much.' I crossed my arms as I glanced around to see if anyone was watching us. I wasn't ready to answer prying questions from my parents. I lifted my chin. 'Why?'

'You're not one for conversation, are you?' He studied my expression, and I could see amusement flickering just behind those charcoal eyes. Eyes that I'd spent far too much time imagining. But I wasn't amused. At last, he exhaled loudly. 'Honestly, I'm not exactly sure why I came. I probably shouldn't be here at all. But you intrigue me, and I had to see you again.'

'You saw me last night, but I didn't *intrigue* you then. You barely noticed me.'

Max hesitated, frowning. 'That's not true. I noticed . . .'

He lowered his voice as his hand slipped to my arm. It was a quiet warning. 'You should be careful about who you keep company with.'

I raised my eyebrows, daring him to finish his thoughts, but he didn't need to; I'd noticed the way he looked at Xander. 'Is that why you pretended not to know me?' I wrenched my arm from his grip.

He took a step closer, and my ribs crushed my heart, threatening to stop it from beating. I wanted it to be fear, and that's what I told myself it was, that I felt threatened by Max. But I knew better, I knew it was something more. And then he surprised me by softly asking, 'Why did you leave so early that first night?'

I was afraid to speak, but he just stood there, waiting. I tilted my head back, so I could meet his stare. I wavered, trying to decide how to answer him, and then I simply said, 'I wasn't feeling well.'

He gazed down at me, and I had the strangest feeling he knew I was lying. But he only sighed, a reluctant smile pulling at the corners of his mouth. 'Will you walk with me?' he asked at last.

It would have been easier to answer if I could breathe, and if my pulse would stop fluttering so wildly. I shook my head, unable to stop staring. 'No.' I finally trusted my voice. 'I need to get inside. I have work to do.'

'*What are you so afraid of?*' He said it so tenderly, so gently, that I almost didn't realize he hadn't spoken in Englaise. Yet it wasn't Parshon, either, which was the only other language I could have responded to.

I'd heard those sounds – that dialect – only one other time, that night at the club, when his friends had spoken about Brooklynn.

And the law was clear.

I blinked once, keeping his dark gaze in view for an instant too long, and then I dropped my head. This time my heart crashed within my chest for entirely the right reasons: fear, terror, dread.

'I don't understand what you're saying.'

I prayed that he believed me. He reached across, inching my chin up so he could look at me.

There was a scowl on his face, or was it something else? I wished that I could decipher his expressions as easily as I'd translated his words.

And that was when we heard it – the cheer coming from the square at the center of the marketplace. An execution.

I didn't move, didn't blink.

But Max did. He flinched, as violently as if he'd just been slapped in the face. And then his eyes filled with such sadness that I felt like he was reading my most private inner thoughts.

The thoughts that said, *How can anyone celebrate*

such an event? Why would anyone want to be there to witness it?

It was the reason I avoided the central square each and every day.

I glanced around, nervous that someone might have seen his reaction. The law didn't dictate that we show joy at such an event, but it was best not to draw unwanted attention by showing revulsion, either, not with so many citizens willing to turn on one another.

After all, whoever had just been hanged in the square was considered a criminal – an enemy of the queen, possibly even a spy.

Or maybe just someone who refused to look away in the presence of a language that wasn't her own.

His hand reached for mine, his fingers grazing the sensitive skin at the back of my hand where the hand stamp was still healing. 'Are you sure you won't change your mind and walk with me? I'd really like to get to know you better. I think there's more to you than just a pretty girl with a sharp tongue.' He smiled fully then, his eyes crinkling – boyishly charming. I did my best not to notice.

'There's not. I'm just a simple vendor girl. And I'm late for work.' I turned on my heel, my head throbbing as I left him standing there on the sidewalk. I rounded the corner at the alley, wanting to get away from him as quickly as possible, and when I reached the back entrance and stepped into the familiar kitchen, I immediately felt the tension in my muscles seeping out in a rush.

I hadn't realized that I'd been so stiff in his presence, practically stonelike.

Or that I'd been holding my breath almost the entire time.

The sirens that shattered the still of the night felt like they were coming from inside my darkened bedroom. I sat upright in my bed, my body jolted from sleep far ahead of my brain. Beside me, I felt Angelina's body start, and then her fingers were digging into my side, clinging to me.

I blinked, trying to clear my thoughts, to make sense of what was happening as the sirens continued to blare from the streets outside.

An attack, I was slow to realize. *The city was under attack*. These were not the sirens of a drill.

My bedroom door crashed open, battering the wall behind it. I jumped again.

My father marched across the room in two long strides, handing me my boots and a jacket. My mother was already scooping Angelina off the bed and stuffing her into her own coat.

There was no time to be sleepy or sluggish. I shrugged into the sleeves of my jacket.

'*Take your sister down into the mine shafts.*' My father's voice was brisk, no-nonsense.

My mother handed my sister over to me, and I took her, my feet trembling as I stepped into my unlaced boots.

'What about you? You're not coming with us?'

My father dropped to his knees and tied my laces, while my mother petted Angelina's hair. She kissed us both, tears in her eyes.

'*No, we'll stay here, in case the troops come. If your mother and I are here, maybe they'll believe that it's just the two of us, that we live alone.*' He stood as he finished, meeting my worried expression. '*Then maybe they won't come looking for you and your sister.*'

His words didn't make sense to me, but none of this did. Why would the troops be interested in us at all, with or without our parents? Why would they bother searching for two girls, children who'd escaped into the night?

I shook my head, wanting to protest, to tell him that I wouldn't go without them, but couldn't find my voice.

'*Go, Charlaina. Now.*' He pushed me toward the door. '*We don't have time to argue.*'

I dug in my heels, but he was stronger than me and pushed harder than I could. Angelina clung to me, her arms wrapped tightly around my neck, Muffin dangling from her white-knuckled fist. Her eyes were wide and terror-filled.

I relented as the sirens outside assailed my ears; I had to get Angelina to safety.

'We'll come for you when it's safe.' My father's voice softened when he realized that I was moving, finally, toward the door.

Behind me, I heard my mother's sobs.

When I hit the streets, I drifted into a sea of hundreds – maybe thousands – of others who were also evacuating their homes. I was pushed and shoved from every direction, and I could feel panic coming off the crowd.

The siren's blast was earsplitting out here in the open – the loudspeakers were set up every hundred feet or so, and in an emergency like this they were converted to an alarm system. Angelina buried her head inside my jacket, trying to shield herself from the shrill noise. Above the blare, I could hear cries of fear and desperation, but nothing that indicated the city was under siege. There was no roar of engines overhead, no bombing, no sound of gunfire in the distance.

It didn't matter, though; the sirens were enough to keep me moving.

There were designated bomb shelters throughout the city, in churches, schools, and even abandoned passageways beneath the streets. That was where most of the people were headed. That was where families had arranged to meet in the event that the battles came close to home.

Yet Angelina and I wouldn't go to the shelters like the others, because our father feared that the shelters were too exposed. He worried that there was nothing secret about those hiding places. Safe from attack maybe, but not from the troops that could march into the city from the east, or from rebel forces fighting to overthrow Queen Sabara. And sometimes men – at least those in the midst of war – were to be feared more than any weapons. Men could be brutal, ruthless, deadly.

We were to hide someplace else. In the mine shafts just outside the city.

My boots pounded heavily against the ground as I shoved my way through the crowds, gripping Angelina as I leaned forward, battering body against body at times. The farther we moved away from the city's core, the thinner the masses grew, until it was just the two of us, and the occasional straggler, who remained in the night.

I knew we were close. I could see the walls that encircled the city – walls that had been constructed to keep us safe, to keep our enemies at bay, yet now contained us and trapped us inside. They were the only thing separating us from the mine shafts beyond.

I watched as others climbed those walls, others who probably had mind-sets similar to my father's.

We reached the perimeter, where the tall concrete barricade stood between us and our destination, and I untangled Angelina from my arms, forcing her to stand on her own two feet. 'You have to go first,' I insisted.

She stiffened, but did as I told her. I lifted her up the wall as high as I could and then I shoved with all my strength. I didn't have time to feel guilty as I listened to her land on the other side of the wall.

I scrambled up after her, using my boots to dig into the cement as I strained to pull myself up. When I was almost to the top, my foot slipped and the right side of my face slammed into the punishing concrete. The taste of fresh blood filled my mouth, and my eyes burned with unshed tears. I was sure I'd just shattered my cheekbone. But I refused to fall back to the ground behind me, and I clung to the wall, pulling until my arms burned. Finally I hooked one of my legs over the top and dragged myself the rest of the way up.

It was dark on the other side, with none of the light from the city finding its way through.

'Get out of the way,' I called down to Angelina, not sure exactly where she was.

I leaped from the wall, landing heavily on my feet

and crouching low, my hands splayed in the damp grass in front of me. Angelina scrambled forward, finding me in the darkness, her small hands reaching for me just moments after I hit the ground. Behind me, the sirens never relented.

I didn't waste any time; I reached around her waist, ignoring the fatigue in my arms and the fiery pain in my cheek, and I hauled her up again as I raced toward the mines ahead of us.

Brush and vines that grew around the mouth of the shaft looked like the shadowy outlines of jagged teeth. I barreled forward, not bothering to glance around to see who might be watching us. I needed to get inside, to find cover.

In the shaft, the blackness was almost complete, but I didn't slow. I reached out, using the chiseled walls to guide me. I knew these tunnels; Aron and Brook and I had passed many long days inside these passageways as children, exploring and setting up camps and pretending that the mines were our own private queendoms.

And now I prayed they would provide shelter for me and my sister.

We stayed hidden within the caverns long after the sirens had stopped screaming. My cheek continued to throb, finding rhythm with my pulse until I knew my eye would soon swell shut.

I let my lids drift closed, fatigue settling through me. I felt fingertips brush over the bruise that was already forming – Angelina's fingertips – and before I could stop her, her lips brushed over it too, kissing it lightly. So much like a mother might do.

My own fingers closed around hers, my eyes wide now, alert. But it was too late. Already I could feel tingling in the wake of her touch. Already I could feel the ache beginning to fade.

'Don't,' I whispered, thankful it was dark in the cavern, and that no one could see us. 'You can't do that. Never. Do you understand?'

She stared back at me, and I hated the flash of hurt I saw on her face in the gloom. I didn't mean to frighten, or even to scold her. I just wanted to protect her and keep her safe. But her touch reminded me of why I was here, of why I'd been injured in the first place, and it forced me to forget about the sirens, the panic, the pain.

We couldn't risk exposing our secrets in front of anyone. Ever.

'It's okay. We're safe now,' I soothed, squeezing her until I felt her relax again in my arms.

Eventually, Angelina drifted into a fitful sleep, but there was little chance that I would sleep tonight. I was tired – exhausted even – but the fear kept creeping back in, keeping me vigilant. That, and the nagging discomfort.

Beneath my jacket, my thin nightdress provided little warmth; Angelina provided the rest. I squirmed against the unyielding wall, trying not to disturb my sister, but my arm was cramped and my back and shoulders ached.

I couldn't stop thinking about what my father had said, about staying behind to stop an advancing army from searching for me and Angelina, and I wondered why it felt like something was lacking in his explanation.

It was a lantern's flame that shattered the darkness, casting a painful glow that scorched my eyes. But in that moment I saw Aron, and he saw me, and suddenly Angelina and I were no longer alone.

I could see the others now too. There were families who clung to one another for support, and people who had no one. Some I recognized, some were strangers. But we were all united now, seeking asylum within the cavernous underground walls.

Aron grinned as he scurried away from his family, rushing to where my sister and I were huddled. His father was too busy gossiping with those around him to notice his son's absence, his stepmother too meek to point it out.

'I was hoping you'd come here,' I exhaled gratefully when Aron reached us. I scanned the darkness behind him. 'What about Brook?'

Aron shook his head. 'She's not here. Her father

126

probably took her to one of the city shelters.'

'Speaking of . . .' I glanced dubiously at Aron's father. 'How did your dad get outside the city's walls?' I tried to imagine Aron pushing his father over the wall, the way I had Angelina.

'You'd be surprised how spry he can be with the threat of war at his heels.' His eyebrows were raised, but I could see he wasn't kidding, and I was mildly impressed.

Aron settled down beside me and I leaned heavily against him, more relieved to have his company than I could possibly express.

'How is she?' he asked, nodding toward Angelina.

I bristled, even knowing that there was no underlying meaning behind his words. I knew that if I looked into his eyes I wouldn't see the unspoken questions about why she was always silent, about why Angelina couldn't speak the way other children her age could. Questions that always worried me, and made me wonder if maybe they suspected something more, if maybe they'd realized she was different in other ways as well.

'She's fine,' I said a little too harshly. And then with less hostility: 'Just tired.' I knew Aron would understand that.

We stayed quiet, listening to the hushed voices around us that speculated on what might be happening in the city beyond the walls. There was no class division in those moments, yet I could distinguish variations in voice, in tone, in language. And even though I couldn't share what I heard with Aron, I understood every word of it.

People wondered aloud about the possibility of an all-out assault on the city. Others spoke of a malfunction in the city's defenses.

I hoped and prayed for the latter, unable to imagine anything worse while my parents were still out there.

Then, from somewhere in the darkness, I heard a voice echoing against the unyielding stone. And then another, and another, and soon everyone around us was rising to their feet out of respect, repeating the familiar words of the Pledge.

I lifted Angelina, refusing to release, or even to wake, her as I joined the others.

My breath is my pledge to worship my queen above all others.

My breath is my pledge to obey the laws of my country.

My breath is my pledge to respect my superiors.

My breath is my pledge to contribute to the progress of my class.

My breath is my pledge to report all who would do harm to my queen and country.

As I breathe, I pledge.

The words held more meaning now, on this night, than they ever had before. I wasn't sure if it was fear or patriotism, but in that moment I truly was making a vow to my queen. Beseeching her for protection that only she could offer.

Eventually, as we settled down again, and talk wore thin, the night became heavy. I succumbed to the fatigue and curled protectively around Angelina, Aron's body warm beside mine.

And somewhere, at some point, sleep became not just an option, but an inevitability.

Voices echoed down the interior caverns, jubilant and loud. The cries woke me, and I shrugged my weary shoulders, trying to work out the aches in my arms and neck. Angelina was already sitting up, pretending to whisper secrets into Muffin's ear.

I reached for her, touching her leg. 'Are you okay?'
She nodded.

It was light outside, and easier to see inside the passageways with daylight reaching down into them.

I looked up at Aron, who was still by my side. 'Has anyone come in here?'

He nodded, and I glanced around, realizing that almost everyone had gone, his family included.

I smiled at Angelina, who was still playing with Muffin.

'What was it?' I asked him. 'What caused the sirens?'

'Queen Elena's army breached the defenses of several of the smaller cities to the east. The sirens were set off as a precaution, just in case her forces came too close.'

That was good news; it meant that the Capitol was still safe. And, almost as importantly, that the alarm system had not malfunctioned: The warning had been deliberate. We could trust the sirens.

Even better, it meant that my father would be coming for us soon.

'You didn't have to stay, Aron. You could have gone home with your family.'

Aron wrinkled his nose, looking at me as if I were speaking nonsense. He shook his head when he answered, 'I wouldn't have left without you, Charlie. You know that.'

I did know; his words weren't even necessary.

I grinned then, and shrugged. 'Funny. I'd have left you in a heartbeat.'

But Aron didn't hesitate. 'Liar. You'd never leave me behind.'

When he found us, my father captured me and Angelina in a huge embrace, threatening to never let us go. Even Aron had earned a hug, whether he wished it or not. My father kissed both my sister and me, and he alternately whispered his gratitude and apologies into my ear. Angelina beamed as he tossed her into the air, catching her before she fell all the way back to the ground. It was like watching a grizzly playing catch with a feather.

We were safe, and that was all that mattered.

For now.

VII

Just because there hadn't been an actual attack on the city didn't mean that everything went back to normal. Not right away at least.

A curfew was imposed. It wasn't particularly early, or even strict, it was just another show of the queen's authority. It told us all that her power was unaffected by the rebels and their allies.

Each night now we heard three short bleats that were sounded through the city's loudspeakers. They were the signal that it was time, that everyone must evacuate the streets to seek shelter indoors. We were told it was only temporary, merely precaution.

It was one more change we would eventually grow

accustomed to, just as we had to so many others over the past days, weeks, months. Acclimation was the key to survival.

I'd tried to question my parents about that night, about why they hadn't gone with Angelina and me. About why they'd thrust us into the streets during the threat of a war. My father was indifferent to my frustrated inquiries, claiming I was overreacting, reminding me time and again that there'd been no real danger, that everything had been fine. But he'd had no way of knowing that would be the case. My mother simply changed the subject whenever it was broached, until eventually, I just let it drop.

Activities resumed in the wake of the sirens' warnings that night. Daily life continued, but for several days following, there was a feeling in the air, a sense of menace lurking like an unseen peril that stoked our fears and made each and every one of us a little wary.

It affected me in the same way it did everyone, consuming my thoughts and dictating my actions. I gave more forethought to everything I did, calculating risks, both real and imagined.

But that vigilance could only be maintained for so long before it wore thin, its veneer becoming unstable and then splintering, giving way to more usual behaviors and thoughts. Soon I found myself thinking about things less frightening than the threat of war, less intense than being awakened by sirens that cut through the night, and more . . . intimate. Although no less worrisome.

Max.

I wasn't certain at what point he'd begun to find his way back into my thoughts, but there was no longer any doubt that he was there. Distracting me.

I found myself thinking about him when I shouldn't be, wondering where he was and what he was doing.

I hadn't seen him again, not since that morning at the restaurant, when I'd all but demanded that he leave me alone, but I'd taken the time since our meeting to dissect those moments, to think and rethink his words, his actions. I replayed the sound of his voice in my head, time and time again; it was quite possibly my favorite part of our brief encounter.

I loved voices, I always had. Words held meaning, but voices held emotion.

I considered other things about him too, those that I could clearly recall. He was handsome and tall and proud, and even when I'd been frightened, I'd been drawn to him. Apparently, attraction knew no class limitations.

Yet I knew enough – even without being told – to know that Max was not of *my* class. Or rather, I of his. I was certain that he outclassed me.

But it wasn't his dialect that gave him away, because

even though it seemed impossible, I'd never heard his language before.

Not that it mattered; laws were laws. In the real world, the world outside of my childish fantasies, we would be permitted to interact, but only in the most superficial – or subservient – of ways.

Besides, I could still recall the other things about him, the things that were less appealing. He reeked of overconfidence.

That part of him, that kind of pride, reminded me of the Academy kids, and I found it difficult to tolerate arrogance like that.

I pushed aside all thoughts of Max as I faced yet another day of school and work. Daily routine made it easier to forget my country's troubles and the war waged upon us.

Made it easier, also, to forget the war waging within myself.

Brooklynn and Aron waited for me in the plaza before school, and when I handed my bag to Aron, I smiled to myself. Things were already getting back to normal.

As we walked, Aron nudged me, frowning apprehensively. 'Who is that?' he asked, his voice surprisingly low.

I shot him a quizzical look. 'Who?'

'Don't look now,' Brooklynn buzzed, hooking her

arm around my elbow. She leaned her head in close, only pretending to lower her voice the way Aron had. 'But over there' – she nodded – 'you seem to have attracted the attention of a delicious little something who can't take his eyes off you.'

Aron glowered, his voice slipping into Parshon, presumably to narrow the pool of people who could listen in on our conversation. *'It's not funny, Brook. He's been following us since we left the plaza, and he's only been watching Charlie. Do you want me to tell him to piss off?'* He said the words, but his feet continued moving toward our school, giving no real weight to his threat.

I glanced across the cobbled road, to where foot traffic was heavy.

Faces blurred together, making it impossible to see who they were talking about. I scanned and searched, trying to find someone who was looking my way, but there was no one. Everyone's eyes were focused on their own tasks, watching their feet as they walked, talking with their companions, admiring wares in the open booths they passed. But none of them were noticing me.

Just as I was turning away, deciding that Aron's overactive imagination had gotten the better of him, I caught a fleeting glimpse of the man they'd meant, hidden within the crowd.

It was Xander.

His face appeared so quickly that I'd very nearly missed it. But that brief glimpse was enough. I was almost positive it had been him. I shifted on my feet, trying to get a better view, but he was already gone.

I thought about crossing the street to go after him, to ask him why he'd left so suddenly that night at the club . . . and to ask him what – if anything – he knew about Max. But those were just thoughts, and I knew that I wouldn't act on them. If he'd wanted to talk to me, he wouldn't have vanished when I'd spotted him.

Finally I spoke in Englaise, hoping that Brook and Aron couldn't hear the disappointment in my voice. 'Well, whoever it was, he's gone now.'

Brooklynn tugged on my arm. 'Come on, Chuck,' she said, trying out a new nickname for me. 'We gotta go, or we'll be late.'

And despite his tough words, Aron had already gone ahead without us, so we were forced to run to catch up with him.

It couldn't have been Xander, I finally decided, convincing myself that I'd only seen what I'd wanted to see, that he'd simply been a figment of my imagination. Why would Xander be here? Why now?

He didn't exactly strike me as a marketplace kind of guy.

'Hey, Brook,' I said when at last we caught up with Aron. 'Don't call me Chuck.'

* * *

After the last bell of the day, I stood beneath the huge shade tree in front of the school and waited for Brooklynn and Aron. Its gnarled branches twisted above my head, casting dark shapes over my fair skin and protecting me from the glaring sun overhead.

The voice that interrupted my thoughts was like delicate silk to my ears and coarse sandpaper to my nerves. 'I hope you were waiting for me,' Max said.

I jumped, backing into the tree trunk; he was the last person I'd expected to see at my school. 'What are you doing here?' I asked as I turned to face him, but I stopped short when I saw him.

'Why do you always ask me that?' The hint of laughter stayed buried deep in his voice, never quite rising to the surface. No one else would have noticed, but I could hear it clearly. After all, voices were my thing. 'What? What's the matter?'

'You're in the military?' I asked, nodding toward his uniform, unable to tear my gaze away from it. It was the dark green of a soldier, its gold buttons gleaming even in the shadow of the tree.

His smile vanished. 'Yes, I'm in the army. It was the best way I could think of to rebel against my family.'

My heart was thrumming, yet I was intrigued by his answer. I looked up at him, finding those dark gray eyes. 'Your family didn't want you to join?'

'No, they were most definitely opposed.'

I weighed that, along with his knowledge of a language I'd never heard before. I wondered who he really was, and where he was from.

And then I frowned, confused as I recalled the way he'd reacted when we heard the applause coming from the gallows in the square. 'If you're in the army, what about that morning? At my parents' restaurant? You jumped when the crowd cheered.'

His response wasn't at all what I'd expected: He grinned. 'Do you think being in the army makes me heartless?' he answered.

'No, but I—' I what? I was surprised that someone in the military didn't support the queen's decision to have people hanged or beheaded for breaking the law? Was he not allowed to have his own thoughts, his own feelings?

I glanced around, nervous that someone might overhear us, on the verge of debating the queen's policies. It was not something we should be discussing in public, shielded only by the low-hanging branches of the tree. But instead I saw something even more startling. Across the street were the other two men who had terrified me so much with their strange language – giants among a normal human populace.

My pulse quickened beneath the surface of my skin. 'Why are they here?' I tipped my head in their direction, accusation thick in my tone.

'It's okay.' His dark eyes watched me closely while he answered. 'I asked them to wait over there. So you wouldn't be frightened.'

I straightened my shoulders. 'Why would I be afraid?' But my question was absurd. Their presence, even from across the busy street, terrified me.

'Don't worry about them, they're harmless. Really,' he replied, his hand crossing the space between us. I watched it move toward me, to where my fist clutched the strap of the book bag hanging from my shoulder, and his fingers brushed lightly across the tops of mine. I told myself I should take a step back – through the tree trunk if necessary – to create some distance between us, but somehow I couldn't move. 'I was hoping I could walk you home. And please, don't say no this time.' He kept his voice low.

I *wanted* to tell him no – I meant to, since it seemed the wise thing to say, but instead I heard myself answering, 'I-I don't even know who you are.' I tried to ignore the longing I felt to move closer to him rather than away.

This time his smile was easy to read, as if he'd just won a minor victory. 'You know more than I know about you. I don't believe you've even told me your name.'

My breath hitched in the back of my throat, and when I tried to speak my voice came out on a whisper. 'Charlie Hart,' I finally responded. It felt strange, introducing myself to him.

'Charlie? As in Charlotte?'

He held his hand out for mine, and this time I let him take it, folding it into his palm and wrapping his fingers around it. It wasn't an actual greeting; it was more like he was holding my hand. But still, I didn't stop him.

I shook my head, almost unable to speak at all. 'Charlaina,' I answered.

And then his thumb moved, the slightest caress, almost imperceptible.

Except that it hadn't gone unnoticed. I had most definitely felt it.

I pulled my hand away, startled by the reaction he'd set off deep in the pit of my stomach.

'Max,' I said for the first time, trying out the sound of his name on my lips. And then, worried that I sounded too infatuated – too like Brook – I asked, 'Why do you keep showing up? Are you following me or something?'

Aron interrupted us then, with Brooklynn right behind him.

Brook didn't seem to remember Max from that night at the restaurant, or the club, but nothing was stopping her from trying to get to know him now. She cast a direct glance his way, raking her eyes over his uniform, her gaze filled with so much enticement and appeal that I wondered how any male could ever resist her.

'Who's your friend, Chuck?' She cocked her head, but she wasn't really speaking to me at all. I'm not sure she even cared that I stood right beside her or that I'd been asking her all day long not to call me that.

I should have felt nothing, Max was virtually a stranger, yet I recognized the flash of jealousy that coursed through me in an instant. It was an unfamiliar sensation, entirely unwelcome.

Aron took a different approach, ignoring the newcomer altogether. 'Are you guys ready to go? I told my dad I'd be at the shop right after school.'

'Your dad's an ass,' Brook pointed out, her ravenous gaze never leaving Max. She held out her hand. 'I'm Brooklynn.'

'Max,' he introduced himself, taking her hand, but the movement was brief and controlled, and I wondered at the guardedness I suddenly saw in him.

Still, my spine remained stiff.

Aron didn't relent; he cast a sidelong glance at Max. 'Regardless of what you think of my father,' he said to Brook, 'I still have to be there. Are you coming or not?' He reached for my bag.

But Max beat him to it, taking the strap before Aron had the chance as he slid it from my shoulder. 'Actually, if you don't mind, I'd like to walk with Charlie today.' He said my name as if we were old friends, in need of catching up.

Aron glared at Max but spoke to me. 'What do *you* want to do?'

I glanced at Max. Where he seemed cautious with Brooklynn, I felt him opening up as he looked back at me. I wasn't sure that was a good thing.

But I shrugged anyway. 'It's okay. You two go ahead.'

Brooklynn's shoulders fell, and I realized she would probably be mad at me again. Still, I watched them go, Aron dutifully carrying her book bag.

'You ready?' Max asked, as he slipped my bag over his shoulder. It looked ridiculously small on him, and I was almost amazed that his arm even fit through the strap.

When he started walking, I fell into step beside him, wondering what his friends – who also wore the dark green uniforms of soldiers – planned to do while we walked. But then they started moving too, matching our pace while maintaining their distance from across the street. It was eerie, like having a long-distance shadow.

'Do they always follow you?' I asked, watching as people moved out of their path.

Max shrugged beside me, as if his answer meant nothing. 'We usually stay together, but I've asked them not to bother us. I told you, they're harmless.'

Examining the two men, I doubted the truth of his words but trusted the sincerity in his tone. As long as they stayed away from us, on their side of the street, I supposed that their presence was nothing but odd. Besides, it was far too easy to forget their existence at all whenever I looked at Max.

I would have to stop doing that: looking at him.

His hand slipped through my elbow, resting just inside the crook of my arm as he led the way. It was a familiar gesture, as if we were comfortable with each other. But that wasn't true . . . I could feel electric currents shooting up to my shoulder and all the way down to my toes. There was nothing *comfortable* between us.

And touching him – I would have to stop doing that as well.

But not now. Later, perhaps.

I wasn't sure how, but I managed to remember the questions I'd meant to ask him. I turned my head to the side and studied his profile. 'How did you find me? How did you know where I go to school?'

He didn't hesitate. 'There aren't that many vendor schools in the city, and this was the closest one to your family's restaurant.'

He was right, School 33 was one of only three inside the Capitol's walls; the rest were scattered throughout the country.

'So, why then? Why me?'

'I already answered that. You fascinate me.' He

gazed down, and with his free hand reached over to brush a strand of stray hair from my cheek. His fingers left a fiery path on my skin. '*You are beautiful,*' he breathed in that unfamiliar language. And, of course, he had no way of knowing that I'd understood what he'd just said.

'You can't do that.'

'What?'

'Speak to me like that.' I refused to look away now that he'd challenged me with his words, even though the meaning made me flush.

'Why not?'

'Because it's illegal. I'm a merchant; you force me to break the law when you speak to me in anything other than Parshon or Englaise. You know that.' I glared at him, daring him to argue.

'I don't force you not to look away. You make your own choice; any lawbreaking is your own decision.' I couldn't tell if he was mocking me, and I felt suddenly trapped by my own actions. His uniform stared back at me.

I stopped walking, and his hand fell from my arm. I narrowed my eyes. 'You know exactly what you're doing,' I accused. 'You came to me. I didn't seek you out. I didn't find you *fascinating*—'

He stopped too. 'Charlie, I was only teasing. Relax, I'm not worried about what you hear and what you don't. I just want to know you.' His eyes flashed with something real, something honest. Something intense. Then his lips curved into a sly grin. 'And are you trying to tell me you aren't a little bit fascinated by me?'

I was confused. Normally I felt more in control of myself, of my emotions. Yet with Max it was different. I was unsure of everything, because he was right. I *was* fascinated. And it went far beyond attraction.

But before I could question him about his language, he caught me off guard, turning quickly and ducking his head low as a group of men passed us on the sidewalk. I glanced at the men, wanting to see why Max would avoid them.

They were military men, five in all, dressed in the blue wool uniforms of the guard. They were lower ranking than Max's soldier grade, and they straightened in a show of respect as they passed, despite the fact that Max refused to acknowledge – or even look up in – their presence.

He kept his head, and his eyes, averted, an action that had nothing to do with his class, since men of the military didn't abide by the class system. As long as they were enlisted, class held no meaning; rank was the only true divider.

One of the men's eyes fell on me in a way that made me squirm inside – in the same way the bouncer's gaze had that night at Prey. Although in Max's presence, the glance was brief, and for that at least, I was thankful. I wasn't like Brooklynn in that regard. I preferred to go unnoticed.

For several moments we stood there, waiting in tense silence, until the men had gone.

Once they were past us, Max gripped my elbow again and pulled me away from the busy sidewalk, leading me toward the less traveled paths of the alleyways.

I should have been frightened to be alone with him, away from the busier streets of the plaza – in truth, he was a stranger. But I wasn't afraid.

'What was *that* all about?'

'What was what all about?' He frowned, nearly dragging me along until we were far from the foot traffic. Finally he slowed.

'Why wouldn't you look at those men?' I stopped walking, crossing my arms and refusing to take another step.

He raised an eyebrow. 'I don't know what you're talking about.'

'You know *exactly* what I'm talking about.'

Clearly agitated, he raked his hand through his hair. 'Can we just go? Claude and Zafir are going to notice that I've lost them and come searching for us soon.'

The hair on the back of my neck prickled at the mention of the other two men. But I didn't care. I wanted to know why he'd gone out of his way to avoid the guards we'd just passed. 'Not until you answer my question.'

'Your imagination has gotten the best of you, I think. Let it go.'

He was lying. I didn't know how I knew, but he was lying and I wanted the truth. 'Why should I? Is there something dangerous about you? Are you some sort of criminal? What are you hiding?'

He scowled. 'You're the only one who's broken the law. You're the one who refused to look away when I spoke to you in—' He stopped himself before he finished his thought. 'You're the one who needs to be more careful. Especially if you *actually* understood what I said.'

My heart raced and my hands shook; his allegation was no longer masked, and I could no longer pretend that he *might* suspect something.

He knew.

I shouldn't have trusted him; I should never have allowed him to drag me away from my friends and off the crowded walkways at the center of the city.

Suddenly Max was my enemy. I turned away from him and ran, not sure where I was heading; I only knew that I couldn't risk seeing his two enormous friends again either. So instead I moved in the opposite direction, running down a long, barren alleyway.

'Charlie, wait!' Max called, his voice filled with

frustration, but I could hear that he wasn't coming after me. 'Charlie! Don't go! Can we please talk about this?'

But I kept running, my feet pounding heavily beneath me, until I could no longer hear his words. Especially the ones I wasn't supposed to understand.

VIII

It was hard to work that evening, to pretend to be polite and to smile thinly at the customers who came into the restaurant. Making small talk was nearly impossible.

I was too caught up in my own sullen mood. Angry, and more than a little frightened as well. The implications of someone knowing my secret were almost too much to even consider. No one, aside from my parents, had ever understood what I was capable of.

No one had ever been allowed to know.

But Max had ruined all that, and I had no idea how he'd done it, what exactly I'd done to give myself away. I hadn't responded to his foreign words, and I'd certainly never admitted to understanding them.

And, most of all, I still wasn't certain which language he was speaking when he slipped into his class tongue. I shouldn't even be able to differentiate one from another. All I should be aware of was that it wasn't mine, and that it wasn't Englaise.

Yet he'd figured it – *and me* – out. How had he done that?

He said that I intrigued him, but why was that? Had he seen something in me that spoke of my unusual aptitude for deciphering words, for my understanding of all languages?

I must have been too obvious that night at the club, my fear too apparent.

But why did he care? Why had he come looking for me?

My father's voice shattered my daydreams, embarrassing me for being so foolish, and I was grateful that he couldn't possibly know what those dreams had been. '*Charlaina*? Did you hear what I said?'

'Sorry, what?' I shook away thoughts of Max. I needed to stop thinking about him. I couldn't trust him. I couldn't afford to let my defenses down again.

'There's someone here to see you.' He was irritated to be repeating himself; he balanced plates of food in both his hands. 'He's waiting by the alley door. You'd better hurry, though. This isn't a break.'

My stomach clenched. Max wouldn't come here, would he?

But I couldn't think of anyone else. Neither Brooklynn nor Aron would come to the back entrance. They were both comfortable enough to come through the front, and then act like they owned the place. My mother would usually show them to a table and feed them while they waited.

I tried to decide what to do, whether I should even go back there to find out, but my father was watching me – glaring, more like it – and I knew I had no choice. If it was Max, I needed to get him out of here. I needed to make it clear that he couldn't come back.

I slipped through the kitchen doors, feeling light-headed. The familiar smells did nothing to dispel my uneasiness.

The back door was closed, and I realized that only my father was rude enough to actually shut the door on someone while they waited in the alley. It was probably meant as a lesson for whoever dared interrupt me while I was working.

I took a deep breath, wrapping my fingers around the doorknob. I wasn't sure I was ready for this.

I tugged it open.

I could have been blown over by the barest of breezes.

Claude – Max's giant of a friend – stared back at me.

Or rather, *down* on me. And scared the hell out of me as I stumbled backward, nearly falling over my own feet. My heart practically exploded inside my chest.

I caught myself and tried to pretend that it was nothing as I looked around to see if anyone had noticed.

Everyone in the kitchen was watching me, including my mother, who wiped her hands on her apron, her mouth agape.

I glanced back at Claude, forcing myself to look somewhere in the vicinity of his vivid green eyes – to at least pretend I was brave enough to meet his gaze – when I finally spoke. 'Can I help you?' My voice shook so much that it was nearly unrecognizable.

'I was told this was yours.' Through the opening of the doorway he thrust my book bag at me. It dangled there, looking flimsy and insubstantial hanging from his enormous hand. 'Max asked me to deliver it to you.' His voice boomed, filling the kitchen as if it were too large for the small space. There were no other sounds, and without even looking around, I knew that everyone was still staring.

I reached out to take it and wished that my hand wasn't trembling. 'Thank you.'

He didn't respond to my words; he just turned on his heel and strode away. I half expected the ground to rumble beneath his footsteps as he retreated, but of course, it didn't.

He was just a man. A very large man.

I watched him go, not yet ready to face the curious stares of my coworkers. Or my mother.

I was still trying to sift through my jumbled feelings: the disappointment over seeing Claude standing there instead of Max, and the confusion and frustration with myself for feeling that way.

I tried to tell myself that it was better that Max hadn't come. Obviously he must have known that too or he wouldn't have sent Claude in his place.

But telling myself as much didn't make me feel any better.

That night in my room, I opened my bag. Angelina was supposed to be sleeping, but like so many nights she was still awake, hoping I would read to her.

'Only if you promise to be quiet. I don't want to get in trouble for keeping you awake,' I whispered, knowing my mother would separate us if she knew how often I read to my sister at night. 'And no complaints if you get nightmares,' I warned as I pulled out my history book.

Angelina nodded, her clear blue eyes filled with assurance.

I smiled at the expectant look on her face. 'Lie down, then. At least try to go to sleep,' I said, and then I explained to her what I was studying, like one of the teachers from my school. 'The Revolution of Sovereigns was the brief period of time in Ludania's history when the monarchy was overturned by the people, when we were self-governed – ruled by leaders of our own choosing.'

I read directly from the text now, which was written in Parshon: '*It was a concept sparked of idealism, and favored heavily by the masses who had risen up against Queen Avonlea and the rest of the Di Heyse family. It was a time of great violence, when the royal family was forced into hiding only to be hunted down and captured, slaughtered in public arenas so that the bloodlust of the people could be satisfied.*'

I peeked at Angelina. I would feel bad telling a four-year-old such tales if she hadn't already known them. We'd grown up hearing these stories, indoctrinated from an early age. Revolutionaries were not new in our history; it was important we understand that our survival depended on having a queen.

I shifted closer to Angelina, shuddering as I tried to imagine what it must have been like for those of noble birth during those times, to know that they must escape or be executed by their own countrymen, their own subjects. To be cast aside as rulers, only to be set on fire, or hanged, or beheaded.

I continued to read, knowing she was waiting. '*Their fortunes were plundered, their homes and lands divided among the new leaders, and all reminders of the former monarchs – statues, flags, paintings, monies – were destroyed, leaving no evidence of their existence.*' There was an image on the page, an artist's depiction of the former reigning family, since no photographs remained.

Angelina reached out and touched the drawing, her finger outlining the image of a girl about her age – a girl who'd presumably been executed simply because of her bloodline.

My skin tightened; it had been a dark time in our country's history.

'*But despite the idealism of the time, there was no real relief for the people under the new government. Old taxes were abolished only to have new ones created. A queen with too much power was replaced by a president who held even more influence.*' Angelina glanced up at me, her expression confused. I stopped reading and tried to explain what it meant, this time in Englaise. 'Because anyone could be a leader, regardless of their birthright, corruption was widespread. Elections were tainted, and taxes were raised to subsidize those who were in command. There were even more bloody overthrows.

'Queens from the other realms – those with *real* power – refused to cooperate with the new regime because the leaders were not of royal descent.' I looked at her as I explained. 'Since we didn't have a queen, our country was isolated from the rest of the world. We were denied essential trade, and the people soon learned that our country was *not* as self-sufficient as we believed, that we needed what those other countries had once provided. It had been foolish to believe that a mere mortal could be a ruler.

'First famine set in, followed almost immediately by disease.'

I curled against Angelina now, not needing my book; this was the part we'd been told countless times, words I'd memorized. Her breathing deepened, becoming heavier, and even though she still listened, I knew she was growing sleepy. 'This was the turning point for Ludania,' I whispered against her cheek. 'Dissatisfaction over the new regime became too much to bear, and the loss of lives was too great. Bodies overfilled cemeteries, and as the surplus of dead had to be burned, they created black clouds that choked the countryside. The people called for another uprising of sorts, a call back to the regents of their past.

'Only there were none. They had all been sacrificed at the altar of a revolution.' I spoke the last words slowly, quietly, as Angelina's eyes fluttered, succumbing, at last, to sleep.

It didn't matter; she knew how it ended. We all knew.

The other countries were petitioned by covert factions who sought to overthrow the new 'democracies', and spies were sent forth to look for those of royal lineage closely related to that of the old throne.

We needed a new leader. We *had* to have a queen.

Eventually, one was found. One who was willing to take her place on the throne and lead our country off its own path of self-destruction.

She was a strong woman – so history tells – of royal blood and regal bearing. When her forces arrived, easily overtaking the complacent and poorly skilled armies of the presiding government, she showed mercy to her predecessors only in that they were killed as privately and as painlessly as possible.

A queen that powerful was easily accepted by the monarchies of the surrounding countries, and soon sanctions were lifted, trade and communication were re-established. The people of Ludania had food once more.

That was when the class system was first imposed. It was designed to discourage future uprisings, to keep people living apart so ideas of rebellion could not be comingled.

Language became a tool, a way to complete that division. It became illegal to speak – or even to acknowledge – another class's language. It was a way to keep secrets, a way to exert power and control over those who were . . . less.

That had been centuries ago – back when cities had names – and even though some things had changed, both the class system and the monarchy still remained intact. Stronger now than ever before.

Words had become the ultimate barrier. The law made it criminal to communicate in anything other than our birth tongue or Englaise. Anyone who showed any aptitude toward language was executed. Persecution kept anyone else from trying.

After hundreds of years, the ability to decipher the words of another class had been lost, making it impossible to master a language other than our own. We'd become resistant to the nuances of foreign dialects.

Yet even if everyone were equal, I would still be on the outside, because I understood *all* languages. And my ability didn't end with the spoken word. I could decipher all manners of communication, including those that were visual or tactile.

My father had once taken me to a museum, one of the few that hadn't been burned to the ground during the Revolution, and he'd shown me the way the world had once been, the way our country had once lived as a single unified nation. Maybe not always at peace, but not divided into a caste system either.

In the museum, we'd seen beautiful drawings that had once been used as a form of communication by ancient civilizations . . . artfully crafted sketchings that our tour guide explained had been translated by scholars into Englaise.

Yet when the tour guide read their meaning to us, I knew he was mistaken, that the translation was faulty.

I'd understood what the beautifully drawn words really said. I knew the true meaning behind the art, and

I'd told him so, revealing the correct message of our ancestors.

The outraged guide had insisted that I renounce my lies and apologize for my rebelliousness. My father masked his fear with embarrassment and made excuses to the infuriated man, maintaining that my childish imagination had simply gotten the best of me. He'd argued that I was fanciful and difficult, and he'd dragged me away. Away from the lovely words, and away from the museum, lest the man discover that I was accurate in my interpretation.

Lest he turn me in for understanding a language that was not my own.

I was first scolded for my outburst, and then hugged tightly out of fear and relief. My father reminded me how unsafe it was for me to share my ability.

With anyone.

Ever.

I was six years old, and it was only the second time I'd seen my father cry.

The first was when I was four and he'd killed a man.

The door to my room opened, and my mother's shadowed silhouette slipped inside, carrying with her the smells of baked goods that seemed to permeate her skin after years of working in the restaurant.

She nodded her head toward Angelina. '*You should*

be sleeping too, Charlaina. It's a school day tomorrow.'

'I know, I'm almost finished.' I answered her in Englaise and closed the book, which I could no longer concentrate on anyway.

She sat down on the bed beside me, smoothing my hair from my face and then stroking my cheek with the backs of her fingers. *'You look tired.'*

I didn't tell her that she was the one who looked tired. That her golden features had grown faded, her proud stance weary. I was never convinced that my mother had been born to work such a hard life.

Maybe no one was.

I nodded. 'I am.'

She bent to kiss my forehead, and the familiar scent of warm bread filled my nose. It was the scent of my mother. She reached for the book, taking it from my hands.

As she lifted it, a slip of paper drifted from between the pages, settling on top of the heavy covers that blanketed me. My mother didn't notice it, and as she turned to set the book on my bedside table, I reached for the note, unfolding it.

I knew immediately that I wasn't the one who'd hidden it there.

And when I read the words written on the page, I drew in a sharp breath.

'What is it, Charlaina?' she asked, turning back to me.

161

I shook my head but kept the note hidden beneath the covers, clutched within my fist.

She raised her eyebrows, as if she was going to ask again, when we heard the three familiar bursts of the siren coming from outside, reminding all that it was time to take cover, that the streets were now off-limits. When she turned back to me, her curiosity was forgotten and she reached for the lamp, turning the flame all the way down. 'Good night, Charlie,' she said, this time in Englaise, surprising me, since she normally refused to speak it within the confines of our home.

'*Good night, Mom*,' I answered with a sudden mischievous grin, surprising her by speaking her favored language.

When the door closed and I was certain she was gone, I turned the flame back up.

I had to read it again.

Or maybe two . . . or three . . . or fifty more times, I thought, pulling out the rumpled note and carefully unfolding it.

The paper was now creased in places that it hadn't been before, where my fingers had squeezed it, hiding it from my mother's view.

I looked at the words scrawled there, wondering at them, trying to decide exactly how I felt about them.

Every muscle in my body tensed. The hairs on my arm stood on end.

I read it one last time, committing the words to memory so I could recall them later. Then I tucked it away again inside my book before turning off my lamp once more.

I listened to the sounds of my little sister's sleeping breaths as I wondered what it would be like to *hear* those words rather than just to read them. To listen to them quietly whispered in the night.

In any language.

IX

I couldn't bring myself to look at it again. Not once over the next few days did I even allow myself to peek at the note nestled inside the flap of my schoolbook.

I was too afraid. Too worried about the words I'd read, words heavy with meaning and laced with the promise of things not said.

I was terrified of him.

I tried to concentrate on my lesson, on the professor lecturing us from the front of the classroom. He was passionate, even after years of teaching the same subject, the history of our people, the Vendor class.

Our lessons were divided into blocks that included three hours in history – one hour of Vendor history and how we fit into our society; another about the history of our country; and yet another about world history, which was filled with stories of ancient aristocracies, democracies, and dictatorships that had risen and failed before the Time of Sovereigns.

Because we were vendors, there were also classes in trade, accounting, and economics. Our one discretionary hour could be fulfilled by anything in the arts, sciences, or culinary skills. Still, these elective classes had a purpose that served a vendor's skill set. Even art involved learning about textiles, potteries, and graphics that could be packaged and sold. All of it training, preparing us to take our place in society.

I took halfhearted notes on the lecture, pretending that what the teacher said was more interesting than the letter concealed inside the book beneath my desk.

When I shifted my foot, I inadvertently bumped my leather bag, spilling its contents onto the floor. I bent over to pick up the mess, ducking my head beneath my table, gathering pencils and sheets of paper that had slipped out. I took great care to arrange everything, placing it all neatly inside. I saw the folded note peeking up from behind the cover of the book in which I'd hidden it.

I brushed my fingertips across the lineny surface, my skin sparking with electricity, my fingers itching to pull it free.

I shouldn't, I told myself, even as I held my breath and watched myself withdrawing it from the book. I tried to tamp down the feeling of anticipation coursing through me at the same time I argued that it was a mistake to look at it again.

It didn't deserve any more of my time. *He* didn't deserve the space he *already* occupied in my mind.

I glanced around to see if anyone had noticed me there, tucked beneath my desk, reading a note that I'd already memorized.

No one paid me any attention.

I held the letter, vividly picturing the six words written inside the folds. Six words that I already knew by heart. Six words that meant more to me than they should.

I unfolded the top third of the paper, then the bottom, purposely keeping my eyes unfocused for just a moment.

My heart stopped.

And then my eyesight cleared.

I pledge to keep you safe.

I spent the rest of the day trying to forget the note, trying to undo the damage I'd done in the moment that I'd allowed myself to read it just one more time. The words now felt inescapable, as if they'd somehow been etched into me and the letters were traced, ragged and raw, into my very flesh. The meaning behind them made my head ache.

He was asking too much from me with that simple pledge.

How could he vow such a thing? How could I take

such a promise seriously? He barely knew me, and I certainly didn't know him. Not well enough to trust him. Not with the kind of information he already knew, or at least suspected he knew, about me.

The kind that could get me killed.

I couldn't allow myself to consider his words, so I decided to ignore them. Decided to forget about the note. To forget him.

I gave up trying to concentrate on my schoolwork and busied myself with other tasks instead. I went to the restaurant after school, even though it wasn't my day to work. I stocked the kitchen, and did dishes, and cleaned tables and countertops. I inventoried supplies that had already been inventoried, and I helped my mother chop vegetables until there was nothing left to occupy my restless hands.

Even then my mind refused to stop fixating on the letter he'd written.

Finally I decided I had only one choice.

I grabbed a candle and marched through the kitchen, out the back door, and into the alley behind the restaurant.

I found a spot in a darkened corner, away from the view of passersby on the street beyond, and I crouched down, cupping my hand around the candle's wick as I lit it. I reached into my pocket and pulled out the folded note.

I thought about reading it again – just this one last

time – but I didn't need to. I would never need to look at it again; those words would haunt me forever, even in the absence of the paper they were written on.

I held the corner of the sheet above the candle, hesitating only slightly before letting the fire claim it. I watched as the flames consumed it, and I dropped it to the ground before they could reach all the way to my fingertips.

Ash flickered in front of me, first orange, and then black, and then pallid shades of gray, caught in the slow currents of air that carried it away.

I felt better once the paper had disintegrated, once it could no longer tempt me.

And that was how Brooklynn found me, in a darkening alley, squatting over a candle as I stared at its tiny flame, feeling free at last.

Brooklynn was a master at convincing me to do things I didn't want to do; she always had been. When I was barely older than Angelina, Brook had talked me into cutting my own hair and pretending to be a boy. She thought it would be funny, a joke to play, tricking the other kids at school into thinking there was a new boy in our class.

Unfortunately, my parents didn't get the joke.

And, even worse, I really did look like a boy with my newly shorn hair. That was the year the kids stopped calling me Charlaina and started calling me Charlie.

The nickname was fine. It suited me better anyway, and the hair eventually grew back. That was also the year I learned that I couldn't always trust Brooklynn to put my interests ahead of her own.

It wasn't because she was a bad friend . . . she wasn't. It wasn't even because she was vindictive or spiteful . . . she was neither. She was just . . . reckless.

Needless to say, I was forced, at times, to stand my ground with Brooklynn in order to avoid doing things that weren't best for me.

Fortunately, this wasn't one of those times, and in this instance, Brook had come along at precisely the *right* time. A time in which I most needed her particular brand of distraction. When I most needed to be pulled out of *my* world and into *hers*.

A night out with Brooklynn was exactly what I needed to take my mind off of . . . other things.

The rally at the park would be the perfect distraction.

We had to promise my father that we'd stay together – a promise I thought was meant more for Brooklynn's benefit than for mine – and my mother that we'd be home in time for curfew. I'm not sure where else she thought we would be that late – the park would be emptied long before the sirens sounded. The last thing anyone wanted was to get caught breaking the law.

And, as always, I kept my Passport pressed safely against my chest.

I knew what to expect long before we arrived at the riverfront gathering. Back when the 'rallies' had first begun, they'd been something else altogether, their name evoking an entirely different response. They'd originated as events intended to show support for those who'd been recently enlisted, a celebration of our newest troops as the threat of war from enemies, both inside and outside our borders, became imminent.

But as weeks became months, and months stretched into a year, the rallies had taken on an entirely different meaning. Now they were simply state-sanctioned parties. Events for the young to gather at the riverfront park under the pretense of patriotism, using the excuse to come together in the night, to dance and shout and sing and rejoice.

Only once had the rallies become dangerous, as a drunken crowd became restless and belligerent under the leadership of a man calling for dissent. Violence had broken out, spilling into the streets of the city.

Several of his activists had been killed by the very same military that the rallies had been designed to honor.

But that was many months ago, and now guards were set up to patrol the monthly gatherings, maintaining order before chaos had the opportunity to erupt. Before party became protest.

And tonight, as spring crested toward summer and the nighttime temperatures grew warmer, revelers were filled with cheer. The air along the banks of the river carried the promise of song and drink and dance. The sound of instruments, played together in practiced harmony, stretched well beyond the lush landscape of the park and into the streets beyond. It was hopeful and intoxicating.

Brooklynn gripped my hand, making sure I couldn't change my mind and bolt. But she didn't need to. I was happy to be here, grateful for her presence and for the distraction of the celebration.

We passed a group of men playing a variety of instruments beneath a dense cluster of leafy trees. They were singing, both loudly and poorly. I laughed at their efforts to draw our attention as their voices rose. Brooklynn giggled and encouraged them, waving and winking and swaying her hips. They shouted at us to come back, for *us* to sing for them, but Brooklynn pulled me along, ignoring their discordant pleas.

We stopped at a flowering bush, and while she was humming, her body moving to the sounds around us, Brooklynn plucked a flawless red flower and slid it into my hair, tucking it neatly behind my ear.

She leaned in and kissed my cheek. 'You look beautiful,' she said, this time winking at me.

I grabbed both of her arms and narrowed my eyes,

letting the hint of a smile curve my lips. 'You're drunk already, aren't you?'

Her face broke, and she grinned. 'Maybe just a little.'

She took my hand, and again we were moving. Torches lined the winding pathways as we got closer to the center of the park, to the center of the rally, where the festivities were well underway.

Several people greeted us, some we knew and some we didn't. Brooklynn knew many more than I did, especially among the guards dressed in blue. She did her best to introduce me, but I knew eventually she would forget I was even with her and she would wander away from me. It was in her nature. I understood that.

Someone gave us drinks, and the cool liquid traced fiery fingers down my throat, relaxing my body and quieting my mind. Brooklynn probably didn't need another, but she took it anyway.

Finding her way into the crowd beneath the canopy of blossoming trees, she went off to dance while I watched her go. She raised her hands high above her head and twirled in hypnotic circles, her eyes – and her actions – inviting others to move closer to her.

As always, I wished that Aron were here. He would have stayed with me. He would never leave my side.

But Aron was against Brook's rules. She didn't like to take him with us on our outings. She was content to compete with him for my attention during the daytime hours, the way it had always been, but only because she had to. At night it was supposed to be just the two of us.

Her rule was absurd, really, considering she found new friends every time we went out and was quick to abandon me if the opportunity arose.

I glanced up in time to see Brooklynn dancing with a partner now, a boy with scruffy hair who pulled her close, his arm wrapped around her waist while she gazed boldly into his eyes as if they were the only two who existed within the crowded space.

Before I could roll my own eyes, a steely voice from behind intruded on my thoughts, causing me to shiver even in the balmy night. 'You shouldn't be here. The park isn't safe after dark.' And then I felt his hand – his palm – lightly stroke the length of my bare arm, a tender gesture, at odds with his tone.

My stomach plummeted, and I felt sick at the very same time that I noticed a distinct spark of something else flickering through me. Something far too close to hope. I quelled that part of me, responding instead to the warning in his voice as I set my jaw, refusing to turn around.

'Fortunately for me, it's not your decision where I go after dark. Or who I keep company with.' I pulled my arm away, ignoring the hairs that prickled in the wake of his touch. I stalked away, to the other side of the dancers, keeping my eyes focused on Brook so I wouldn't lose her in the crowds. And also so I wouldn't have to look at Max. So I wouldn't have to face his unsettling gray eyes.

I could hear his footsteps following right behind me. 'Charlie, wait. I didn't mean to tell you what to do.' His voice was gentler this time, begging me to listen.

I shook my head – my stubborn refusal – but it was more to myself. I doubted he'd even noticed the slight movement in the flickering torchlight.

A part of me wanted him to follow me – I was almost certain I did – even though I was very nearly running away from him. My heart was speeding, and the confusion of my own reaction made me feel dizzy and unsure.

My entire body was tingling as if it had never been more alive.

Then his hand covered mine, pulling me to a stop as he stood before me. The battle within me surged until I was overwhelmed with frustration.

I wanted my hand back. And I didn't.

It seemed as if it belonged in his, yet I refused to even look at him.

'Charlie.' Just that one word, that one whispered sound, and he had my complete attention.

I tried to breathe around my pride, but it was too thick in my throat. His thumb moved, ever so slightly, releasing a floodgate of currents that rocked through me.

My shoulders slumped.

'Go home. I can't keep my promise if you put yourself in harm's way.'

His promise. The reminder of his note sent chills over my entire body, and still, I felt myself straining to be closer to him.

'I'm not leaving,' I insisted, afraid to raise my eyes. Afraid to see him, and to let him see what I was trying so hard to hide. That I wanted to keep him near me.

He dropped my hand, and it fell to my side feeling strangely cold and empty. When he spoke again, his voice was hard, clipped. 'What if I insist that you go?'

My eyes shot upward, staring at him in disbelief. 'You can't do that!'

But as soon as I looked at him, I knew that I was wrong. I knew he could do *just* that.

His uniform was crisp, immaculate, commanding. It was all the authority he'd need to have me escorted from the park, to have me taken back to my home.

It wouldn't matter that I wanted to stay; Max could force me to leave.

My jaw tightened and I scowled at him, taking a step closer. The only conflict I felt now was toward him. 'You wouldn't dare! I have every right to be here. I haven't done anything wrong, I'm not the one harassing people, you are! You're the one who should leave.' I reached out and tried to shove him out of my way, but he didn't budge. He didn't even flinch. 'I just want to be with my friend tonight,' I rasped, my voice verging on hysteria. 'If I'd known you would be here, I wouldn't even have come.' I tried to step around him, but his arms reached out and were around me before I realized what had happened.

My face was pressed against his chest; I could hear his heart thrumming beneath the thick wool of his jacket. I could feel the warmth of his body straining toward me, the way mine yearned to be near him. And the spicy scent of him, as I breathed it in, made me light-headed. I craved more. So, *so* much more.

My resolve slipped, and then crumbled. I took harbor within his arms.

'And if *I'd* known you were going to be here, I'd have come just to see you.' Max's voice rumbled beneath my ear. Then he spoke again, in a language that should have been foreign to me. '*All I want is to keep you safe, Charlie. It's all I've ever wanted.*'

Just like that it was over, the brief and idyllic moment in which I'd come so close to letting down my guard. I stiffened before I could even respond, wishing he hadn't just said that.

Not in that way.

I shoved away from him, untangling myself from his arms.

When I glared at him, I could see that he knew what he'd done, that he understood where he'd gone wrong. He should have spoken in Englaise.

'Charlie, I'm sorry.'

But I was already disappearing into the crowd, and this time he didn't come after me.

Even though a part of me still wanted him to.

Brooklynn was breathless by the time she found me, and even though I was no longer in the mood for her jubilance, she brought it with her anyway. She was intoxicated off both attention *and* drink. It was her perfect high.

She reached for my hand, drawing me from the spot where I'd been hiding, among the trees that stood along the river's edge. What the foliage didn't conceal, the darkness had taken care of, keeping me out of sight.

But Brook had been determined, and I'd heard her calling my name long before she'd discovered me there, tucked into the dark space where I could sulk in silence.

'I just met the most amazing guy. You've got to come meet him. Trust me, Charlie, you're gonna love him!' Her hands over mine didn't feel comforting or strong the way Max's had. Her skin felt warm and soft, but her fingers dug insistently into mine.

I took a few steps but only because she was pulling me, and I stumbled onto the path. 'If he's so great, why don't you hang out with him? You don't need me.'

Brooklynn grinned, her eyebrow raised. 'Because he has a friend. A really cute friend.' She pulled again and dragged me another couple of steps. 'Come on, you don't want to miss this.'

I shook my head, digging in my heels. 'I'm not in the mood to meet anyone. Not tonight, Brook.'

She let go of me and put her hands on her hips. Her posture was defiant, her brown eyes glittering. 'Why not? Because of your little soldier boy?'

I stared at her, not sure I understood her meaning.

She shrugged. 'Yeah, that's right; I saw the two of you. So what, Charlie? I also saw that he didn't come after you. Why waste your time sitting here alone and letting him ruin all your fun?'

I might have hated Brooklynn at that moment, or as close to it as I ever had before.

She'd watched me argue with Max and had let me wander away by myself, knowing I was upset. She was more worried about getting back to some guy she'd just met than she was that I might have needed her.

But there was something else, too, something about the way she'd said 'soldier boy', her voice dripping with venom.

Was Brook jealous?

I thought about that afternoon at the school, when Max hadn't paid attention to her, even after she'd tried her best to make him notice her. Brooklynn wasn't used to being ignored.

And she certainly wasn't used to being ignored for me.

Suddenly I wondered if that was why she liked having me around – if it made her feel better knowing that men would almost always notice her before they would me. I wondered if that was why Aron couldn't come with us, if it was because he had seen through her outward appearance and had decided that he liked me better.

Yet, still, I guess I really wasn't mad at Brook. I wasn't even envious that when we returned to the rally so she could introduce me to the guys she wanted me to meet, their eyes would be on her and not on me.

I should be, I supposed. I should be angry and hurt and petty, the way she was.

Instead I just felt sorry for her.

Max was still there. I couldn't see him, but I knew he was nearby. I could feel his presence as surely as I could feel my own.

I played along with Brooklynn, pretending to have fun, if only for Max's benefit, to let him know that I didn't care if he thought I should leave.

I met Brook's friends, and she was right, the boy she'd met – the one with the messy hair who she'd been dancing with before – seemed very nice. His friend, Paris, was cute too. Plus, they were Vendors. They wore the simple fabrics, in shades of brown and gray, that were familiar to me. And with them I wouldn't have to pretend not to understand their words, no matter which language they spoke in. These were the kind of people I *should* be keeping company with.

But I wasn't wrong when I'd guessed that both of them would spend the evening watching Brooklynn. Even Paris, who did his best to make me feel at ease, couldn't keep his eyes off her entirely.

It didn't really matter, though; I didn't want to be there with him, either. Every fiber of my body strained to locate Max's presence among the revelers, until I felt anxious and tense. Still, I laughed at the boy's jokes and took the second drink he offered me, ignoring the fact that my head was already starting to spin.

When his hand was at my hip and he was pulling me toward the dancers, I followed, our shoulders bumping against each other as he led the way. He pulled me closer than I was comfortable with, and I was shocked by my reaction, considering that not so long ago I had wondered what it might be like to press myself up against Max. With Paris, it was just the opposite; I was repelled by his touch, my body resistant to his.

Still, his arms were strong, his hands insistent, and he leaned in close.

I glanced around, trying not to feel nervous as his alcohol-laced breath mingled with mine. His body was moving with the music, and rather than cause a scene I decided to go along with it, only half dancing, and only half following the beat. I wondered how far into the song we already were, and how soon I could make an unnoticeable escape.

'*You have pretty eyes,*' he complimented me in Parshon. His words were hot and sticky against my face. I almost laughed, trying to remember at what point he'd stopped staring at Brooklynn long enough to notice *my* eyes.

Instead I smiled weakly, leaning my head away from him. 'Thanks,' I answered loudly above the music, wishing the song would hurry up and end already.

But it wasn't a pause in the music that interrupted the awkward dance; it was something I wasn't prepared for. Something I could never be prepared for.

The roar of the sirens exploded as if the sound was echoing from inside my own head, its shrill din shattering the night. These weren't the bleats of the curfew.

I felt frozen in place, my mind numbed by the sudden chaos breaking out around me.

Screams erupted, although I could scarcely hear them above the noise. I felt myself being shoved from every direction as people tried to flee, crushing against one another in an effort to escape the park, to seek cover. To find refuge.

I searched for Brooklynn. *I had just seen her!* But now I couldn't locate her amid the confusion and the press of bodies.

'Brooklynn!' I yelled out, but my voice was lost in the commotion around me.

I watched as a girl, about my own age, fell to the ground in the crush to get away. A man ran over the top of her, his heavy boot kicking her square in the head. She tried to get out of the way of the others, crawling across the ground toward the edge of the path, her fingers clawing at the dirt beneath her, but she couldn't move fast enough.

She glanced up, looking dazed as blood trickled down the side of her face.

The moment her head lifted I realized that I recognized her.

It was Sydney, the Counsel girl from the Academy who taunted us when we passed on our way to school each day. The one who had come into my family's restaurant that night and mocked me, thinking I couldn't understand what she'd said.

Before I could tell myself otherwise, I was running, racing toward her. I was jostled and bumped, shoved and pushed, in my effort to get to her, each individual on a mission to save only themselves.

By the time I reached her, I almost stepped on her myself. Body was pressed against body, and I was nearly swept past her.

I thrust myself as hard as I could through an opening in the crowd, forcing my way through. A hand reached into my hair and yanked. My scalp felt like it was on fire, yet I leaned forward, jerking my head away and crying out in pain.

No one heard me. Or even cared.

I could see Sydney, still struggling to drag herself out of their way. She looked broken. I staggered a little, but I was determined, and I reached down to grab her, gripping her beneath her arms and hauling her backward, farther off the pathway. Farther from the punishing feet that battered her.

The wailing sirens were constant, but I didn't have time to worry about what they meant.

I leaned down and yelled right next to her ear, hoping she could hear me. 'Can you stand? Can you walk?'

She looked confused as she blinked up at me, and I wondered if she'd even understood what I'd just asked. Then slowly, almost too slowly, she nodded, reaching out her hand for me, allowing me to help her to her feet.

She was wobbly at first, swaying, and I held on to her, waiting for her to steady herself. She opened her mouth and said something, but I couldn't hear her. The words were swallowed by the roar around us.

I shook my head and shrugged.

She stepped closer, her mouth nearly at my ear, and tried again. 'Why are you doing this?' Her voice was pinched.

I wasn't sure what to say, how to answer her question, so I didn't try. 'We have to get out of here! Where do you live?'

She just pointed east. It was where I'd suspected she would need to go, where a Counsel family would live, in the upper-class neighborhoods of the east side of the city.

But I needed to head west, toward my end of town. Toward my family. Toward Angelina.

My heart squeezed. I needed to find my sister.

'I can't go with you!' I screamed as loud as I could. 'Can you get there on your own? Do you know where to meet your family?'

Her hand shot out, grasping mine, and I realized that she was giving me her answer. She didn't want me to leave her. She didn't want to be left alone to find her way.

She was coming with me.

The crowds had thinned; most of the people had already escaped into the night, in search of shelters where they could hide. We were no longer in danger of being trampled, but there was something else to fear as strange new sounds popped in the distance, one after the other, rising above the ever-present shriek of the sirens.

Holding my hand, Sydney recoiled beside me, her body shuddering after each new explosion.

I recognized these unfamiliar sounds, even though I'd never actually heard them before.

Bombs.

They were the sounds of bombs.

This wasn't a drill, and it wasn't a warning. The city was under attack.

I had to get to Angelina.

We hadn't gotten far when I felt myself being yanked from behind, and before I could wonder who was pulling at me – or why – I was already stumbling backward, thrown wholly off balance.

I fell into Max's arms for the second time that night, although this time I had no intention of pushing him away. And from the feel of his arms around me, like iron bands, I doubted he would have allowed it.

'I was looking everywhere for you!' He was yelling, but even if he hadn't been, I would have heard those words. 'Where were you?'

I could barely breathe, so when I tried to answer it came out muffled against his chest.

He relaxed his grip so I could tilt my head back, and as soon as I saw the look on his face, any anger I still felt dissolved.

He was worried about me! I hated that it was this moment, with the sirens threatening and the sound of weapons crashing through the night sky, that I felt my heart softening.

I reminded myself that Angelina was still out there

as I squashed these new and unwelcome feelings. This wasn't the time for infatuation.

'I need to get to my family! I need to find my sister!' I called out, wiggling free from his arms and running again, leaving them both to decide whether or not they would follow.

I couldn't hear their footsteps, but I knew they were there with me. Max kept up easily and ran beside me. I worried about Sydney, though. I thought she might fall behind, but I didn't stop. I couldn't stop. And every now and then I would catch a glimpse of her out of the corner of my eye, assuring me that she was, somehow, keeping up.

The sirens were everywhere, but I couldn't tell which direction the explosions were coming from. At times I felt like we might be running toward them, while at others they seemed to be very far away, on the other side of the city.

Maybe it was both.

Men and women, children and the elderly, had been swarming the streets since we'd left the park. But by the time we'd reached the west end of the city, the streets were all but abandoned. I worried that we were already too late, that my family had taken shelter somewhere and I'd be unable to find them in the night.

I didn't allow myself to consider the other possibility . . . that the war had come too close to our home.

I almost cried with relief when we turned the final corner and all the houses on my street were still standing, unscathed by the bombs that were pummeling other neighborhoods in the city.

There was the flicker of candlelight coming from inside my house.

'Stay here!' I yelled to Max and Sydney.

Sydney's face was creased with pain, and I knew it had been too much for her to run so far, so fast. Blood dried along her left cheek, crusting in her hair. She seemed grateful for the moment's rest.

I rushed to the front door just as it was opening from the inside. My father nearly ran into me, carrying Angelina in his arms.

'*Oh, thank heaven! Magda! Magda!*' he called to my mother as he pulled me against him. '*She's here! She's safe!*'

He squeezed me tight, Angelina smashed between us. My mother pushed past my father, grabbing me, touching me, ensuring herself that I was all in one piece.

Then my father handed his squirming bundle over to me; Angelina tangled her fingers into my hair, wrapping her arms around my neck.

'No!' I shouted, understanding his intentions. 'You have to come with us! You can't make us go alone!' My voice was hoarse from yelling, but I needed him to listen to me.

The crushing sound of a bomb rattled the air nearby and I jolted, ducking my head without thinking. The explosions seemed to be growing louder. And closer.

He shook his head, and I could see his answer written on his face. He'd already made up his mind. 'We're staying. You girls are better off without us.' This time he spoke in Englaise . . . so unusual for my father, so out of character. I wasn't sure which surprised me more, that he was casting his daughters out into the war-torn streets of the city, or that he'd not spoken in Parshon.

My mother handed me a pack and I took it, slinging it over my shoulder. '*There's food inside. And some water!*' She was yelling her words at the same time my father was pushing me down the front step. '*When this is over, we'll come for you. Until then, protect your sister, Charlaina.*' She stepped onto the street, gripping my shoulders and staring me hard in the eye, serious in a way that I'd never seen her before. Her words were tough – harsh. '*And don't come back to the house until you know, without a doubt, that it's completely safe.*' She shook me once. '*I mean it, Charlie. Stay away from here and avoid the troops – on both sides. And whatever you do, never, ever reveal to anyone what you can do.*' When her hands tightened, they conveyed something else – something softer – as her face contorted, her eyes welling with tears.

She kissed each one of us on our foreheads, taking just a moment to breathe us in, to memorize our smells.

Then my father shoved me, forcing me to take the first step away from them. I turned, clutching Angelina to my chest as I ran back to the corner where Max and Sydney awaited us. Bitter tears stung my eyes as I obeyed.

It felt wrong. All of it.

I worried for my parents and for my sister. But worse than that, I worried for myself, and I felt selfish for it.

X

Max took the pack filled with food and offered to take Angelina as well, but she clung to me. It was just as well; I needed her as much as she needed me.

'We can go to the mines!' I called above the constant wail. 'We can hide there until the fighting ends.' I led the way, wondering which was the right way to go. Above the tops of buildings in the distance, I could see intermittent flashes that could only mean the ruin of homes, businesses, and schools. Flames beat at the sky, smoke darkening the night.

And, still, the sirens screamed.

Almost no one ventured out now; the streets were desolate. The power grids had fallen, and as we ran, the lights flickered and then vanished all around us. I didn't know how the sirens continued, but I guessed that they were tied to another system – some sort of emergency backup power – that kept them operating even when the rest of the power failed.

The blackness felt like it was reaching down into my lungs, suffocating me.

Angelina must have felt it too, because she dropped her face to my neck and refused to look up.

I envied her. I wished that I could hide my eyes, bury my face, and choose *not* to see the world crumbling around me.

Thankfully, Max had a battery-operated pocket light. It wasn't much, but when he turned it on, we could at least see the ground at our feet so we wouldn't stumble as we ran.

My legs were already burning, and my arms quivered from the weight of my sister, but hugging Angelina to me made me feel safer. And as much as I hated to admit it, having Max at my side made me feel better as well.

Sydney didn't slow us down, and that, at the moment, felt like a minor miracle in itself.

But that was when everything changed, and my plan of making it to the safety of the mines disintegrated, like so many pieces of a written promise set to flame.

Ahead of us, the white flash of an explosion, followed by an earsplitting crash, rippled through the air. I could practically taste the concussive shock wave as it rattled the night.

Angelina jolted in my arms as I stopped running and curled myself around her, doing my best to protect her. Her fingernails dug into me. Max grabbed my arm and dragged me closer to the cover of a building at the other side of the street, away from the blast.

My ears were ringing, and I could no longer distinguish the sound of the sirens from the humming that came from inside my own head. The two became one, and I knew it wasn't just me as my sister reached her hands up and stuffed her tiny index fingers into her ears. She was shaking all over, and I squeezed her tighter, trying, without words, to comfort her.

A second explosion detonated somewhere close to the first one.

But Max was already pulling us in the opposite direction. Away from the mines, and away from the latest assaults on the city.

I wondered briefly how long it would be before the blast of bombs would not be our only concern. How long until enemy ground troops marched into the streets, wreaking their own brand of havoc and killing with reckless abandon?

How much longer until none of us was safe?

For some reason the words of the Pledge drifted through my head at that moment, and I tried to find the line that spoke of protecting the people, of keeping one another from harm. But of course, there was no such line. The Pledge was meant only to safeguard the queen.

Max's grip on my arm tightened, and I realized he was speaking to me. I tried to focus, concentrating on his lips and the muffled voice that made its way through the buzzing in my head. His eyes were focused and intense, his black eyebrows drawn together as he leaned closer to me, his breath warm.

'Where is the nearest shelter?' he was yelling.

I looked over and saw that the fingers of his other hand were laced together with those of Sydney, who cowered beside him.

I told myself that it didn't matter. Not now. I just needed to get Angelina to safety. Max, and his hands, were not my concern.

I tried to think, to remember all the places we'd been told to go during the countless drills. Churches and schools. But all of them were above ground, and they all seemed too exposed, too at risk during the bombings.

Another explosion ricocheted through the air, and this time I felt the ground rumble as I dropped to my knees, covering Angelina's head with my arms. I heard her whimper – or maybe I only felt it – and I made sounds to soothe her, although I doubted she could hear them.

Then I remembered a place we could go, safer maybe than the others. Hopefully.

'The tunnels!' I cried out, lifting my head and meeting Max's intense gaze. We were just inches apart. 'Beneath the city, where the subways used to run! They're being used as shelters!'

I didn't wait for his approval, I just stood and ran. I kept my head as low as I could, wrapping one arm over Angelina as if I could somehow shield her.

The passageway wasn't far ahead, and I prayed that we weren't too late, that they hadn't been sealed up already. *Please let us gain entrance!*

When we reached the stairs that led beneath the street, Angelina and I went first, with Sydney right behind us. Max waited at the top, making certain that we'd all made it safely below. I didn't wait for him to catch up.

Ahead of me, I could see the set of double doors already sealed shut, a pair of uniformed men in blue standing guard before them.

For the first time, I thought of Max's uniform and wondered why he was still with us, if there wasn't someplace else he should be while the city was under attack. I wondered if he had abandoned his duty to be with us.

I rushed forward, practically falling over my own feet in my panic to get to the shelter beyond the doors. The burning muscles of my arms were screaming at me to set my sister down, to force her to walk on her own two feet, but again, I couldn't make myself do it. I needed to feel her against me. She was all that kept me going.

Before we could reach the doors, one of the men stepped forward, holding out his hand in warning, motioning us to stay back. 'There's no more room. You'll have to find shelter elsewhere.'

My heart twisted and despair strangled me, making it difficult to speak. 'We – we can't go back out there. It's too dangerous on the streets.' I took a step closer, hoping they could hear me.

The second guard, a man with copper-red hair and sallow skin, fingered the trigger of his weapon, a rifle that he held across his thin chest. It was a grave warning. 'That's not our problem. The tunnels are full.'

My mother's words haunted me, her pleas that I take care of Angelina at all costs.

I ignored my instincts and took another step in their direction. 'At least let her inside,' I begged, pulling Angelina away from me. She fought me, struggling to hold on, but I was stronger than she was, and I pried her fingers free. 'She's small, and she won't take up any space at all. Please.'

Angelina's breath caught as I shook her off. My heart was breaking, but I couldn't let her see that. I had to be strong.

The red-haired guard, the one with the gun, moved so suddenly that all I could do was watch in stunned silence. He shifted his rifle to his shoulder, readying and aiming it with lightning speed. I didn't have time to stoop out of the way. All I could do was reach for Angelina and drag her back to me.

Sydney gasped, reminding me that she was still with us.

I stared at the weapon, blinking, my chest squeezing as I lifted my hand. 'I – I'm s-sorry.' My voice shook as violently as my hand. 'We d-don't want trouble.'

I heard Max's footsteps rushing up behind me, but I didn't turn around, even when I felt his hand grip my shoulder. I kept all my attention on the rifle instead, as I took first one, and then another, cautious step backward, easing Angelina behind me.

But it was the actions of the first guard that confused me most of all, as a look of alarm flashed briefly across his face, and then he moved even faster than the red-haired man had. His arm shot out sideways, his fingers curling over the shaft of the gun as he twisted hard, disarming the red-haired sentry in one swift motion. The guard, who had just moments earlier held a weapon aimed at my heart, looked stunned by the sudden turn of events.

He opened his mouth to say something, to protest, but the first guard cut him off with a scathing glare, making it more than clear which of the pair was in charge.

And then the first guard reached for the door. He opened it and stepped aside, indicating that we could pass. All of us.

I snapped my head around to glance at Max, to see if he understood what had just happened, but he was already shoving Sydney through the doorway, and I could no longer see his face.

I picked up Angelina and followed the two of them, casting a wary glimpse at the guards as we passed.

Behind us, the doors closed again.

The first thing I was aware of was the darkness. It wasn't complete, this darkness, but it was broken only in places by the flicker of lanterns and the pale glow of handheld lights. Definitely not enough to see where I was walking.

Once again, I was thankful for Max's pocket light so we could pick our way through the overcrowded platforms in search of a place to rest.

That was the second thing I noticed: the people. Everywhere. Crammed together.

It was quieter down here, below the streets. Away from the sirens. But there was a hushed desperation that filled every ounce of space, every recess, making even the air feel thicker and harder to breathe. I could smell the worry.

We stepped carefully, avoiding legs and feet in our path, the small light's beam scanning for an opening where we could stop and rest. When I could bear it no longer, I set Angelina down, squeezing her fingers tightly in an unspoken assurance that I wouldn't release her.

I pushed her in front of me, keeping her back pressed against me, my free hand on her shoulder to guide her.

When it became clear that we wouldn't find a spot on the platforms, Max turned his light downward, onto the oily, dirt-caked tracks below. Faces stared back at us from the shaft of light, and Max moved it quickly over them, scanning, searching.

'There,' he finally said, pointing the light toward an opening. Although it was less an opening than it was a slight gap in the mass of people huddled atop the gravel on the far side of the unused tracks.

I agreed, it seemed the best we'd be able to do. And even though it would be a tight fit, at least we could all stay together.

Max dropped down from the platform, his feet crunching in the loose rocks below as he found a narrow space to stand between the bodies. He reached for Sydney's hand, and I hated the twinge of jealousy I felt at seeing them touch again.

But I didn't have time to dwell on it, because next he was reaching for Angelina. She went to him, this time without hesitation, and I was surprised by her willingness to trust him so easily, so soon. She was normally reserved, careful with whom she let down her guard. Yet her instincts were infallible.

Even in the shadows, I saw the sliver of a smile on her lips as Max set her gently to the ground. And then she reached for Sydney's hand while she waited for me.

If not for the fear of stepping on someone below me in the darkness, I wouldn't have waited for Max to help me down – I would have jumped myself. But I couldn't see where I would land, so I was forced to place my hand in his.

He pulled me toward him and I landed in his arms, my body sliding down the length of his. Suddenly I was aware of everything about him, his strength, the heat of his body against mine, his hands at my hips as he gradually drew me down – far slower, I thought, than necessary for the task. Fire burst from the core of me and shot through my veins as I told myself that none of this mattered. None of it was real.

My hands were at his shoulders, and my thumbs brushed against his neck, and even that simple contact, that stroke of bare skin against bare skin, made me blush all over. A wanting shiver clutched me in its grasp.

When my toes touched the gravel beneath me, a sigh escaped my lips that I fervently prayed he hadn't heard, although I wasn't sure how he could have missed it. He was only a breath away from me.

For several beats too long, he continued to hold me pressed against him, his palms flat against my back, and I didn't move away. I vaguely wondered what we looked like to anyone watching us – to Sydney and Angelina. But still, I stayed rooted where I was, feeling his heartbeat thundering beneath my cheek.

Someone near my feet coughed, and then I heard whispers, sounds that had been there all along, but that I had only just noticed.

I shuffled backward, just one tiny step, but that space between us felt infinite. His hands dropped from my back and mine fell from his chest, and we parted as I went to join Angelina, taking her hand from the other girl.

I was too ashamed of myself to make eye contact with either of them.

Max took the lead again, directing us to the small opening on the ground. It was smaller than it had looked from the platform, but several people moved aside to make a little more room for us. Thanks to their shifting, there was just enough space for one person to lean against the rough brick wall. The rest of us would have to sit up straight in the gravel or lean against one another.

One look at Sydney, and there was no question that she was the one who needed to rest. Dark rivers of drying blood crept down the side of her cheek, and her skin looked gray even in the gloom. She fell into the spot, letting her head collapse back against the bricks. I eased myself onto the crushed rocks with my legs crossed, creating a nest for Angelina, who slipped easily onto my lap. Max sat beside me, his shoulder pressed right against mine.

I could feel every breath he took, could feel the strength in the muscles that rippled down his arms.

On the other side of me, I brushed against a man's back as he guarded over a woman and three small children.

I shot a sheepish glance Max's way, feeling suddenly speechless and uncomfortable, neither of which I was accustomed to. Angelina tipped her head back, looking first to me and then to Max, watching each of us silently in turn.

When she was satisfied – and comfortable – she leaned against my chest, and I saw her pull Muffin from her inside jacket pocket. She tucked the doll beneath her chin, using it as a makeshift pillow, and her breathing slowed.

'She's tough, isn't she?'

I narrowed my eyes at Max's statement, a small smile finding its way to my lips. Angelina was tiny and fragile-looking, and she never spoke, but all of that was deceiving. She was whip-smart and took in everything around her. I'd always known that about her, even when everyone else underestimated her.

She never missed a thing, and she *was* strong. In my mind I thought of her as a fighter, a scrapper. Little, but wily and resilient.

Funny that Max had noticed it too.

'Yeah, she is,' I answered. 'As long as we're together, I think she'll be okay.'

'I want to thank you.' Sydney's voice interrupted us, surprising me because I half expected her to be sleeping already. She looked worn, battered. 'For back there, at the park . . . when you saved me from being crushed by those people.' She glanced down at her hands, guilt evident on her face. 'You didn't have to do that. I'm not sure I would have done the same if I were you.'

I didn't know what to say. I still wasn't sure why I'd done it; it wasn't as if I hadn't fantasized about worse things happening to her and the other kids at her school. It wasn't as if she'd done anything to deserve my sympathy.

Except that she was still a person. Cruel and nasty, perhaps, but no one deserved to be trampled like that.

Not even her.

She turned her eyes toward me, tears making them glisten in the faint glow of a far-off lantern, and somehow I forgot to hate her. Somehow I managed to erase all the terrible things she had said to me in the past, how she'd reminded me, time and time again, that I was of a lower class than she and her Academy friends.

'I'm so sorry,' she whispered, a tear slipping free and tracing a path to her chin. She swiped at it, frowning. 'I hope you'll forgive me.' Then she leaned forward, her hand extended to me. 'I'm Sydney. Sydney Leonne.'

I chewed the inside of my cheek, trying to decide if I should respond, but wondering whether there was really any decision to make. Hadn't I already made my choice when I'd pulled her to safety instead of running away?

I accepted her hand, startled that her fingers felt so much like my own. She was just a girl. An ordinary girl, alone and frightened. 'I'm Charlie. And this,' I explained, pointing to the bundle in my lap, 'is my sister, Angelina.'

Angelina lifted her head, letting us know that she was still awake . . . still listening. Then she settled back down without saying a word.

'I'm sorry. About everything. I didn't know you. I didn't realize—' Sydney was nervous, and I was glad it made her uneasy to admit to what she'd done in the past.

I didn't say anything to make it easier for her, I just waited.

She shrugged. 'If I could change things . . .' I could almost hear her sigh; I could feel the tension of her regret. 'Anyway, I'm really sorry.'

I just nodded; it was all I could do. I couldn't tell her that it was okay, because it wasn't.

Max sat quietly, and I wondered how much he knew, or at least suspected. Up until now, he'd been more perceptive than I cared to admit. Did he remember that Sydney was the girl from my parents' restaurant that night? Or did he pick up on the fact that we had a history that went back farther than that? Did he recognize all that her quiet apologies meant?

If he did, he kept his opinions to himself, and for that, I was grateful.

Sydney watched me for several seconds, silent currents of understanding passing between us, before she eased back again, settling against the wall behind her. I felt bad that she couldn't lie down completely, to recover in comfort. The solid wall was the best we could offer her at the moment. She closed her eyes, too exhausted to complain.

Now it was just the two of us, Max and me. And about a thousand other people around us.

XI

'Do you want to tell me what happened back there? At the entrance?'

Max shifted closer, as if to tell me a secret. As if he wasn't close enough already. His charcoal eyes looked almost black in the darkness. 'I don't know what you're talking about,' he answered, his lips very nearly brushing against mine.

I jerked backward, bumping into the man behind me.

'I think you know *exactly* what I'm talking about. Those guards didn't let us in here out of the goodness of their hearts – they made themselves more than clear that the shelter was closed. That guard even had his gun pointed at me,' I hissed. 'Yet *something* happened to change his mind.' I tried to lean forward the way Max had, wanting to appear confident, meaning to intimidate him. Except that he didn't retreat, and instead I found myself dangerously close to him once more. I hoped that he couldn't hear the sound of my heart pounding. 'I think *you* had something to do with that.'

The corner of his mouth twitched, and then he reached out and laid his hand against my cheek, enjoying himself far too much. I was certain that *everyone* could hear my heart now. 'It was my uniform.' He said it so quietly that I almost couldn't hear his words at all.

I shook my head in denial, not yet ready to believe it was that simple, but his hand stayed against my face, his fingertips inching their way into my hairline. His thumb moved down to the corner of my mouth, and I closed my eyes. I should have shrugged his hand away then. I told myself that I didn't want him to touch me . . . that his touch meant nothing, less than nothing.

His hand remained where it was, his thumb poised beside my lips. I opened my eyes, watching as he gazed at my mouth.

'You are so beautiful.'

'Stop it,' I breathed. 'That's not an answer.'

His thumb moved, ever so slightly, tracing a sensitive path along my lower lip. Goose bumps shivered along my spine. 'You didn't ask me a question.'

I stared at him and I asked, 'Who are you?'

It was as if I'd jolted him with a shock of electricity. His hand dropped away from my mouth, from my face. 'What do you mean?'

'I mean, where do you come from, Max? What class were you born into? What language is it that you speak?' I tried to think of all the questions that I'd been saving, and all the things I'd been afraid to even wonder. 'And why are you here when the city is under attack? Isn't there someplace else you need to be?'

His jaw tightened, the muscles there leaping. 'I am exactly where I need to be.'

'You know what I mean. Shouldn't you be with your battalion? Won't you get in trouble for *not* being with them?' I hadn't realized that I was practically shouting until several heads turned in our direction. I bit my lip and shot an angry glare at Max for embarrassing me like that, silently blaming him for my outburst.

This time when he leaned close, the danger wasn't imagined, and it wasn't desire that stoked my fears.

His teeth were clenched. '*How about we swap secrets, Charlaina? I'll answer your questions, if you answer mine.*' He raised an eyebrow as he slipped easily into that same dialect he'd spoken before . . . the one I'd never heard until the night I'd first laid eyes on him. The one I shouldn't be listening to.

I didn't like where this was going, and my stomach clenched painfully.

'Never mind,' I threw back at him, this time keeping my voice whisper soft. 'I don't care what happened back there. I don't want to know anything about you or where you're from. In fact, the sooner we get out of here, the better, and then you don't ever have to worry about me snooping in your life again.'

'Come on, Charlie, it's just getting interesting. You don't want to stop now, do you?'

'Leave me alone,' I hissed, turning my head away, my cheeks burning with anger and shame and regret.

No one had ever confused me the way he did.

I remained silent, and he didn't try to goad me further. The hush around us was thick, but it was the sounds from above, coming from the city, that reminded me – reminded all of us – of why we were down here, huddled and hiding.

At times it seemed like the violence – the blasts that would cause the ground beneath us to quake – was right on top of us, making me worry for myself and my little sister, who I knew wasn't actually sleeping but lay motionless in my arms. At others, the sounds were farther away, making me worry for my parents, for Aron and for Brooklynn. For everyone who wasn't here.

It was easy not to speak to Max. Fear consumed me,

making me raw, eating away at me from the inside out. I would rather not be angry on top of the fear, but that was his fault. His choice.

All his secrets and lies made it impossible *not* to be mad at him.

At some point during the night, sleep had won. I couldn't recall the exact point at which I'd finally succumbed, but I knew that the exhaustion had been there, tugging at me, trying to close my eyes and making me weak with fatigue.

Angelina had given in long before I had.

I leaned against something warm . . . or rather, someone, I thought vaguely. A strong arm held me, a hand stroked mine.

And lips.

Someone had kissed the top of my head.

Or had I only dreamt that?

Somewhere in the back of my mind, whispered warnings insisted that I wake, insisted that this was all a mistake.

Yet I continued to sleep, refusing to pay attention to that cautionary voice.

I was sure it was the shouting that woke me, but it just as easily could have been the murmuring. Or the lights that were starting to fill the tunnels, infiltrating my eyelids and invading the darkness.

Or it could have been the fact that I'd just realized my head was resting on Max's lap, my hand draped casually over the top of his thigh.

Whatever it was, I bolted upright, clinging to Angelina and trying not to disturb her. I was startled that I'd allowed myself to get so comfortable.

Around me the whispers grew, becoming frenzied.

Something was happening.

'What's going on?' I questioned Max, who was watching the commotion near the entrance.

His lifted his finger to his lips. 'Nothing,' he answered softly. 'Just stay quiet and keep your head down.'

I glanced around, trying to make sense of things.

Near the entrance, voices rose to shouts, and lanterns were being lit all along the platform. Still, it was hard to see anything from where we sat.

'I know you're down here!' a man's voice bellowed, like a growl, rippling through the shadows.

There was silence for a moment, as everyone stopped to listen. And then a smaller voice – another man – responded, but I couldn't hear what he said.

More lanterns were ignited.

I craned my neck, trying to get a better view.

'Charlie, stay down,' Max warned, pulling me back.

Angelina was awake now, sitting noiselessly on my lap. I squeezed her arm but spoke to Max. 'Who is that? His voice, it seems . . . *familiar.*'

Max shook his head, so many emotions crossing his face. He looked at once trapped and defeated, and his shoulders sagged. He watched me closely for several long seconds before answering me at last. 'They're here for me.' He reached out and ruffled Angelina's hair, smiling at her wistfully. 'I should have known they'd come looking for me.'

My eyes widened. *I knew it!* I'd worried that Max should have been somewhere else, that he was supposed to be with his platoon instead of helping a pair of merchant girls escape into the tunnels beneath the city. Even Sydney, as a member of the Counsel class, didn't warrant the kind of protection he'd provided us.

I wondered what the penalty was for desertion.

I reached for his hand, clutching his fingers. 'What can we do? There's no place to hide.'

The voice boomed again, coming from atop the platform. 'I know you're down here! You might as well come out now!'

I knew this time, without a doubt. I knew who was speaking – yelling, rather – through the passageways. His deep voice rumbled off the walls and vibrated in the air. I glanced up again. More lanterns had been lit, and he was closer now as people stood hastily to get out of his way.

It was Claude, sounding and looking imposing in his uniform, even in the gloom of the tunnels beneath the city.

And he wasn't alone. Behind him marched a small army of soldiers, including the other man I recognized, the second man from the club that night, the darker-skinned Zafir. Neither he nor Claude were the kind of men I could ever forget.

Max grinned at me, an odd response, I thought. Then he leaned close, his mouth almost to mine, stealing my breath and capturing my awareness. 'Whatever happens, promise me one thing?'

I wanted to nod, but I was afraid to move. Afraid that if I did, our lips might actually touch, and then I'd be lost, unable to think, or speak, or promise him anything at all.

I blinked slowly instead.

Max's smile spread, his lips parting.

Footsteps landed in the gravel somewhere nearby, and the light from a lantern came closer still. They were almost upon us, and I knew that time was running short.

'Promise me that no matter what happens right now, you won't be angry with me.' I was still holding on to his hand, and his fingers crushed mine, as if securing my oath.

The man on the other side of me stood and moved his family out of the path of the approaching soldiers.

The grinding of a thousand feet seemed to stop right in front of us, but Max held my gaze, sharing my breath.

'Get up.' Claude's voice cut through the silence that had

settled in the air while everyone in the tunnels watched. Then, impatiently, without waiting for a response, he spoke in a language that I doubted anyone around me had ever heard before. '*Get up now, or I'll drag you up. The queen won't like this when she hears of it.*'

The queen? Why would the queen need to hear about the desertion of one soldier?

But I didn't get a chance to ask the questions that buzzed within my head.

Max just sighed, still not turning to face the others. He held my face between his hands and pressed the gentlest kiss to my lips – reminding me of my dream, of the kiss I'd imagined in my sleep. I told myself that this wasn't the time to indulge such fantasies, that this was serious. Max was in trouble.

But he didn't seem to notice.

I watched as he stood, his demeanor too casual for the situation at hand. '*How did you find me?*' he asked Claude, who was scowling at him.

Claude raised his lantern, illuminating Max's face, and I watched as the light danced over Max's handsome features. I could still feel his lips against my skin as if he'd scalded me with his brief kiss. My cheeks felt like they were on fire.

Every muscle in my body tensed as I waited to see what was going to happen to Max.

'*You're not that hard to track. People notice you. One*

213

of the guards at the door knew exactly who you were,'
was Claude's gruff response.

And then, from somewhere in the distance, I heard
one of the soldiers barking an order to the people in
the tunnels. I wanted to know what he'd said, but his
command was swallowed by a chorus of gasps, first
one . . . and then another. And another. The whispered
utterances that passed from person to person rose to a
deafening roar as the soldier's words spread throughout
the crowd. A command that still hadn't reached me. A
command I had yet to hear.

I glanced to Sydney, to see if she understood what was
happening, but she looked just as confused as I was.

Then all around us, people began to fall to their knees,
and I wondered what was being said that made them
suddenly too feeble to stand.

The other giant of a man, Zafir, smirked. *'How long
did you think you could remain hidden?'* he asked Max,
his voice nearly as thunderous as Claude's.

Max looked down at me, his expression serious now.
He reached out a hand and I took it, letting him help
me to my feet. 'Long enough,' he answered, this time in
Englaise.

I frowned at Max, wondering why they were all acting
so strangely. Why he wasn't being arrested. Why they
were standing there, chatting, while everyone around us
was suddenly unable to remain on their feet.

And then, from right beside me, the man and his family knelt down, and I heard the man utter as he dropped to the ground, bowing low, 'Your Highness.'

It took far too long for those two simple words to register. And even when they did, I couldn't imagine who he could possibly be speaking to.

But as soon as they were out there, Max turned to watch me, scrutinizing me. Awaiting my response.

And it came. Far too slowly, but it came nonetheless.

The secret language. The fact that Max seemed to come and go as he pleased despite being a member of the military. The mention of the queen.

Everyone in the tunnel being ordered to their knees, forced to bow low out of respect.

Not to Claude or Zafir, or to any of the men in uniform.

But to Max.

They were bowing down to Prince Maxmillian, grandson to Queen Sabara.

His Royal Highness.

I turned around in a circle, gravel crunching beneath my feet as I stared at the people on the ground. Angelina stood beside me, watching me, watching everything.

Silence filled the underground caverns; hush echoed off the walls. Not even the soldiers made a sound.

My tongue felt thick in my mouth, as if it might choke

me should I attempt to swallow. Or speak. The air in my lungs felt too warm and arid as I stole shallow breaths to sustain myself.

Time seemed to stand still.

I blinked once, my eyes feeling gritty. I frowned at Max, pleading at him with that stare to tell me that I was wrong, that they were all wrong, that he was no one . . . just a young man who'd deserted his post.

I'm sorry, he mouthed, no sound escaping his lips . . . lips that had just touched my own. Lips that had lied and betrayed me.

Max was royalty. That was who he was. That was why I'd never heard his language before. It was the language of the Royals . . . a language very few would ever have the occasion to hear.

Especially a simple merchant girl.

I reached for my sister's hand and pulled her down with me as we, too, dropped to our knees. We couldn't afford to draw any more attention to ourselves than we already had. We couldn't afford to appear disloyal.

I wondered how I hadn't seen it before, how I hadn't recognized him for who he was. But how would I have? He was a prince – a male. There were no monuments constructed in his honor, no flags or monies depicting his likeness. And I had no particular interest in the royal lineage. There was no reason for me to recognize his face.

In a rush, the sounds around me were back, as if they

had never been absent in the first place.

Claude reached for my arm, gripping it too tightly as he hauled me up to my feet once more and began dragging me toward the entrance.

I jerked away from him, suddenly furious. 'I'm not going anywhere with you. I'm staying right here.'

He didn't touch me again, but he towered over me, glaring, intimidating. When he spoke, he didn't address me, but rather turned to Max. '*We need to find out what she knows.*'

Angelina clutched my hand, and I wondered if she'd somehow understood the meaning of his actions, if she'd sensed the tension in his voice.

I wondered what he meant exactly by '*what she knows*'? Was it possible that Max had confided his suspicions in Claude?

I lifted my chin, refusing to give him the satisfaction of knowing how hard my heart beat or how cold my blood ran.

Fortunately, at least in that single moment, Max's was the only answer that mattered, and he shook his head. '*She stays here with her sister,*' he stated in a voice that was unyielding – and regal. And I couldn't believe I hadn't picked up on that before.

I narrowed my eyes, refusing to look at any of them as they departed, Max leading the way and never looking back.

I simply remained quiet, ignoring the conflicting emotions that warred within me, refusing to entertain the thousand questions that swirled in my head. I concentrated instead on keeping Angelina tucked safely at my side.

PART II

PART II

XII

I don't know how long I stood there, or how long the people around me planned to remain on their knees, but for far too much time none of us moved. This time when I heard the sound of footsteps, they came from an entirely different direction and carried with them none of the thunder that Max's army had.

All I knew for certain was that when I looked up to see who approached, I saw the last person I'd expected staring back at me.

Xander. And he stood before a motley group of men and women who remained behind him, hidden within the darkness the underground passageways provided.

Whatever I'd felt about Xander before was now overshadowed by Max's deceit. I wasn't sure I felt anything at all for the moment, save a dull glimmer of relief.

We were no longer alone, my sister and I.

They'd come not from the entrance, but from the rear of the tunnels, from the deserted channels that had once been traveled by trains that ran beneath the city. Xander strode forward with quiet confidence to where we waited, his own army small in contrast to the one that had just vacated the tunnels. Angelina huddled against me, squeezing my leg.

'What are you doing here? How did you find us?' I asked when Xander was almost upon us.

But he just lifted his finger to his lips, silencing my questions. 'Just come with me.' There was no other explanation. He held out a hand, and I had to make a decision. It wasn't a difficult one, though. I didn't want to stay where we were, surrounded by all those people who'd just witnessed what had happened with Max. I couldn't bear to see the questions in their eyes.

When I stepped forward to take his hand, I felt Sydney at my back and realized she had no intention of being left behind, and we followed Xander as he drew us into the passageways that cut a path through the blackness.

* * *

224

I had no idea *where* we were, but it was magnificent. Breathtaking.

It was more like an underground city than a tunnel by the time we'd finally reached our destination. People – Outcasts, I assumed – moved freely around us, their lanterns creating near-daylight conditions even in the middle of the night.

Like the clubs, color filled nearly every space, but here the colors came in the form of carpets, mismatched clothing, and blankets that were strung everywhere, creating barriers that were used in place of more permanent walls and doors, a means of privacy amid the confusion. I smelled rich spices and tobacco, and smoke and food, as well as the moist earth that surrounded us. The acoustical sounds of stringed instruments melded together with shouts of laughter and crying babies.

A small boy scooted past us, squeezing between Sydney and me as he ran from an older child – girl or boy, I couldn't be certain, the chin-length curls could have gone either way. I watched as mothers rocked their babies while toddlers played at their feet, and as men gathered to play games of chance. There was the familiar bustle of commerce and steady chatter. It was a little like standing in the middle of the crowded marketplace, save the absence of a blue sky overhead.

The activity was ceaseless. And the only language I heard spoken was Englaise.

I felt instantly at peace.

'What is this place?' I breathed, setting Angelina on the ground to walk beside me as I marveled at the chaos all around.

We stopped to see an older girl drawing lines in the dirt, while a group of children dressed in what I could only describe as patchwork clothing began dividing into teams, readying for a game. The girl's fingers were coated with layers of grime, and her cheeks were pink with exertion as she concentrated on creating the large, perfectly shaped squares.

Xander smiled. 'This is my home.'

A woman marched up to meet us – or rather, to greet Xander – and I realized that I'd seen her before; she was the bartender from Prey. Her blue hair was evident even in the unnatural glow of the gas lamps.

'Charlie, this is Eden.' Xander introduced the two of us, and I nodded at her, trying to recall if I'd ever before seen eyes so black. I was sure there were no others like them in all the world.

I had the strangest feeling that the bartender – *Eden* – didn't smile often. Her teeth were bared just a little too much as she attempted to appear hospitable.

Yet another reason the Outcasts didn't live within the rules of normal society, I thought as I tried to smile back at her.

Angelina stayed close, as always, and Sydney was practically on top of me.

Xander pulled us along, with Eden following right behind. 'Don't worry, you're safe here.' Then he smiled kindly at Sydney when he said, 'We'll take you back home once the sirens have ceased.'

I stopped walking, my heart stock-still within my chest. 'How do you know it's not an attack on the city? How do you know that the sirens will just . . . stop?'

Xander's grin had the same predatory quality I'd seen at the club. 'Because we were responsible for the attack on the city. We made them go off.'

I couldn't believe what I was hearing. It didn't make any sense. Almost less sense than a subterranean city. 'Why? Why would you do that?'

He sighed. 'Come with me, Charlaina. We need to talk.'

It wasn't hard to convince Angelina to stay with Sydney in the room that had been prepared for us. From what I could tell, there were very few individual accommodations, so I was grateful that one had been set aside for us. It was dank and smelled of cellar dirt, but at least there were suitable sleeping pallets.

I was still worried about Sydney's injuries. She looked more and more like she might need medical attention, and I could only hope that some rest might do her good.

Before I left them alone, I pressed a gentle kiss against Angelina's cheek. It was a chance to speak to her with no one overhearing. 'Don't do anything to help her, Angelina. I need you to keep your hands to yourself.' But when I pulled back, I could see worry in her eyes, and I knew she didn't want me to go. 'I'll hurry back as fast as I can. I won't be long,' I promised.

Angelina knew I spoke the truth. I could never lie to her, and she quieted down at last, silently agreeing to remain with the girl.

As I passed, I studied the armed woman who stood guard outside the small chamber's entrance. She was more intimidating than any soldier I'd ever seen. Yet another extravagance afforded us by our host.

'Who are you? Who are all these people down here?' I asked, now that Angelina was no longer around. 'I mean, I get that they're Outcasts, but how did you all end up together?'

Xander settled down behind a makeshift desk, a sturdy-looking wooden table with pockmarks and peeling varnish. On it, an odd assortment of colorful maps and charts were strewn haphazardly. We were in an office of sorts, another chamber carved into the ground around us. 'They're not all Outcasts, Charlie. Many of them have chosen to be here. Yes, some have left their class, deciding they'd rather live freely among the Outcasts than adhere to the strict rules of society, but others . . . well, let's just say that others are leading double lives.'

'What do you mean? Why would they want to live in two places at once?'

'This isn't just an underground city, where people are free to come and go as they please, a place with no rules,' he explained, sitting forward, his elbows on his desk. 'You still don't get it, do you? These are people with strong beliefs. We've all come together because we have a common goal – a common enemy. You're sitting in the headquarters of the resistance.'

He was watching me, and I knew he was waiting for my response, but my brain felt suddenly sluggish, and my thoughts were slow to process what I'd heard.

Finally Xander broke the silence. 'Do you understand what I'm telling you, Charlie? *We* are the revolutionaries.' He grinned then, his teeth flashing white and his scar stretching taut. 'And I'm their leader.'

His words dangled in the air. 'What are you talking about?' I finally scoffed. This was some sort of elaborate hoax. But then I looked at him, really looked at him. And I noticed the sense of power he wore, radiating off him like heat, and I wondered why I hadn't noticed *that* at the club. Maybe I'd been too preoccupied by his strange silver eyes. Or maybe I'd been too concerned with Max. Whatever it was, Xander waited for me to catch up. 'You're . . . you're not joking, are you?'

He shook his head solemnly. 'I'm really not.'

'How many of you are there?' I asked, still trying to make sense of everything he'd just told me, my head reeling with nebulous, unformulated questions.

He studied me as intently as I did him. 'Here? Thousands. The underground city stretches for miles, we have access points hidden in every part of the Capitol, and we have nearly as many escape routes as we have soldiers willing to die for the cause.' He smiled at his boast, and then added, 'Outside the Capitol, we have encampments in almost every major city in the country. We're bigger than you realize. Bigger than the queen realizes.' His eyebrows drew together, his expression was grave. 'I can't fail, Charlie. I can't let these people down. They're counting on me.'

I didn't know what to say.

It didn't matter that his reasons seemed sound, or that he truly believed his cause was just. It didn't matter that I thought Xander was a decent man trying to make a difference in this world.

He was a criminal. He was the leader of a rebel movement bent on destroying the very foundation of our country. If he succeeded, if by some inconceivable stretch of the imagination he was truly able to overthrow Queen Sabara, then the country would be thrown into chaos. Everything we believed in, everything we'd ever been taught, would become obsolete.

It had been tried before. And it had failed.

Without the kind of magic that only a queen was born with, we could never survive.

THE QUEEN

The queen waited in hushed anticipation. She did not appreciate the calm.

When, at last, the door to the chamber opened and Baxter strode inside, she breathed an imperceptible sigh of relief.

'Has he spoken?' she demanded to know. 'Have you broken him yet?'

Baxter hesitated, not a good sign. 'No, Your Majesty,' he apologized, ducking as low as his belly would allow. 'Not yet. We believe we're close, however.'

She weighed his statement, his sugared reassurance of triumph, against the very real possibility that they would kill the boy before securing his cooperation. At the moment she needed all the information she could get about the resistance; killing anyone who might have valuable information would be counterproductive.

'Bring him to me,' she finally stated.

Baxter raised his head. 'Your Majesty?'

Her eyebrows lifted, and her lips tightened.

Baxter cleared his throat, clearly recalling his position. 'Yes, Your Majesty.'

She watched as he clumsily exited the room, and she wondered how much longer he could possibly be of use to her. He'd outlived his predecessors by years, but he was beginning to cross lines now too, to question his queen, even if only in thought. That in itself was treasonous. Cause enough for a death sentence.

Maybe, she thought, the new queen would have room for a traitor like him among her ranks. A sly smile found its way to her lips as she ignored the ache in her bones.

If only they could find a *new* queen in time.

The boy had to be carried into the room. He was incapable of standing before his queen, and she questioned whether he would have stood even had he been able to.

She had first received word of the boy from her spies, an intricate network laid throughout the city. They were distributed among every walk of life: the Counsel class, vendors, servants, and even within the ranks of military personnel. They knew how to gather information, using rewards and the promise of glory to coax her subjects into turning on one another.

She knew that the boy himself was no threat to her, that he was a nobody. But he had information to offer, or so she'd been told.

She gave the signal, and he was released by the guards. He dropped in a heap at her feet, whimpering softly as he clutched his ribs. His eyes were swollen, mottled with dark bruising, his lips gashed and bloodied. And these were just the injuries that were visible.

She did her best to sound gentle and reassuring. A difficult task, since her heart felt nothing for the boy. *'You're a fool. You'll tell us what we want to know if it kills you,'* she uttered.

He didn't look up, and she took that as an indication that his wits were still intact, since she'd spoken in the Royal tongue. She dismissed the alternative, that he was already too damaged, that he was no longer capable of responding to words in any language.

She tried again, this time in Englaise, in hopes of gaining an answer from him. 'We don't want to hurt you,' she lied. 'We just want the girl.'

His head inched up cautiously. He opened his mouth to respond, but only an arid whisper escaped his mangled lips. His expression bore defeat.

Fury quivered through her. 'Idiots! Give him water! You bring me a prisoner without preparing him properly?'

Baxter gave the signal, and a serving girl rushed out the door to fulfill their queen's command. As she waited, the queen watched as her grandson entered the chamber, followed by his loyal guards. He looked smug, as always. And ineffective, as was to be expected of any male heir.

She was enraged that he'd slipped away from his guards yet again. He might only be male, but he was still a member of the royal family. There were rules to follow, precautions to take. It was bad enough he'd stooped to the ranks of the military.

She stopped herself from narrowing her gaze at him, reminding herself that personal matters were best handled in private. An insubordinate grandson could be dealt with at another time.

Maxmillian knew his place, of course, and he waited silently at the back of the room as she attended to the matter at hand.

The boy drank greedily, water dribbling from his lips onto his bloodstained shirt. When he was too weary to swallow any more, the queen resumed questioning him. 'We know you've been associating with a member of the resistance. I promise you that all of this ends if you'll only give us her name.'

His head lolled unsteadily as he tried to meet his queen's gaze. 'I don't know who you're talking about,' he rasped.

A sliver of a smile settled over her thin lips. 'Come

now, boy, your denials are pointless. Our information is accurate, I assure you. If you're not sure which friend we speak of, then name them all. We'll find her ourselves.'

He shook his head; it wobbled from side to side. 'I won't. You're asking me to implicate everyone. I can't do that.'

The queen jumped up, towering over the boy's crippled body. She was quivering now, as rage consumed her. Of course she was asking him to incriminate his friends! She *needed* to find the revolutionaries, to squash them before they could cause further damage to her country. She needed to stop them. She needed names!

'Tell me! I command you to tell me!' she shrieked, spittle foaming at the corners of her mouth. She held out her hand in front of her, pointing at the boy's throat and then balling her crooked fingers into a fist. She was surprised by the sudden show of emotion, surprised that she was eliciting the use of magic, but she was unable to check herself in time.

She could feel the current of her own power tingling from the tips of her fingers and stretching toward him, wrapping around his throat like a taut ribbon of electrical wire.

The boy's body went suddenly rigid, every muscle contracting as he struggled for air. His hands clawed at his neck as his eyes rolled back in his head. His fingers dug into his flesh as if they could excavate an opening through which he could breathe. He had no idea what he was up against.

His queen watched dispassionately, unimpressed by his display of self-preservation and momentarily exhilarated by her demonstration of power.

The boy was a fool. He would rather die than confess the names of his friends? He would sacrifice himself to protect those who stood against his queen? A fool *and* a collaborator.

At last, when she was sure he'd learned his lesson, she closed her eyes and dropped her hand, releasing him. She settled back against her throne as she struggled to hide her exhaustion.

The boy's loud gasp filled the room, followed by a second and a third. Fresh blood seeped from the nail marks he'd left along the length of his own throat when he'd fought to break free from her invisible grip.

'Take him away,' she finally commanded, turning her head as if unable to look upon him any longer. 'Tell them to get the information I require. At any cost.'

MAX

Max didn't blink, but it took every ounce of resolve to remain still as he watched. He understood the need to maintain order, but he could never approve of the way in which his grandmother – *his queen* – went about her business. How could she justify this kind of torture?

Beside him, Claude and Zafir stood just as motionless. It would do none of them any good to interfere.

However, it wasn't the boy who held Max's attention as the queen took her throne once more, releasing the boy from her spell. It was she who he studied from beneath his lowered gaze.

She was still powerful; she'd just proven that, still as potent as ever. But a display like that used up valuable energy, and observing her, Max wasn't sure it was energy she had to spare.

She was far too old for such shows of strength. Even if no one else noticed, he could see that she was fading right before their eyes.

Guards lifted the boy from his place on the ground, a man taking position on either side of him, and Max inwardly cringed as he caught the barest glimpse of the boy's ravaged face. Not for the first time in his life, he was grateful that he'd been born a male and that the duties of ruling Ludania would never fall on his shoulders.

As he was being dragged away, the boy raised his head, only slightly, but it was enough. He saw Max. And Max recognized him almost immediately, making his pulse hammer in warning. He knew how badly this could end.

If only they'd been alone, Max would have cautioned the boy, would have warned him to remain quiet, to keep his words to himself.

But they weren't.

And the queen – along with everyone else in the room – heard the boy's accusations as he realized where he'd seen Max before.

'Where's Charlie?!' Aron screamed as he struggled against his guards, straining to break free from his captors, never even realizing that he'd just given the queen what she wanted: a name. 'Is she here, you son of a bitch? What have you done with Charlie?'

XIII

'You can't win,' I explained, even though I had no idea if what I spoke was the truth. But it made sense; he was talking about defeating an army.

'We can, and we will,' Xander insisted, his metallic eyes flashing. 'Sabara has spent too much of her energy fighting us in inconsequential conflicts; she never even realized we were enlisting help from outside the borders. Now it's too late. There are many queens who'd like to see Sabara's rule end. We're strong, Charlie, much stronger than she knows.'

I still didn't understand, there was so much to process, and my mind was elsewhere, consumed by worries and fears. 'How could you harm your own people? How could you attack the city like that?'

Xander's face crumpled, and I felt his guard slip. I had no idea why he was so quick to reveal his secrets to me. 'We were as careful as we could be, but violence can't always be avoided. The places we bombed, the buildings we set on fire, were strategic for the most part. They were military installations and checkpoints. We stayed as far as we could from the shelters and didn't start striking the neighborhoods until well after the sirens should have cleared everyone out.'

'And if they didn't? If there were still people in their homes?' I tried not to imagine my parents as I asked the questions.

His finger absently drifted over his whiskered cheek, following the pale line of his scar. 'I hope that there weren't.' It wasn't an adequate answer, and we both knew it.

'I need to go back. I need to make sure that my family is safe. And my friend . . . I couldn't find her at the park . . .' I had no idea if Brooklynn had made it to a shelter, and my skin crawled with regret.

Xander didn't respond in the way I'd expected. His defenses went back up, his guarded expression slipped back into place. 'Are you talking about Brooklynn?' he asked, stealing my breath and making it hard for me to swallow.

He knew her name.

I nodded, blinking once, twice, and then again. I

remembered meeting Xander, that night in the club. He'd known my name then; I shouldn't be surprised that he knew Brook's as well.

Xander lifted his hand, gesturing to Eden, who stood just outside the circle of our voices, watching us with her polished black eyes. I never actually saw her move, but I was certain she had somehow given a signal of her own.

From out of the shadows, a group of Xander's soldiers marched toward us in unison, dressed in mismatched uniforms and carrying unpolished weapons. They were the antimilitary, but clearly just as formidable. They approached in measured steps, giving their disorganized-looking group a sense of order.

Then one girl stepped to the front of the militia, leading the way, a combat rifle slung over her shoulder.

It was Brooklynn.

I knocked my chair over in my rush to reach her. I gripped her shoulders, momentarily forgetting to be alarmed by her sudden appearance as I pulled her against me, whispering against her dirt-smudged cheek. 'You're okay. Thank heaven, you're okay.'

But somehow, she felt different in my arms, like a different Brook from the one I'd known all my life. She certainly looked different.

She pulled away, and I surveyed her face. It was harder than I remembered it, tougher. Stronger.

'I was never in danger, Charlie.' Even her voice sounded unusual to my ears. That was something I knew I hadn't imagined.

I wasn't sure how to respond; my head ached and my heart squeezed. So much had changed in just one short day.

Xander came to stand beside me, and that was when I saw it, a flicker of the old Brooklynn – my familiar friend – behind the cool exterior she now wore. Her eyes seemed to brim with adoration as she glanced at him.

'Send your team to the surface,' Xander told Brooklynn. His voice was no-nonsense, a leader giving a command. 'Tell them to check on Charlie's parents, and to let them know that Charlie and Angelina are safe, that they're under our protection now.' He squeezed my shoulder. His hand was strong, his words comforting. But like that, with that single gesture, the light faded from Brook's gaze.

Xander. Brooklynn had a thing for Xander.

THE QUEEN

Queen Sabara waited until the room had been cleared, until it was just she and Max and his two guards, before she spoke again. It gave her the time she needed to compose herself.

But her voice, when it found its way to her lips, was like unyielding steel. 'Who is she, Maxmillian? Who is the girl that vendor boy spoke of?'

Her grandson stepped forward, his expression earnest. But his voice rang false, giving her pause. 'She's no one, just a girl I met in one of the clubs.' His loyalty was now in question.

She studied him, holding his gaze and clutching her armrests until her knuckles ached. She would need to choose her questions carefully. 'Which club? Perhaps it was the one in which the resistance was last headquartered? Was it *that* club?'

His eyebrow lifted, likely unintentionally, and she had her answer even before his measured words hit the air. 'I don't recall exactly. It's possible that was the club.'

'And the girl, was she keeping company with anyone you recognized? Members of the resistance, perhaps?'

He bent at the waist, dropping into a gentlemanly bow, and she knew immediately that this was not a gesture of respect – it was meant to hide the deceit on his face. 'No, Your Majesty, she was not.'

One of the guards cleared his throat, and the queen's brows snapped together. She lifted her chin, forcing her words to resonate. 'I remind you all that committing perjury to your queen is punishable by death. If you've anything to add, now is the time to do so.'

The only answer she received was that of Baxter's untimely entrance into the throne room, interrupting her warning. She locked gazes with her grandson, a boy she'd scarcely noticed before this moment, a boy whom she now suspected of withholding information, pertinent or not. Subversion could come in many forms.

'I caution you, Maxmillian, should this *girl* turn out to be a member of the resistance, I shall not hesitate to send you to the gallows right alongside her.' The blood left her lips as she pressed them tightly together. She meant what she said.

'Of course.' His response was so casual, his voice no more serious than if they'd been discussing a feast spread before them, or a painting, or the weather . . . anything other than the threat of his execution. He bowed again before exiting the room.

Only when he and his guards were gone did Sabara lean back in her throne, feeling suddenly breathless, her skin prickling with cold sweat. It took several moments before she acknowledged her adviser.

'I don't care what it takes, Baxter, I want you to find this *Charlie* before sunup. If she has information about the resistance, I insist on knowing what it is.'

Baxter straightened, clearing his throat. 'Yes, Your Majesty. I'll send some men out to retrieve her immediately. If she knows anything, we'll find out.'

The queen glared, unable to purge the image of her grandson's insolence from her mind. She shook her head and skewered Baxter with a fierce glare, glad to see *someone* squirm in fear. '*No!* Bring her to me. If she knows anything, I mean to discover it myself.' Then her lips parted in a cruel smirk. 'Besides, I find myself curious about the girl my grandson is willing to risk his life to protect.'

MAX

Max strode into his chambers and waited to hear the sound of the door closing behind him. Even without looking back, he knew he wasn't alone.

'You would damn us all for a girl?' It was Claude who made the accusation.

Max kept his back to his guards, not caring that they were angry with him. He didn't have time to concern himself over their feelings. He'd always been loyal to his country and his crown, but he couldn't stop thinking of Charlie . . .

. . . and what his grandmother – *his queen* – would do should she find her first.

'I don't have to explain myself to you,' he answered

flatly. And then, because he knew he wasn't being fair, he turned on his heel, his eyes narrowing. 'Besides, when did you become such a child? You were never in any danger. I didn't lie. I don't know where she is.'

'But you know as well as I do that she's acquainted with Xander; we all saw them together at the club. And whether she's a part of the resistance or not, keeping company with their leader is dangerous business. The queen would want to know as much.'

'No!' Max snapped. 'It's irrelevant. She's no more involved with the resistance than I am.' He turned his back again, ending the conversation.

Claude was right, of course. He'd wondered about that night, about seeing Charlie with Xander. But he knew something that even Claude didn't.

His thumb slid over the smooth gold chain hidden within his pocket.

A truth he couldn't risk his grandmother discovering.

'We need to get out of here.' Max strode toward the door once more, knowing full well that Claude and Zafir would follow. 'We need to find her before the queen does.'

He needed to keep Charlie safe.

He'd made a pledge.

XIV

There was nothing more I could do but wait on word of my parents. And the waiting was excruciating. Up until now, protecting Angelina had been my most immediate concern, and for the moment, she was out of harm's way. Xander had made certain of that.

I squeezed in close to her on the pallet we were sharing as I pressed my chin against the top of her head. It was the same way we'd slept so many times before. Sydney was restless in her own bed, and I did my best to ignore the thrashing sounds that came from her side of the room. She was accustomed to more luxurious accommodations: soft mattresses, finely woven linens, heat.

Harder to ignore were the noises that came from

beyond our chamber. There was no door, just an opening carved through the very earth itself. Only a blanket pegged into the chiseled wall separated us from the activity outside. There seemed to be no differentiation between day and night down here, no curfew to abide by.

It was cooler below the city, and Angelina shivered. I pulled the musty wool throw over her shoulder, tightening my embrace around her.

Unlike Angelina and Sydney, there was no hope that I'd sleep, not without news of my parents. Not until Brooklynn returned.

Brooklynn. Odd how the name seemed to no longer fit the girl.

Brooklynn – *my* Brooklynn – was carefree and self-centered.

This Brooklynn, the one I'd met today, was someone else entirely. She was a soldier.

How had I not known that this other Brook existed? How long had she been here? And which one was the true Brooklynn?

Laughter trilled loudly somewhere beyond our walls. A sound that joyous seemed oddly out of place within the chilly underground caverns of a city under siege. In a country at war with itself.

But these people, these Outcasts who spoke only one shared language, seemed happier than those of us who lived above ground. Those of us who were segregated by words and ruled by fear.

I closed my eyes, and not for the first time I pictured Max, and I wished – once more – that he would cease to occupy my thoughts. I had no business worrying over his deceptions while I awaited information about my parents.

Yet he was here, forcing his way into my mind.

A prince. Born to a life of nobility, yet trying to pass himself off as something . . . less. No wonder his family objected to his post in the military. No wonder he was shadowed, wherever he went, by Claude and Zafir. They weren't his comrades or his friends. They were his guards, sworn to defend him with their lives. Every Royal had them, even a merchant girl knew as much.

So why me? Why the interest in a common vendor's daughter?

He'd said I intrigued him.

Intrigue wasn't cause for impractical entanglements, not of the romantic kind. Intrigue was too close to curiosity, to oddity.

Yet still, the skin of my lips burned.

I brushed them against the top of Angelina's head, hoping to erase his touch.

It was unfair. He could have chosen any girl, anyone other than me, and she would have gladly fallen under his charms, even knowing that it could only be a temporary pairing.

But I had been the one who'd intrigued him.

XANDER

Xander paced the dark, untraveled corridors where he could be alone with his thoughts.

He worried that he'd revealed too much to Charlie about who he was, about who they all were. If only it could end there.

Soon he would have to tell her the rest, and he worried about losing her trust.

She would resist, he was almost certain of it. How could she not? She was reasonable, and no reasonable person would simply accept what he knew.

'X, the team's back.' His thoughts were interrupted by Eden, and when he turned to face her, he saw that she was joined by the dark-haired beauty he'd put in charge of the mission.

Brooklynn had been a valuable asset to the resistance; she'd been a competent spy, understanding that her looks gave her the unique talent of loosening a man's tongue. Members of the military were not immune to a beautiful girl's attention. And most people underrated her intellect.

Xander knew better than to underestimate her. She was both ambitious and cunning, a deadly combination. One that could be advantageous when navigated with care.

'And?' Xander asked, when neither of the armed women spoke. 'What of Charlie's parents?'

Brooklynn stepped forward, her full lips set in a hard line. She didn't speak immediately, drawing out the anticipation, and he wondered if the pause was calculated – like so many things she did – for effect.

But Eden, ever impatient, wasn't one for premeditated suspense. 'They were too late,' she told Xander, her shoulders squared, her jaw tight. 'The girl's parents were already gone.'

XV

Breakfast was *interesting*. The dining hall was run less like my parents' well-organized restaurant and more like a frenzied free-for-all. The 'kitchen' was set up at the end of a blocked passageway and was surrounded by rows and rows of mismatched tables, chairs, crates, and boxes, all used as places to eat. Several people ate standing up, scooping their food from the bowls directly to their mouths, hardly bothering with things like utensils or manners. Others squatted on the ground, staying on the fringes of the crowded space, finding a spot wherever they could in corners and against walls, seeming to favor the solitude over being crushed between the bodies that packed the tables.

Eight huge vats were lined up along one entire wall, every one of them filled with steaming breakfast grains that had been cooked to a pasty mush. The men and women who worked kitchen duty were supervising the distribution of the hot cereal, and made sure that no one took more than their allotted single bowl.

Angelina, Sydney, and I waited silently in line for our turn, as Angelina stared in wide-eyed awe at all the sights and sounds and colors. The man standing behind us chatted continually with Angelina. I couldn't see a single tooth in his mouth, and his lips curled inward, hugging his gums. He asked Angelina how old she was, where she was staying, and what her doll's name was, although he scarcely took a breath between words and didn't seem to notice that she never answered any of his questions in return.

When it was our turn, we politely took our bowls, allowing a large woman in a checkered apron to slop her overfilled serving ladle into each of them, and then we wove our way in and around the tables until we found three seats together.

What the soggy bowl of grains lacked in odor, and even color, it made up for in substance. It was thick and hearty, and I encouraged Angelina to eat even though she didn't want to. I wasn't sure how long we'd be down here, or when we might have our next meal.

Everything felt uncertain at this point.

I stared at Sydney, sitting across from Angelina and me, and I wondered at her overnight transformation. Last night her skin had been sickly and gray, a pallor closer to death than to life. I knew because I'd lain awake listening to her sleep, worrying over her every breath. This morning, however, after an unsettled night's sleep, her cheeks were pink again, and her eyes clear, despite the blood that was still caked in her hair and alongside her face.

'Tell me a doctor visited you and Sydney while I was out last night,' I begged Angelina in a whisper that only she could hear.

But Angelina just shook her head and gazed guiltily at her bowl.

I tugged her hand beneath the table, forcing her to look at me instead. 'I told you not to help her,' I warned, moving as close as I could so Sydney couldn't listen. 'You can't go around healing people. What if someone had seen you? What if Sydney realized what you'd done?' I sighed, resting my forehead against hers, suddenly weary. 'You have to be careful.' I recited the words my father had repeated time and time again. 'Always careful.'

Sydney didn't know that Angelina was the reason she

was feeling better this morning. I could tell by the way she ignored the two of us as she took a hesitant bite of her breakfast. She didn't bother to hide her distaste for the meal before her.

'It's not *that* bad,' I assured Angelina, who was watching Sydney, horror-struck. 'You just have to get used to the texture. Come on, try it.'

Sydney closed her lips around the flat utensil – a makeshift spoon – and scraped another bite into her mouth. She tried to smile for Angelina's benefit, letting her know that it really wasn't half-bad, although she wasn't all that convincing, even to a four-year-old.

Angelina's lips tightened even more.

Brooklynn surprised us all when she sat down on the other side of Angelina, setting her own bowl on the table. 'Here,' she offered, pulling out a small container of syrup from her pocket and pouring it generously over Angelina's bowl. 'It makes it better. Not good, just better.'

My sister grinned up at Brook, our old friend, someone she'd seen nearly every day since she was a baby. Brooklynn grinned back at her. The old Brooklynn. The real Brooklynn.

'So, what is this place exactly?' I asked Brook.

Angelina was in better spirits after she'd actually eaten, swinging my arm as we walked. Not that I was surprised; sleep and a meal were general cure-alls for the under-ten crowd.

Unfortunately, I fell into a different category altogether.

'For me, it's sort of a home away from home, but for many of these people, it *is* home,' Brooklynn explained as she led us through the tunnels, showing us around.

Sydney had opted to go back to our chamber to lie down after offering up a poorly executed fake yawn, attempting to convince us she was exhausted. But I guessed it had more to do with getting away from Brooklynn, who glared at the Counsel girl every chance she got.

'Most of these passageways haven't been used in years; some didn't even exist before the Outcasts began to move down here. We've even created new channels that connect the old subway lines to the mines outside the Capitol. It's like our own city down here.'

'Don't you worry about getting caught? About the queen's men finding you?'

Brook made a face as if I was speaking nonsense. 'She'd have to know where to look to find us. Even if they could find an entrance, the tunnels are long and winding. They'd get lost before they ever reached us.' Her teeth flashed, dazzling and white. 'We've been down here for over a decade; no one's found us yet.'

Angelina let go of my hand when we came to a group

of children playing. She stood silently, watching them.

The same checkerboard pattern we'd watched the girl drawing in the dirt when we'd first arrived was also outlined in the dirt before us. Their game was already underway, and they took turns as they tossed pebbles into the squares. Then the players took their places in the square in which their stone had landed. When the last pebble was tossed, they would use their bodies as game pieces, trying to eliminate the other players.

I recognized the game immediately as princes and pawns, a game of strategy that every child in the realm knew.

The children were giggling, something Angelina rarely did.

But she reached again for my hand, jerking it, asking me without words if we could get closer, asking me to help *her* get closer.

'Go ahead,' I whispered, squatting in front of her so that we were eye to eye. 'See if they'll let you play.'

I grinned at Brooklynn as Angelina left me, easing her way toward the energetic group at play.

'So, what about you, Brook?' I finally broached the subject, once I was certain Angelina could no longer hear. 'How did you end up here?'

She didn't hesitate. 'I've always been here, Charlie, you just didn't know it. I was practically born here. My mother was part of the resistance long before Xander was around to lead us. She believed that things would be better if there was no class system at all.' Brook's brown eyes warmed as she spoke of her mother. 'It wasn't until I was older – just before she died – that she confided her true beliefs, and her passion for the cause. By then, I knew these people; I'd spent so much time down here that I felt like I belonged with them. No one has to pretend down here. There is only one language, one class.' Her voice drifted off. 'Sometimes, when I'm supposed to be at home, I come here to sleep. My father never even notices I'm gone.'

I felt ashamed that I hadn't realized how lonely she'd been. 'So your dad, he's not part of the cause?'

She made a face. 'He doesn't have a clue. He was always happy with his lot in life; he would never want to cause trouble. Besides, he would never cross the queen.'

'And you would?'

She shrugged as if her answer was inconsequential. 'I think if my dad had ever known about my mother, he probably would have turned her in himself.'

'Really?' I was shocked by her statement. 'But he was devastated when she died. He doesn't even seem like the same person anymore.'

She raised her eyebrows. 'I didn't say he didn't love her.'

'Were you ever going to tell me?'

'No,' she stated, and even though her denial was absolute – final – I couldn't help thinking I'd heard just a trace of regret in her voice.

Then she turned her back on me and walked away, leaving me feeling deceived and abandoned. And in need of some answers.

XVI

I pounded my fist against the wall, my frustration bubbling over. 'What do you mean, you're having a hard time finding them? You told me yourself that the fighting is over. How hard could it be? They must have returned from the shelters by now.' I hated the feeling that he was holding something back, that there were things he was leaving unsaid. 'They checked our house? And the restaurant?'

Xander nodded, folding his hands in front of him so casually that it took everything I had not to run over and shake him, to scream in his face that they'd made some sort of terrible mistake. That they'd gone to the wrong places.

Except I knew that they hadn't. Brook had been in charge of the search team, and she knew *exactly* where to look for my parents, exactly where they should be.

'We'll keep looking, Charlie. I swear we'll find them. Until then, you need to get some rest. Did you sleep at all?'

I didn't answer his question; I wasn't in the mood to discuss my sleeping habits. 'How do you expect all of this to end?' I threw my hands up in exasperation. 'Even if you can overthrow the queen, what then?'

Xander grinned, and I got the impression this was a topic change he wasn't opposed to. 'What are you asking me, Charlie?'

'What becomes of the queen? Who do you expect to lead the people once your revolution overthrows the throne?' I leveled my gaze on him. 'You? You can't possibly expect to rule without a queen's power. It's been tried before.'

Xander's voice was calm; he didn't seem to share my doubts. 'I'm not sure what becomes of the queen.' He shrugged. 'I suppose that's up to her. If she wants to make things difficult, I imagine she'll have to die—'

'Be killed, you mean?' I challenged flatly.

He nodded, eyebrows raised. 'That's exactly what I mean.' Why was I relieved that he didn't try to lie to me? Why did that simple acknowledgment elevate my trust in him, even if only a little? Behind me I heard footsteps, and I turned to see that Brook had joined us. 'As far as a new ruler, you're right; we must have a queen to take her place.'

I scoffed at his response. 'You're insane! Where do you think you'll find another regent willing to come to our country to take the queen's place?'

'We don't need to go to another bloodline. We have one here, in this country. Descendants from the original line, who survived the overthrow more than two hundred years ago.'

'So where have they been? Why does no one know about them?'

But Xander didn't even blink; he had a quick answer for all my questions. 'They've been hiding. And why wouldn't they? Their very existence would be a challenge to the monarchy. Surely if anyone had known who they were, they would have been captured and executed by the crown.'

'And what's changed?'

'Time is running out. Sabara is growing old and needs an heir soon. She's been searching as well, hoping to find these descendants before we do, to infuse her brand of evil into them before we can convince them that our way is better, that the class system is no longer necessary. If she finds them first, I worry about what type of spell she'll cast on them.'

I was confused; he was talking nonsense. Besides,

I questioned, 'If they truly are descendants, wouldn't they have the will of the people to back them? Why wouldn't they have sought to regain the throne long ago? Why has no one tried to put them back into power?'

'It's simple. There's never been a female child before. There has to be a princess to inherit the realm.'

I gave him a dubious look. 'And now there is?'

Brooklynn shifted behind me but remained silent.

'We believe so.'

I hesitated, wondering why there was a sudden charge in the air, why the hairs on my arms were suddenly standing on end. 'How do you know?'

Brooklynn cleared her throat, and I turned to look at her, as she – not Xander – answered my question. 'Because, Charlie, we think we've found her.'

They were wrong. This was all wrong. There was nothing royal about my family – or me. I'd been born into the Vendor class, plain and simple.

We were merchants who worked hard in service to the crown.

I studied Angelina as she slept, wisps of her silver-blond hair sticking up from her head, creating a soft halo even in the darkness. I tried to imagine her as anything other than what she was, but it was ludicrous. She was no more a princess than I was.

'Wake up.' I spoke as quietly as I could, leaning close to her ear. I shook her gently.

I felt bad waking her after so little sleep, but we needed to leave. I needed to go in search of our parents, and after everything Xander had confided – his suspicions about who we were – I was certain he would try to stop me if he knew what I planned.

Her sleepy eyes blinked up at me.

'You have to get up. We're leaving,' I explained, slipping her jacket over her shoulders and tucking Muffin into the inner pocket.

She took my hand without hesitation and we crept from the chamber, careful not to disturb Sydney, who slept more soundly now. I was grateful that the woman who had been positioned at the door the day before was no longer standing guard over us.

It was easy for us to blend into the ceaseless activity in this city below the streets; no one paid any notice to the two of us as we moved quietly among them. Angelina kept pace with me despite the weariness that was apparent in the dark circles beneath her eyes. Her pale skin hid nothing from me.

I scanned the walls again – just as I had before retiring to our chamber for the night – looking for possible exit points. In my head, I'd mapped out several promising options. The people who lived down here seemed to come and go freely, and I could see no shortage of tunnels and doorways leading to the world above.

What I wasn't as sure of was whether we would draw more attention using any particular route. Attention was something that Angelina and I needed to avoid at the moment.

I pulled Angelina out of the way, our backs pressed to the wall, as we watched three drunken men staggering toward us from one of the darkened passageways. They were loud and unruly, clinging to one another as they stumbled over their own feet and then laughed at their missteps. I kept my eyes lowered, relieved that we didn't earn so much as a second glance from any one of them. I was certain they had just come from above ground.

I dragged my sister in the direction from which they'd come.

Once we were away from the ever-present gas lamps of the main chambers, the channel we stepped through grew darker and narrower. From somewhere up ahead, I could hear the constant sound of water dripping. The fetid smell that assaulted us made me wonder if we were traversing some sort of sewage line. Angelina squeezed my fingers tightly, although whether she was afraid of the dark or repulsed by the odor, I couldn't be certain.

'I'm here,' I assured her, taking each step cautiously, feeling my way with my toes. With my free hand, I brushed my fingertips along the wall, which was slick in places, making my stomach recoil even when my fingers could not.

Every step felt dangerously uncertain.

We walked like that for over seventy paces, the entire time listening for any sounds that we were being followed, until at last, a splinter of light fractured the near-total blackness. But it was enough, and I could see a set of crude steps that led up to a fissure in the ceiling above us. I wasn't sure where the opening would lead, but it seemed our best chance for escape.

I thought I should go first, just in case, but I knew Angelina would never allow me to leave her alone in the sewers, so I pushed her ahead of me. 'I'm right behind you,' I vowed.

She scrambled up quickly, faster than I could manage, and she disappeared through the gap before I could insist that she wait for me. I was less steady on the uneven steps, and I released a relieved breath when I finally surfaced on the other side.

Angelina was already reaching for me.

'I'm not sure where we are.' I looked around. 'I don't recognize anything.'

The area we found ourselves in was more industrial than residential, with large darkened warehouses and storage depots. I couldn't see any of the destruction from the bombs in this section of town, so I assumed that there were no military facilities nearby. The crevice we'd emerged through was just that, a crack in the ground, but thankfully there was no one around to witness our emergence from the opening.

I had no real grasp of time, other than that it was late, which was confirmed by the curtain of night that surrounded us. I didn't know if it was before or after curfew, so we'd need to be cautious. I had to assume the worst, that the sirens had already sounded and that we were breaking the law by being out here.

The first thing I was aware of was that electricity had been restored and that streetlamps glowed brightly in the night. I figured our best bet was to just choose a direction . . . eventually *something* had to be familiar.

Angelina was tired, and I would have carried her, but I was afraid she would fall asleep in my arms, and then I'd be unable to put her down again. For now, it was better that she walked.

After a while, we began to see wholesale markets and retail shops, places that, had it been daylight, would have been open for commerce. I knew when we saw people in front of a small café that we were safe to be out. The café was loud, teeming with activity.

I heard the familiar intonations of Parshon among them, and I realized that we must be near the west side of the city. These were *my* people.

No matter what Xander said.

When we rounded the corner, I got my first glimpse

of the devastation caused by Xander's bombs; almost an entire city block had been annihilated. The acrid scent of smoke crept far beyond the perimeter of the damage, while black plumes still smoldered, climbing toward the night sky. I silently prayed that no one had been wounded – or worse – in these explosions.

Soldiers and guards, their blue and green uniforms now covered in soot, worked to clear away the rubble. I knew it would be faster if we navigated through the debris, but instead I tugged Angelina's hand, signaling her to keep pace with me. I didn't want to take the chance that the military men might notice us, so we cut left, taking the long way around the wreckage.

When we reached the other side of the decimated block, I had my first real dawning of recognition.

We were near the restaurant now – *our* restaurant – in the alleyways that ran behind the marketplace.

After a wrong turn, we finally found ourselves standing in the central square. I almost never came there, but I knew the place immediately, and I dragged Angelina close to me, wrapping my arm around her head to shield her eyes. I didn't want her to see the place where men, women, and children were regularly executed, even though *I* couldn't stop staring at the simply constructed scaffolding of the gallows. The hangman's noose dangled limply, lifelessly.

'Just a little longer,' I promised once we were past it,

recognizing that her steps were growing sluggish. 'We're almost there.'

Angelina said nothing in return.

As we approached the plate-glass window of our parents' restaurant, I squeezed my sister's hand. We could see only darkness inside, not even a flicker of light to ignite my hope that they might be in there. There was no point stopping.

I struggled to contain my emotions so that Angelina wouldn't see my disappointment. What had I expected? I didn't believe Brook had lied about searching the restaurant. Still, I couldn't just give up.

We moved faster now, spurred by the fact that we were so close to our home. When I felt Angelina faltering beside me, I reached down and gathered her into my arms, finally letting her collapse against me.

There were other destroyed buildings, damage that blemished the landscape of the city, but I couldn't take the time to reflect on those things now.

When we reached our street, anticipation made my heart stutter.

I slowed down, my pace hesitant now. I took in every tiny detail. Everything appeared so normal, practically unscathed by the violence that had rocked the city just the night before. It felt like a lifetime had passed since my parents had pushed my sister and me into the battle-scarred streets.

Ahead of us, our house stood silent and still, cloaked in total blackness.

Despair snaked around me, squeezing until I thought my lungs might collapse. At the front step, I set Angelina on the ground once more and tried the door.

Unlocked.

My parents had never left the door unlocked before.

I eased it inward, the creaking of hinges heralding our arrival. I kept Angelina behind my legs, not certain from what I was protecting her, as my throat tightened.

As vendors, our home had never been fitted for electric lights; they were a luxury well beyond my family's earnings, so I fumbled inside the door for the lamp that was always there. But this time it wasn't, and neither was the table it usually sat upon.

Choking on my own fear became an entirely real possibility.

'Stay here,' I ordered softly. But Angelina held tighter, stepping when I did, refusing to peel away from me.

I blinked hard, trying to adjust to the absence of light within the walls of my own home. When I stepped again, glass crunched beneath my foot, and Angelina's grip grew desperate.

Every step I took over the debris was loud, and inwardly I recoiled from the noise I was making.

I groped in the blackness with my hands, searching aimlessly. I jolted when I bumped into the bulky wooden dining table where we ate our meals, but at least now I had a landmark.

My fingers explored its scarred surface, feeling the familiar blemishes that had always been there, and then relief blossomed when they brushed against the candle, exactly where it should be at the table's center. I edged around the table, carrying the candle with me to the sideboard and fumbling through the drawer for the matches I knew I'd find.

That pale flame was more beautiful than any sunset I'd ever witnessed. I sighed heavily at the sight of it.

The light gave me the courage I'd needed to try my voice for the first time since crossing the threshold. It only seemed natural to call out for my parents in the language they preferred. I turned in a circle, Angelina still clinging to me as I searched the room. '*Mom! Dad*—'

The words had barely reached my tongue before I sucked them back down my throat.

My house – *our house* – couldn't have been more damaged had one of the bombs found its way inside. But I knew that wasn't the case. The walls were still standing, still sturdy.

Angelina's fingers pinched my hand.

'I don't know . . .' I answered on a silent breath.

I scanned every corner with my eyes, every place the light could reach, hoping we were all alone, that whoever had done *this* to our house had already gone.

I knew now, without a doubt, that my parents weren't here. That something had forced them away.

The broken lamp beside the door was only the beginning; our home had been ransacked. Furniture was upended. Cushions had been sliced apart and were bleeding stuffing onto the floor. Books and photographs looked as if they'd been blown haphazardly by heavy winds, and, in some places, even the floorboards had been ripped from their joists.

For what purpose, I had no idea.

My first instinct was to flee, to take Angelina away from here, in case those responsible returned. But this was our home, and we had no place else to go. At least not until I had some answers.

And I was desperate to find out what had happened to my parents.

Angelina was sleeping on the sofa that I'd pieced back together, replacing the cushions and as much of the stuffing as I could. I didn't want her in our bed; it was too far from where I worked to restore some semblance of order, repairing some of the damage that had been inflicted on our home. And she hadn't argued; she'd simply curled into a ball, yawning hard and loud, and allowed me to cover her with a quilt to keep her warm. I doubted she wanted to be too far from me, either.

I did my best to put furniture back in its proper

place, and then swept away the shards of broken lamp from the entry before gathering papers and books and photographs from the floors. Most of the things I picked up were familiar items, part of our household: written recipes, childhood storybooks that my father had read aloud, first to me as a girl and then to Angelina, and the small pile of family photographs that my parents had been able to afford on our modest budget.

But there were other items as well, things that were less recognizable. A carved box lay in pieces beside a hole in the floorboards, and I knew that I'd never seen it before. There were documents, many of which looked old – older than my parents' generation – and the papers they were printed on were brittle and curling at the edges, the ink fading with age. I flipped through them but could see nothing significant in their contents. Antiquated land deeds, legal rulings, and personal correspondences, mostly dating from before the Revolution of Sovereigns. But among them were portraits that I didn't recognize, fading as well. Old, but beautiful. And strangely haunting.

I sat on my knees as I sifted through them, tracing my fingers over the faces that stared back at me.

I knew these people – these strangers. Men, women, children. I recognized their posture, their expressions, their features.

I studied the photo of a man, a smile touching my lips as my eyes moved over his mouth, his eyes, his gossamer blond hair. His face was the face of my father. *And of my sister*, I thought as I glanced at Angelina sleeping soundly on the sofa.

I reached up and ran my fingertips over my cheeks and my nose and my chin. *And of me.*

But who were these people? Why had I never seen these portraits before now?

I looked closer, trying to find a clue.

In several of the pictures, the men were wearing sashes of some sort, each bearing a similar emblem. I leaned forward, drawing the photos closer to the lamp on the floor beside me, trying to decipher the wording on the insignia. But the image was too unclear, too faded.

Frustration wept through me, and I squeezed my eyes shut, trying to figure out what it was that nagged me about the image.

I glanced down at the shattered box. I could make out parts of that very same symbol on it, identical to the one the men wore in the photographs, but now it was splintered apart. I reached down and carefully began piecing it together, like a puzzle, using the photographs as my guide.

Outside, in the street, I heard voices. They seemed far away, another lifetime from this moment.

When I was finished at last, I studied the emblem, wondering at it. It was beautifully carved; the woodwork was masterful. But it said nothing, this etching. Just a design. A brilliantly intricate design.

I sighed, running my finger over its lovely, ornate surface . . . and that was when the world around me shivered. My vision blurred, and for an instant I was aware of nothing but the sensation beneath my touch. Time seemed to stop.

I moved my finger again, stroking the details of the carving, feeling my way around each groove as I realized that this was no ordinary design.

This was a language. A tactile language.

And it spoke to me.

I gasped as I drew my hand away, clutching it to my heart, which was pounding erratically within my chest. I suddenly wanted to take back that simple action, that light brush of my skin over the surface of the mended box. I wanted to unlearn what I'd just discovered.

Because it wasn't just an emblem they wore in the photograph, these men who looked so much like my father, and like myself.

It was a seal. A crest.

Belonging to a long-banished royal family.

XVII

The noises I'd heard coming from the street were just outside the door now, practically right on top of me.

I was almost too stunned by the disturbance to breathe, let alone acknowledge that we – my sister and I – were no longer alone. My fingertip felt as though it had been blistered by the flames of a fire, but I knew that it was something worse that had burned it. Knowledge of something that should have remained hidden, buried beneath floorboards I'd walked upon my entire life.

Xander was right. Of that I was almost certain.

My father was a descendant of the throne. *The original throne.*

And that meant that I . . . that Angelina and I . . .

The first female children, wasn't that what Xander had told me?

The door opened, and again, I cursed the fact that the lock had been broken. We were trapped in here, and I jumped to my feet, positioning myself in front of the sofa, reminding myself that nothing else mattered right now except keeping Angelina safe.

Behind my back, I clutched the iron fireplace poker that I'd kept close for exactly this purpose. I was prepared for anything, I tried to convince myself as I readied to fight my way out of here.

But as it turned out, I was not at all prepared to face the person who stood inside the doorway, filling out the frame.

He glanced at the photographs and papers strewn about my feet, his gaze falling to the crest atop the poorly repaired box. Then his eyes landed on me, taking in the defeated expression on my face, and the fireplace poker now hanging limply at my side.

'I'm sorry you had to find out this way.'

'You knew? How many more secrets have you kept from me?' I ducked out of his path, circling the table as he tried to approach, keeping it as a barrier between us. I didn't want his sympathy or his compassion. 'And where are your goons? I'm assuming since you travel in a pack that they're somewhere nearby.'

But Max didn't give up that easily; he eased toward me, taking slow, cautious steps. 'I was worried about you, Charlie. How long have you been here?'

'I don't want to hear how worried you were. I want answers. I want to know what you haven't been telling me. Are we in danger now?' I tried to keep my voice low so I wouldn't wake Angelina, but I felt hysteria creeping in on me. I had so many questions; they were all coming at once.

'I don't think so. No one knows you're here. The queen thinks you're a member of the resistance. She doesn't know that I . . .' He didn't finish his sentence, but I wondered how he would have: *Know you? Kissed you?*

I was thankful that the queen knew neither.

'What about your guards, they didn't tell her? Are they here now? Will they turn us in?'

'They're right outside the door, making sure no one can enter,' Max explained. 'They'll tell only what I allow them to, which is only what you want to reveal. You can trust me, Charlie. I never meant to hurt you. I wasn't trying to deceive you.' He stepped closer, but I shoved my hands against his chest, keeping him away and shaking my head.

'You have a strange way of showing it. So it's true, then?'

I waited, needing to hear it from him. He didn't move

right away, and I wondered if he understood what I was asking.

Then he nodded his head. So slightly, almost imperceptibly.

I closed my eyes. I'd needed his confirmation, more so even than Xander's.

I was a princess. As was my little sister. My father was a prince, a member of the Di Heyse family – which meant almost nothing in a long line of male progeny, even those belonging to a royal bloodline.

Only the girls were born to rule.

'How did you know?' I finally found my voice again, and Max took another slow step toward me, closing the gap.

He shook his head. 'I wasn't entirely sure until now.' His eyes fell on the box again. It was the Di Heyse family crest that should have been destroyed more than two hundred years ago, along with everything else from that sovereignty. But it wasn't. It was here. In my home. 'I first suspected when I saw you in Prey.' He reached into his pocket and pulled out a heavy gold chain – a necklace with a locket, and on the outside, that same royal crest had been engraved into the antique metal. His thumb released the catch, and he revealed the miniature photo inside.

Even in the pale light of the candle I could see the resemblance. Like all the other pictures I'd looked through, it was like looking in a mirror. I lifted my gaze to his. I had so many questions.

'Queen Avonlea,' he explained. 'She was the first to die in the Revolution.' His dark eyes were heavy with sadness. 'My brother and I used to hunt for treasure on the palace grounds . . . I doubt my grandmother even noticed when this went missing.' He held it out for me. 'It seems as though it belongs to you now.'

I shook my head, backing away as if the locket would somehow scald me. 'I don't want it. I can't—'

Max didn't press me; he simply put the necklace back into his pocket. 'And then when I saw you with your friend, you seemed to *understand* my guards . . .' He studied me pensively. 'No one should have known what they said.' It wasn't an accusation, but it felt like one.

I looked away, not ready to admit anything.

'Is it just the Royal language, Charlie, or are there others?' He stepped again, this time standing right against me. If I'd wanted to meet his gaze, I would only have had to tip my head back. But I didn't. I stood stock-still. 'Didn't you ever wonder how that was possible? How a vendor's daughter could understand a language she'd never heard before?' He reached over, his finger nudging my chin to gain my attention. *'You'd never heard it before, had you?'* He didn't bother speaking in Englaise now. And I didn't pretend not to understand.

I shook my head, my eyes finding his. My heart was thundering in my chest, making so much noise I was surprised I could even hear his words.

'*Your parents knew?*'

A slow nod, a simple admission.

'*They never explained what it meant? About why you might have this . . . ability?*'

I glared at him, the only answer I was willing to offer. What did he know of my parents? What right did he have to question their reasons for what they did – or did not – tell me?

'*You know,*' he continued, refusing to relent, even while facing my frown, '*only those who can be queen are born with powers. Only the female royals.*'

I took a step back, bumping into the table behind me. 'It's not a power,' I tried to explain, shrugging it off. 'It's nothing. Less than nothing.'

He smiled then, but it wasn't at all warm or friendly; it was triumphant, gloating. 'Really, Charlie? Tell that to everyone who can understand only the language of their class.' Then he tipped his head toward Angelina, just four years old, a beautiful slumbering angel, oblivious to how her life was changing. 'What about her? Do you know what she can do yet?'

I frowned at him, my head reeling. 'So, what now?' I

finally managed, ignoring his question. I felt dangerously light-headed.

Max reached for my hand, and I was too overwhelmed to keep it from him. I wasn't sure what I thought about him, whether I trusted him or not. But for the moment, he was all I had. Besides, he made me feel things that had nothing to do with trust, and if I was being completely honest, I liked having my hand in his.

'I'm not sure. I suppose that depends on you.' He was speaking in Englaise again, probably to put me at ease. His thumb moved in lazy circles over my palm, as if he were trying to create his own language, trying to communicate with me through his touch. I understood the meaning even if I didn't comprehend the vernacular. 'There are things we need to discuss.'

A loud crash outside the door made me jump, and I pulled my hand away, tucking it behind my back as if hiding the evidence of our intimacy.

'Don't move,' he ordered, even as I was rushing to Angelina, who'd been awakened by the commotion. He shot me a warning look, telling me that he meant it, but it didn't matter – the door was already swinging inward.

Claude stormed inside. *'There's someone outside who insists on seeing the girl.'* I wondered if he actually didn't know I could understand him.

Max played along, keeping his sentry in the dark. *'Who is it?'*

'Xander.' The way he said Xander's name made me shudder. It was dark and laced with menace. There was a history there, I was certain. *'And he's not alone.'* Claude smiled then, and like Max's smile before, there was nothing warm or friendly about it. It was pure daring, and it was chilling. *'Do you want me to handle him?'*

Max glanced at me, sizing up my response before answering. He'd made it clear that he'd seen me with Xander that night at Prey, but I could only guess at whether he knew Xander's role in the resistance.

'No. Let him in. But only him.'

Claude looked disappointed but did as he was told, leaving to fetch the leader of the revolutionaries.

'How much have you told Xander? How much does he know?' Max asked quickly once we were alone again.

'Nothing. I haven't told him anything.' I stood up from the sofa, leaving Angelina behind my back as I tried to recall if Xander had ever questioned what I could do. 'But he's the one who explained who we are. Or at least who he believes we are.'

Max's eyes narrowed as Claude returned, Xander at his side.

I wasn't certain that I'd ever noticed just how large Xander was until that moment; he very nearly rivaled

Claude in height. He was less bulky, perhaps, but still muscular in a leaner, stealthier way. Xander appeared more jungle predator, ready to strike, while Claude bore the presence of a charging bull. Each demanded notice in their own way.

'*Guard the door and make sure no one else disturbs us,*' Max told Claude, dismissing the scowling guard.

Xander didn't even speak to Max, barely acknowledged him at all. Instead he came directly to me. He clasped my hand in his, the one that only moments ago, Max had stroked with tender reassurance. 'You have no idea the danger you put yourselves in by leaving, Charlie. We can't protect you if you won't let us.'

'She doesn't need your protection.' Max shoved his way between Xander and me.

Xander laughed derisively. '*Why? Are you offering yours? She'd be safer in a nest of vipers. You may as well hand her over to Sabara with the noose around her neck,*' he scoffed, surprising me as he berated Max in the Royal tongue.

I took a step back; my world was suddenly reeling. How was it that Xander spoke the language of Royals?

'*And you believe she's safer with you and your band of misfit soldiers? Have you told her who you are? What you used to be?*'

Xander cast a quick glance in my direction, as if his words were veiled, their meaning hidden, and I knew in that moment that my secret was still safe. He had no idea that I understood what he was saying. Angelina was the only one in the room who didn't comprehend. '*Damn right she's safer with us. We have her best interests in mind.*'

'*Your interests are as selfish as the queen's. You need a ruler, and you think Charlie fits the bill.*'

'*She does. She's the One. And you know it too, or you wouldn't be here on the queen's errand.*'

Max's teeth ground together as he took a warning step toward Xander. '*You have no idea why I'm here, and neither does the queen.*'

Xander hesitated, but only for a moment. '*She must know something. Otherwise . . .*' His eyes swept over the destruction inside the house. '*Otherwise she would have no need for Charlie's parents.*'

I gasped, my hand reaching around my own throat as I staggered backward. I settled down on the sofa, where Angelina sat silently.

'You – you think *Queen Sabara* has my parents?'

Xander's eyes grew wide, his anger toward Max momentarily forgotten as he stared at me, finally realizing that I'd understood him. He didn't ask for an explanation; he just frowned, looking sorry. 'I do, Charlie.' This time in Englaise, so there was no room for misinterpretation. 'And you may be the only chance they have. But right now, we need to get you out of here.'

He shot an angry glare in Max's direction as he added, 'Before she sends someone back for you and your sister as well.'

Suddenly my home had become a trap, and we stayed for only as long as it took me to gather Angelina in my arms and rush through the doorway into the street. Brooklynn was waiting there, along with a small contingent of Xander's soldiers, and I was again struck by how at ease she appeared among them. We made an odd assemblage, our traveling party – soldiers and commoners, rebels and royalty; although I doubted anyone looking would recognize us for what we truly were.

Once it was decided that the only place we could safely go was back to the underground city, we traveled in silence. It wasn't a comfortable silence, however; it was strained and filled with unspoken tension.

Claude and Zafir had both made it clear that they had reservations about going with the resistance fighters, while Xander had qualms about allowing the queen's grandson, and his two guards, into his underground operation. But no one could agree on an alternate option, another place where the queen would be unable, at least for the time being anyway, to locate Angelina and me.

Brooklynn walked at my side, and I wondered if it

was simply out of habit or if she was still my oldest friend. I honestly couldn't tell any longer, and I hated that I was questioning her loyalty.

Max stood on my other side, his bulky guards surrounding him as best they could, keeping Xander and his people at bay.

We didn't go back the way that Angelina and I had come, through the tiny fissure in the ground. Instead Xander led us through the back entrance of a restaurant that was closed for the night. We made our way through the shadowy kitchen and through a doorway that should have led to a cellar below, but rather than a cellar, it opened up into a passageway that stretched endlessly before us. There were lamps, already lit, along the way. It was cleaner, and smelled better, than the sewer through which my sister and I had traveled earlier.

Still, whether from fear or attraction, I found myself moving closer to Max. My shoulder bumped against him, and I felt the tension within me unravel with his proximity.

I set Angelina on the ground between Brooklynn and me, my arm aching from the weight of carrying her. On her other side, I saw her reach for Brook's hand, clinging to each of us as she walked. It was reassuring to know that Angelina still trusted her.

Only once we were securely ensconced within the

tunnel, away from the staircase that led back to the restaurant above, did anyone speak.

It was Xander who first broke the silence. He fell back so he could speak directly to Max. 'If you didn't tell her, how did the queen know about Charlie?' His voice echoed along the dim corridor.

There was a brief pause, and I got the distinct sensation that this wasn't a question Max wanted to answer. But I, for one, was anxious to hear his response. I glanced up so I could see his face.

His brow creased when he finally spoke. 'They had no idea who she was until they went to her home and discovered her parents.' Accusation was heavy in the stare he directed at Xander. 'It was you they were looking for, questioning everyone with suspected ties to your revolutionaries. They use force to gain any information they can.'

'But what did I do to draw their suspicion? Why would they believe I knew where Xander was?' I still didn't understand.

'You didn't do anything, Charlie.' Max's hand reached over and slipped around mine, squeezing tightly. I didn't have time to ponder the meaning of the gesture; his next sentence explained it all. 'One of the people they tortured was your friend Aron.'

For a moment, I didn't realize that I'd stopped walking. It wasn't until Angelina tugged at my hand, reminding me that she was still there . . . that they were all still there, watching me.

I looked up, swallowing the anguish that threatened to clog my throat, my eyes stopping at each one of them. At Max and at Xander. At Claude and Zafir, the guards who had sworn their lives to protect their prince. At Xander's well-armed revolutionaries, including Brooklynn, who had sworn their lives to their cause. And at Angelina, who stared back at me with her trusting blue eyes.

Aron. I couldn't fathom it. They had tortured Aron to find *me.* And not because of *who* I was, but because of who I might know?

It was only a bonus, I supposed, that they'd discovered the missing royal family in the process.

I felt sick to my stomach. Max held me up as I swayed, and my fingers clutched his, if only to remain on my feet.

'Did they—' But I couldn't finished my sentence.

Then Brooklynn, who had been silent up until this moment, finished for me, and in her tormented words I heard her, the person she'd been before I'd lost her to a rebellion. 'So it was me they were looking for, not Charlie.' Her voice sounded hollow, and then she whispered her question – *our* question – on a shaky breath. 'Did they kill him?'

'No,' Max answered. 'When I left, he was still alive.'

I felt her shuddering sigh all the way from the other side of Angelina, as if it were my own.

There was something about knowing that I wasn't alone in this, that Brooklynn was still with me, suffering because Aron had suffered, that made me feel stronger, more determined.

I stood upright now, releasing Max's hand just to prove that I could. I held my back straight. 'Then we need to save him. And my parents. Somehow, we need to make this right.'

XVIII

Brook tugged my hand, drawing me away from the others, doing her best to afford us some privacy as we navigated the chiseled corridors, moving farther underground.

'I didn't know,' she whispered, keeping her voice low and glancing around to make certain no one could hear us. 'I never meant for anyone to get hurt. Especially not Aron.' Her dark eyes were sad, filled with regret.

'I know,' I assured her, seeing her differently now. She was no longer the carefree girl I'd known in my childhood, nor was she the hardened revolutionary I'd imagined she'd become. Instead she was passionate, devoted, dedicated. And, still, my friend. 'But you do realize that people are going to get hurt if there's a war, don't you?'

'We don't want that, Charlie. We don't *want* to fight, but we can't just go on like this. We deserve to choose what we want to be, *who* we want to be.'

I didn't disagree with her reasons, but I didn't know how to respond, so I didn't try. 'What about me? How long have you suspected—?' I faltered; the right words were difficult to find. 'How long did you know who I was?'

'We only just figured it out. Your father did an excellent job of keeping his identity hidden. In fact, your parents weren't the only ones being watched . . . there are other families who've been suspected. But then the night the Academy girl—'

'Sydney,' I corrected her.

Brook shrugged, as if knowing her name was somehow distasteful. 'The night *Sydney* came into the restaurant and you spilled water on her, I overheard your parents arguing in the kitchen. Your father was worried that someone might discover the truth if you weren't careful. He was afraid the queen would learn you existed. I was pretty sure then. After that it was just a matter of getting you close enough to Xander so he could decide if you fit the description.'

'The club?' I asked, understanding dawning.

Brook nodded, the trace of a glint in her eye. 'But we

left too early that first night. Xander wasn't there yet.'
No wonder she'd been so mad at me when I dragged her
out of the club that night, insisting it was time to leave.
'You made it easy, though, when you asked if we could
go back.' She nudged me playfully with her shoulder, as
if we were talking about boys, or school, or anything
other than what we were really discussing. 'But even
then I had no idea what your gift was, what power it was
that you were hiding.' She smiled at me then, a wickedly
familiar grin. 'I wish you would have told me, Charlie.
Think of all the cool things we could have done with that
little trick!'

'You're crazy!' I nudged her back, smothering a laugh.
This didn't feel like the right time for laughter, not while
my parents were still out there.

'And the night at the park? Did you know what was
going to happen?'

Brook's head dropped shamefully. 'I knew something
was up. I was told that I needed to keep an eye on you.
I figured the best way to do that was for us to go out.'
She glanced sideways at me. 'I didn't mean to lose you in
the park. When the sirens went off, I looked everywhere.
Eventually, I figured you must have taken off with . . . *him*.'

She didn't say Max's name, reminding me that she was
still bitter, and I wondered if it was ever jealousy after all,
or if she'd known all along who he was. I thought of that
night at Prey, when she'd flirted shamelessly with Claude

and Zafir, and I wondered if it had all been just an act. A calculated way to gain their trust, to try to gather information. I suddenly wondered at Brooklynn's choice in men, always leaning toward those in the military.

I didn't bother asking her.

'We're so close,' she explained. 'To everything we've always wanted, to everything we've worked for.' Her eyes shimmered as she looked at me. 'And you can give it to us, Charlie. You can change everything.'

I shook my head, my eyes filling with tears that I couldn't explain . . . even to myself.

Brooklynn was wrong. I could accept that my father came from a royal bloodline, or at least I could no longer deny it. I'd seen the proof with my own eyes. I could even accept that *that* was the reason I could comprehend the other languages, that interpretation was my ability as a royal daughter.

But I wasn't born to rule . . . I could never be a queen.

'Yes, Charlie,' Brook offered before I could voice my denial. She seized my hands, clasping them tightly in hers as she pressed them to her lips. 'You must.'

I closed my eyes, hating that I would let her down, and not wanting to have this discussion right now. Not when I finally felt like I had her back.

Once we were back in the underground city, Xander took charge of the situation. 'Brook, you take

Angelina back to her chamber, so we can talk to Charlie alone.'

'But shouldn't I be here—'

A fierce look flashed across Xander's face, warning Brook not to argue; she'd been given an order.

'Leave her with Sydney,' I offered. 'And then you can come back.'

Xander and Eden exchanged a meaningful glance. It occurred to me that Eden wore her moods the way others wore their garments; they hovered about her, invading the space wherever she went. At the moment, I could feel a heavy veil of reticence.

'Brooklynn, go,' Xander insisted, and he waited until she and Angelina were out of earshot before turning back to me. 'Sydney's not here, Charlie.'

'What do you mean, she's not here? Where is she?'

'She was feeling better, so we sent an escort to take her home,' Xander explained.

'Aren't you worried that she'll tell someone about you? That she'll turn you in?'

Xander just smiled, a patronizing smirk. 'She won't. She cares about you, Charlie. She's grateful for what you did to help her. Besides, even if she did try to bring someone down here, she'd only get lost.'

I remembered the convoluted pathways we'd traveled, one passageway connecting to the next, twisting and turning. And then I thought about what Brooklynn had said, about how long they'd been down here – over a decade – completely unnoticed.

Yet it seemed a huge risk to take.

'We couldn't keep her here forever, Charlie. She needed to go home to her family.' Xander's voice was more reasonable now, less boastful.

And then I heard Max's quiet voice behind me, his breath tickling the back of my neck. 'I think maybe you liked having her follow you around like a puppy,' he teased, and I grinned at the absurd suggestion, elbowing him as inconspicuously as I could.

Unfortunately, there was nothing inconspicuous about the gesture. Everyone saw that single, simple action.

And all hell broke loose.

Within the span of a heartbeat, the two enormous Royal guards lunged toward me with deadly intent etched in their expressions. Before I could think or react – or even blink – Xander's men had raised their weapons, and were aiming them directly at Claude and Zafir.

Xander came crashing into my side, wrapping himself around me to soften the blow as we hit the ground. Every ounce of breath burst from my lungs when we landed. And at the same time, from between Xander's arms, I could see Max launch himself between me and his determined sentries.

'No!' he shouted, raising both of his hands, his voice hard, angry. 'Stop! All of you!'

I gasped against Xander's grip, struggling for breath, my head reeling. Xander's arms loosened, but not by much.

'I mean it,' Max snarled, and I caught a glimpse of him turning in a circle to glare at the soldiers around him. Yet only Claude and Zafir obeyed their prince's command, each halting where they stood.

No one else complied, and weapons remained readied.

'Are you all right?' Xander whispered against the top of my head.

Somehow I was able to nod, and when I did, I heard his voice rumbling from deep within his chest. 'Stand down, soldiers.' I couldn't see all of them, but I could hear the simultaneous withdrawal of both bodies and weapons. When Xander finally released me, lifting me to my feet, the look on his face was fierce.

Max reached for me, dragging me away from Xander and drawing me against his side, his arm wrapped protectively around my waist. There wasn't a single person in that room I would've traded places with, including Eden, who had shouldered her rifle as well.

When Xander spoke to his soldiers, his voice was deceptively composed. But there was a fury coiled below the surface as he turned on his own. He was a snake, ready to strike as he moved with dangerous precision around the small space. 'You raise your weapons without my order? Do you have any idea the damage you could have done? The danger you put *our guest* in?' I knew he was talking about me; everyone in the room knew it.

I looked first to Claude, and then to Zafir to judge their reactions to Xander's rant. I don't know why it mattered, but I needed to know if they'd been told yet, if they knew who I was.

Zafir appeared bored, his brown eyes glazed over. Claude looked incensed, as if he'd like to personally snap every neck in the room.

I was suddenly self-conscious in their presence, knowing they were still unaware.

'You could have hurt her,' Xander continued, treacherously quiet. 'I expect you to protect her with your lives. All of you.' And then he said the words that made my stomach twist. 'As if you were protecting your future queen.' He reached Eden and lifted his fingers to her cheek, the ropy muscles of his forearm visibly tense. He ran his hand along the side of her face, and she squeezed her eyes shut. 'Do I make myself clear?'

Jumbled emotions surrounded her like a thundercloud: fear, regret, devotion, and something that felt unexpectedly close to passion. A tear slipped from her closed eyes, cutting a path down her face. She nodded, opening her black eyes once more and staring, not at Xander but past him, to where I stood.

'I understand,' she vowed, swearing her fealty to me.

* * *

300

'*How is this possible? She's a simple merchant girl you met in a club.*' Claude raised his voice, shouting now in the Royal tongue. He had refused to look at me since Xander's men had holstered their weapons. Since Xander had dropped the bomb about who I was.

Zafir seemed more open to the idea. '*How do you expect your grandmother to react when she finds out?*'

The reminder that Queen Sabara – the woman who Xander and his revolutionaries were waging war against – was Max's grandmother was jarring. It was something I shouldn't forget, I told myself. I had no idea where Max's loyalties lay.

'*She'll be thrilled,*' Xander interjected. '*Why shouldn't she be? Charlie could be the heir she's been searching for, the one her own family was unable to provide. And I intend to make certain the old woman never gets her hands on her.*'

Zafir tipped his head, as if accepting Xander's cryptic statements. I, however, remained in the dark.

I glared at them all, unable to keep my opinion silent any longer: 'I have no intention of taking the queen's place.'

Only Claude and Zafir reacted to my interruption, reminding me that they were still unaware of my ability to comprehend the Royal tongue.

'*She interprets?*' An expectant smile lit Zafir's stony face.

'She does,' I replied tersely, as if he'd been speaking to me.

He hadn't been. '*What else can she do?*'

Max answered. In Englaise. 'Nothing that she's aware of, but time will tell.'

It was the first time I'd considered that possibility, that I might be capable of more than just deciphering the languages of others.

'*What of the child? Has she displayed a proficiency yet?*' This was Claude, sounding irritated by the discovery. The only difference was that he addressed me directly.

'No.' Max shook his head, and I guessed that he'd taken my silence when we were at my house as a denial.

Xander draped his arm around Eden's neck. It was a brotherly gesture – like comrades – and I wondered how long they'd been fighting together. 'We need to figure out what our next step will be.' He raised his eyebrows expectantly. 'I, for one, think it's time to let Sabara know we have Charlie.'

'What about my parents? And Aron?' I cried, tired of being spoken about as if I were livestock, cattle for them to do with as they chose. 'We need to get them back.'

Xander's expression turned serious, and his words were callously indifferent. 'It may already be too late for them. They can't be our concern right now,' he explained.

'No, no, no! You don't get it!' I shook my head, crossing my arms defiantly. 'They *are* your concern.' I glowered at him and at Eden, and then turned to face Max. 'Do you think it's too late? Do you?' I demanded.

Max moved toward me. 'I don't think they're dead, if that's what you're asking.' He frowned, watching me intently, his intense gray eyes boring into me, delving into my psyche and searching for cracks in my spirit as if the weight of this bit of information – or the next – might be too much. 'But my grandmother is ruthless, and if she thinks there's even a chance they might know where you are . . .'

I spun on Xander once more, not wanting Max to finish his sentence, or even to contemplate the words he hadn't said. 'You see? They're alive,' I rasped, demanding that he pay attention to me. 'I need to go there.' Then to Max, I said, 'I need you to arrange a meeting with your grandmother.'

'It's a bad idea, Charlie,' Xander explained to me, and I took it as a good sign that he was no longer shouting at me. 'Sabara can't be trusted.'

'You can't reason with her,' Claude insisted, repeating the words he'd already stated several times.

'They're right, Charlie,' Max agreed. 'She's both my queen *and* my grandmother, and I don't trust her. She'll say, and do, almost anything if it means getting her way.' He reached for my hands as if somehow he could convince me through his touch.

I was tired of having this conversation. They were my parents – what was I supposed to do? I withdrew my hands, watching as his fingers slipped through mine. 'I have to,' I whispered. 'Please, just make it happen.'

Xander tried once more. 'What if I refuse to let you go?' But there was no real weight behind his words now.

I bristled at the idea. 'What choice do you have, really? You need my cooperation, and unless you help me get my parents . . .' I let the meaning hang between us.

His eyes warmed, even as his brows drew together. 'So are you saying we have your cooperation? That you'll agree to be our queen?'

'I'm saying that you're guaranteed *not* to have my cooperation if you don't help me.'

Xander beamed at me. 'Already I see a promising negotiator,' he lauded me, and I recognized the cunning behind his carefully chosen words. He'd missed his true calling, I thought. He should have been a diplomat. 'You'll make an *excellent* queen.'

XIX

'There are things you should know, then, if you plan to actually meet her in person,' Xander explained, and I wondered why it was Xander offering this lesson and not Max or one of the royal guards. Surely they had more firsthand experience. Yet they seemed satisfied to let Xander take the lead in this instance.

'She's cunning, deceptively so. Don't allow her feeble appearance to fool you into believing otherwise. And she's brutal, don't ever forget that.' He paced, and I had difficulty following him with my eyes. He was making me dizzy. 'I'd feel better if we all went with you. I'd rather you not be alone with her.'

'What if she doesn't agree to meet with us?' Max questioned Xander.

Xander dismissed the notion with a wave. 'Of course she'll want to meet with Charlie. She's been planning this for years.'

Max was as uninformed as I was, it seemed. He shook his head. 'How would you know what she plans?'

'I know more than you realize. More than anyone else, probably.' He laughed derisively, yet no one challenged his statements. Still, I was baffled by how this revolutionary had such intimate knowledge of our country's ruler.

He stopped pacing and stood before me. He stared down at me with such a familiar tenderness that I nearly forgot into whose eyes I was looking. I blinked as I realized that it was Xander – and not Max – gazing at me with such intense adoration. 'She means to force a promise from you, to share the throne.'

'That makes no sense,' Max finally interrupted. 'How can she expect to co-rule? Loyalties would be divided. How would disputes be settled?'

'Her magic is ancient – she's much older than the body she inhabits. This is not her first time on the throne.' Xander's story sounded like a child's fancy, but still, no one disputed him.

'What is he talking about?' I asked, turning to Max instead of Xander.

But it was Zafir who answered, his voice low and almost melodic. 'He's right. The queen's soul – her Essence, she calls it – has been passed from body to body since before she accepted her post on the throne of Ludania. Same ruler, different body.'

Xander took up where Zafir stopped. 'She's powerful, but she must have permission to make the exchange from one body to the next. And she's desperate, she's running out of time. She needs your approval before she can transfer her Essence to your body. Otherwise she'll remain trapped in the body she's in. If it dies, she dies.'

'Why my body? Why can't she find someone else to take her place?'

The answer seemed obvious, but I needed to hear him say it. 'Because your blood is royal. Because you're the only female heir she can find.'

I frowned. 'But am I really? I mean, my mother isn't royal. And my father certainly can't be full-blood, can he? How strong can my blood really be?'

Xander seemed to know everything, and he answered smoothly, easily, without hesitation. 'It doesn't work that way, Charlie. A female's blood, no matter how far down the line, is as strong and pure as if she were born to the first generation of royals. Her gifts will be just as powerful as those of her ancestors.' He raised his brows, begging for more questions, but I had only one.

My eyebrows drew all the way down. 'And if I were

to accept this . . . this *Essence* . . . what happens to me then?'

'Nothing's going to happen to you,' Max interrupted, gripping my shoulders and forcing me to look at him. 'Because you're not going to do it. You're going to tell her to go to hell!'

But Xander ignored Max's outburst, giving me the only answer he had. 'My best guess is that there's room for only one of you in there.'

No one spoke again as silence ate up the air around us. The queen was going to try to bargain: my life for my parents. She was cunning, Xander had said. Well, I would have to be *more* cunning.

'Max is right,' I declared, snapping my chin up and making my decision. 'She can go to hell.'

They were still arguing when I left them, as they tried to decide how best to get a message to the queen. Max wanted to go himself, to ensure there was no miscommunication in the missive, and to force a promise from the queen that I wouldn't be harmed. But Xander wouldn't allow it; he still didn't trust Max. In the end, it was decided that Claude would go, but that he must take one of the resistance fighters with him. Which fighter was going was still up for debate.

Because we were underground, and darkness ruled, I had no sense of day or night as I made my way through the passageways, but I knew enough to realize I was aching and bone weary.

When I reached the chamber, Angelina was awake, and I wondered if she'd slept at all. I dropped to my knees as she rushed into my arms. She smelled like sweat and sleep and dirt, and I inhaled deeply as I pressed her close to me. Her luminous blue eyes belied the nights of fragmented sleep and interrupted dreams. Looking into them, it wasn't difficult to imagine that she was someone special.

My eyes, on the other hand, felt gritty and tender, and I rubbed them with the back of my hand in an effort to keep fatigue at bay.

I glanced longingly at the pallet on the floor, at the pillows and the scratchy blanket. Brook took Angelina by the hand to find some breakfast, while I fell into a restless sleep filled with dreams of soldiers and queens and lost souls.

It was the sound of water that woke me, the whooshing noise it made as it was poured from one vessel to another. It wasn't loud, but I'd heard it nonetheless.

I blinked as I opened my eyes, hoping it wasn't an illusion I was witnessing: the big metal tub with steam rising from it.

A bath. Someone had brought me a bath.

Eden held open the drape that had been affixed over

the doorway, while two men carried in two more oversize buckets of water, adding them to the tub.

'Claude's back. We're leaving as soon as everyone's ready.' Her black eyes met mine, and she raised one brow. 'Xander thought you might want to get cleaned up first.' She turned to leave. 'I'll be right outside.'

'Wait! Where's Angelina?'

Eden nodded, her countenance relaxed for the moment. It was easier to be around her when she was like this. She made me feel the same way, despite the fact that she'd just informed me I was about to meet the queen. 'She's already had her midday meal, but she wanted to stay and play with some of the children. I decided it would be okay. Time can move slowly down here with nothing to do.'

She was right, of course. I didn't want Angelina to be stuck in this dark chamber all day. Or all night, whichever the case may be. 'Okay,' I finally agreed.

The curtain fell behind her, and I eyed the water. Never had I imagined that a bath could look so enticing, especially one in a steel tub. But I undressed quickly and slipped beneath the water.

There was no soap, so I just soaked, enjoying the feel of the water over my bare skin. I felt bruises forming already on my ribs, from when Xander had slammed me to the ground, and I prodded them gingerly with my fingertips. It was a tight fit in the tub, and mildly uncomfortable, but somehow I managed to lean all the way back, drawing my head and face beneath the surface. I ran my fingers through my hair, scrubbing as best I could. It was like a bit of heaven.

When the water was too cool to bear any longer, I finally stood, reaching for the threadbare towel I'd been left. It was then that I saw a pile of clean clothes stacked neatly on the end of the sleeping pallet. My clothes, from my home. There was also a set for Angelina. It seemed a dangerous risk to send someone back to our house for fresh clothing.

I dried and dressed quickly, sitting on the edge of the pallet as I toweled my hair and used my fingers to comb through the tangles.

It seemed like a lifetime since I'd been both clean and rested – luxuries that I'd taken for granted my entire life. It was hard to imagine it hadn't even been two days since the night of the attacks.

A soft tapping came from outside the doorway. 'Charlie?' It was Max's voice, and I was suddenly aware of how very alone I was in here.

My pulse thrummed nervously throughout my body as I cleared my throat. 'Come in.'

He stepped inside, and I smiled broader than I'd meant to. I wasn't certain I wanted him to know how pleased I was to see him.

'May I?' he asked, pointing to the spot next to me on the pallet.

I nodded, my expression earnest, my heart racing as he sat down beside me.

'How are you holding up? You don't have to do this, you know.'

'I'll be okay,' I insisted, but still, I bit my lip. 'Can I ask you a question?'

'Anything.'

'Was Xander right not to send you? Can we – can *I* – trust you?'

His smile was unexpected. He reached up and moved a damp tendril of my hair from my cheek. 'You can trust me, Charlie. And so can Xander, even when he makes me want to put my fist through his face. He knows as much; he just doesn't want to admit it.'

His lazy smirk was pure enticement. I wanted to be immune to his brand of temptation, but I wasn't, and I found myself leaning toward him. The lamp in the corner flickered, casting shadows over his face, changing shapes and colors, but no matter what dance they did, he was still beautiful to look upon.

His mouth inched toward mine, and I watched it, my gaze frozen on his lips, my breath stuck somewhere between my lungs and my throat.

'What time is it?' I asked, hoping it would stop him from coming any closer.

He smiled, and I could see his teeth, every detail, including a tiny chip that would have been indistinguishable from any decent distance. His breath was warm and smelled of promise. 'Why? Is there someplace else you'd rather be?' His voice was rough and gravelly, and filled with something I didn't quite recognize but that made my toes curl.

When his lips reached mine, my heart stopped beating, its cadence lost on our kiss. I closed my eyes, telling myself to pull away from him, but I was incapable of following through with that one simple action.

It was tentative at first, just the slightest encounter of our lips as they brushed ever so lightly together. A feather's touch . . . lighter even. My thready pulse spoke its own recognizable language.

But then I moved – closer, though, not away as I'd warned myself I should – answering his tender request with my own. Telling him that I wanted more.

His fingers laced through my still damp hair then, hauling me against him until we were chest to chest and mouth to mouth. I reached for his shoulders, clinging to him as I parted my lips, unsure of my actions, but needing to be closer. His tongue slipped inside my mouth, and my veins were infused with liquid fire, making me shiver with both need and fear.

Never had I wanted something so badly in all my life.

Never had I been so frightened of my own emotions.

I was still shaking when I finally turned my head away, ending the kiss. It was the hardest thing I'd ever done. My lips felt swollen and raw, and achingly cold in the absence of his.

Max's eyes were glassy, as I was certain were mine. I'd never seen the face of interrupted passion before, but without a doubt it was the look I was witnessing now. Disappointment weighed heavy in my heart.

He was quicker than I was to recover, and within moments he was breathing normally again. It made me angry that he could compose himself so quickly, as if he was well practiced in a skill that I was not. I glared at him, ignoring the stab of jealousy that such a thought had delivered.

'What are we doing?' I asked on a shaky breath.

'I thought we were kissing.'

'*Shhh,*' I insisted, covering his mouth with my hand and trying not to think of what that mouth had just done to mine. I didn't want Eden to hear what he said.

'What's the matter, Charlie? Are you angry that I kissed you? Or that you kissed back?'

I lowered my voice and my eyes. 'I just don't know how this can possibly end. What good can come of this? Of us?'

His finger lifted my chin, a gesture that made my stomach flutter. 'Who says it has to end?' His thumb rubbed my lower lip.

I closed my eyes, so I couldn't see his fathomless eyes, so I couldn't imagine staring into them forever. 'I'm a vendor's daughter, Max.' The heartbreak in my words was nearly painful to my own ears.

Max nudged my chin, forcing me to look at him again. When I finally did, he answered, 'You're a princess, Charlie.'

The world around us froze as Max watched me. Hearing those words out loud was something I would never get used to. It was one thing to talk of meetings with the queen, or to imagine my sister and my father as members of a distant royal blood line. It was something else altogether to hear myself referred to as such. It was far too easy for me to overlook that fact.

He was right, of course. I *was* a princess. In his arms, I'd allowed myself to forget. In his arms, I'd merely been myself.

'Is that what this is about, then?' I didn't want to ask the question, but I needed to know the truth.

Max looked confused. 'What are you talking about?'

I clenched my jaw, bracing myself. 'This. The kiss. The reason you found me *intriguing* in the first place. Is it because you suspected I was a princess?' Who else would be suitable for someone of Max's birthright?

He disarmed me by smiling. Then, tucking a strand of hair behind my ear, his voice rumbled low, caressing my heart. 'I would have found a way for us to be together even if you'd been a servant's daughter,

Charlie. You *do* intrigue me, but not for any of the reasons you suspect.'

He leaned in then and kissed me again, sweet and soft and tender, silencing my arguments and stealing my breath, making me wonder how one simple gesture could be so tragically lovely.

THE QUEEN

The queen held back her smile, a *real* smile, as genuine delight coursed through her. 'You've located their base? The heart of their entire operation?'

Baxter nodded. 'We have, Your Majesty.'

Her lips twitched. 'You're certain? I've no patience for another failure.'

His head dropped at the reminder of his shortcomings, his stout frame trembling. 'Of course not, my queen. This time we're certain. The rebels sent a small group of soldiers out into the city, an escort of sorts into the east side. One of our scouting parties just returned with word that they were able to track the rebel contingent all the way back underground.' He met her gaze, grinning. 'This time, we've got 'em.'

She was practically quivering with anticipation. Her next words were the ones she'd waited so long to ask. 'How long until you can be ready to attack?'

Baxter lifted his chin, daring a quick peek at the woman on the throne. 'On your command, Your Majesty. The troops simply await your order.'

She could no longer contain the grin that broke across her face. 'Good, Baxter. This is very good, indeed.'

She recognized the relief on her adviser's face; he knew he'd evaded a death sentence of his own by bringing her this news. He realized he could no longer afford to disappoint her.

'Oh, and Baxter?' She lifted a gnarled finger to her lip, deciding it was time to make preparations.

'Yes, Your Majesty?'

'Spread the word, and I don't care how you do it, but make sure that no one questions my decree. Tell them that soon we will have a new queen.'

XX

'You have to wait here, Angelina. There's no room for argument. I promise I won't be long.' I leaned close to whisper in her ear. 'If you're good, I'll bring you a surprise.' I smiled at her as I drew away. I was certain I could find some treat to satisfy a four-year-old. 'Eden will stay with you.' I glanced up at the blue-haired woman who watched us. 'She promises to take good care of you. Right, Eden?'

Eden nodded, curt and no-nonsense, a soldier to the bones.

I glanced back to Angelina. 'You trust her, don't you?'

Angelina didn't turn her wide eyes away from me, and at first she didn't respond at all. The delay worried me.

I *needed* Angelina's answer. But then her eyes sparkled, ever so slightly, as she gave me her response, a barely perceptible nod.

No one else could have possibly known how much meaning that single gesture held.

Eden was honorable. Angelina had told me so.

That was Angelina's other ability, I recognized now. What I'd once thought was just a strange intuition on her part – a knack for knowing who could, and who could not, be trusted – I now understood was something more. Like her gift for healing.

We were the reason our parents worried so much, why they sheltered us and taught us to keep our unusual talents a secret. They'd known all along who, and *what*, we were.

I smiled again at my sister, satisfied that the arrangement was acceptable. I kissed her cheek, noting the sticky scent of candy on her breath, and wondered if she'd already gotten a treat from her new babysitter.

No wonder Angelina didn't mind being left with Eden.

I turned to Max, taking a deep breath to steady my nerves, and then made my decision. 'Okay. I'm ready.'

When we were out of earshot of my sister, he repeated, 'You don't have to do this, you know?' And I could hear the doubt traced through his words.

'Yes, I do. It's the only way to ensure that my parents remain alive. You heard what Claude said, the queen promises not to harm them if I come to the palace.'

'What she didn't promise was to release them,' Max argued, reminding me – again – that his grandmother had chosen her words carefully. 'I still think you could get her to agree to meet elsewhere. The palace is *her* ground.'

'This is her country, Max. Everywhere is her ground. Do you think she wouldn't outman us no matter where we agreed to meet? Besides, the farther from Angelina, the better.'

I pulled Max to a stop, using it as an excuse to touch his hand. Max didn't seem to mind, and he drew me close as we slipped out of the stream of traffic in search of a quieter place where we could talk privately.

He looked down, watching as our fingers intertwined, and a thousand butterfly wings beat in the pit of my stomach. I could feel his breath against my cheek, and I wanted to turn toward it, to find his lips with mine. Even the feel of his hand touching mine was distracting, and I had to focus to remember why I'd wanted to get him alone in the first place.

In a lowered voice I finally asked, 'Who is Xander?'

Max's head snapped up. 'What do you mean? He's the leader of the revolutionaries.'

He couldn't possibly imagine I would believe his lie, could he? Even without my sister to tell me otherwise, I knew better. 'You know exactly what I'm talking about,

Max,' I insisted, pulling my hands from his and placing them on my hips. 'I want to know why he can speak in the Royal tongue, same as you. Where is he from exactly? How does he know so much about the queen?'

He wavered then, and the denial that I'd sensed was coming remained where it was, suspended without voice. At last, he released an audible breath. 'He's from the palace, Charlie. Xander is my brother.'

'I should have told you sooner,' Max tried again once we were tucked safely within the shelter of the awaiting transport. He sat beside me, yet he felt miles away. 'But there was never a good time. Besides, I'm not certain it even matters any longer.'

We were alone in back, just the two of us. At Max's insistence, Xander, Claude, and Zafir rode in front. If we'd been speaking at a normal volume, they could have easily overheard what we said, but we weren't. Max kept his voice low, a hushed plea. And mine remained stubbornly lodged within my throat.

It was my first time riding in a fuel-based vehicle, and it was like nothing I'd ever imagined. I felt as if I were floating on a cloud. It was smooth and glided like silk over the stone streets. Automobiles were rare, even on the streets of the Capitol, and people moved out of our way, standing on the sidewalks to watch in awe as we passed. This was an opportunity that someone born in my position was rarely afforded.

Then I remembered what my true position was and realized I was wrong. This was *exactly* the kind of luxury that someone of my status would be allowed.

I might never get used to that fact.

I turned my head to stare out the window, watching as we reached the concrete walls of the city, the vehicle slipping past the pedestrian lines at the checkpoint without even slowing down. Those who could afford the luxury of a motorized vehicle weren't required to submit to the customary inspection and document checks that everyone else was. It was assumed that they were legal, above reproach.

It was a day for firsts, as I had never before seen the countryside, either. I was born and raised within the walls of the city. I'd heard stories of fields and forests and small country villages; I'd even seen drawings. But to experience it firsthand nearly stole my breath. It was very nearly as sweet as a first kiss.

My skin tingled as I thought about Max's lips touching mine, reminding me that he was still sitting beside me.

The quiet within the cab of the transport was thick, and as much as I wanted to continue ignoring him, my curiosity was getting the best of me. Besides, I tried to console myself, he'd already apologized several times.

Curiosity is an addictive drug, my father used to tell

me when I asked too many questions. I wanted to heed the warnings of my childhood about my inquisitive nature, but I found myself lured by my interest. Still, I refused to look at Max when I finally whispered, 'How do you deny your own brother?'

His expression darkened. 'I didn't turn my back on him. *He* was the one who decided that being a royal wasn't good enough. *He* was the one who wanted to change the world.'

I looked at the men in front of me, studying the back of Xander's head and trying to imagine how I'd missed the resemblance between him and Max, not just in looks – their eyes were varied shades of molten steel – but also in build and manner. Even their voices were similar. I'd been so consumed by their differences that I had never recognized just how alike they really were.

Max tried to bridge the distance as he reached for my hand. I jerked it away; I wasn't yet ready for him to touch me. 'Every lie I discover leads back to you.' The words were true enough, but even I understood that I was wrong, that I could trust Max. Angelina would have warned me if he was disloyal.

He inhaled deeply, an impatient sound, and Zafir turned in his seat, his black brows raised as he checked on the well-being of his prince. Max shook his head and waved his guard away.

'Charlie, please. I'm not asking you to choose sides; it's not me or my brother. But you're about to face my grandmother. Let me stand beside you.' His hands closed around mine, his eyes watching me intently. 'Have some faith that I have your best interests in mind, that I'll do everything in my power to keep you safe.' Max was making me a pledge, just as he'd done before when he'd written a note and slipped it into my history book.

But his reminder of where we were going made my stomach tighten.

To the palace. To the *queen's* palace.

I closed my eyes and leaned back against the seat behind me.

The palace was a place like no other. We were on the estate grounds long before the buildings came into view. The green lawns looked like they'd been hand-shorn, every blade a sliver of perfection spread out before us in sweeping verdant waves.

Glittering ponds were stocked with beautifully feathered waterfowl, beyond which forested lands stretched for as far as my eyes could see. If paradise were a real place, I imagined it would look very much like this.

I glanced at Max, nerves and anticipation making it easier to forgive his deception. He was right, I needed his support.

'You'll be fine,' he assured me. 'I'm right here.'

I took a breath as the vehicle passed through gates that stood open, awaiting our arrival. Both sides of the stone-tiled driveway were lined with manicured hedges that obscured my peripheral view and forced all my focus forward, toward the grounds that opened up before us.

Anxious to get my first glimpse of the palace, I raised my head, straining to see above the three enormous men crowded into the seat in front of me. But they were taking up all the space, and I could catch only fleeting glimpses of stone and iron and glass. Nothing to satisfy my mounting curiosity or quell my overworked nerves.

And then everything happened so quickly that I didn't have time to contemplate the view. The vehicle came to a stop, and the door was opened. My pulse hammered recklessly. Max exited ahead of me, and I knew what he was waiting for, but I couldn't find the will to move.

From the front, Xander turned to me, eyeing me with admiration. 'You can do this, Charlie. You're stronger than you think.'

I wondered if he would say such things if he knew how badly my hands shook, if he knew that my skin felt brittle, like ice, as if it would shatter should I move too suddenly. Or if I dared to breathe.

My parents are in there, I reminded myself. *And Aron. They need me.*

It was enough, and I was propelled into motion.

I reached for Max's awaiting hand and let him draw me from the shelter of the transport. I held my teeth together to keep them from chattering as my eyes searched for his. I needed to see his calm, to borrow from it.

The tenderness I saw there thawed my chill and gave me the strength I'd been searching for.

Yet as I emerged from the vehicle, it wasn't the opulence of the palace that captured my attention, but rather the thousand uniformed soldiers who stood before it in faultless, evenly spaced rows. Every muscle in their bodies was aligned as they awaited . . . something. They were vast and powerful and commanding. I was overwhelmed by the very sight of them.

My eyes widened, my breath caught.

Max took my arm and forced me to take a step forward; Zafir and Claude stood on either side of us.

From the field of men, a lone voice barked an order to the hushed crowd, and in an instant a thousand heads bowed, a thousand men fell to their knees in unison, and I was awed by the show of respect, this harmonic display of reverence.

I'd seen this kind of action only once before, in the

shelter below the city the night of the attacks. When I'd learned that Max was a prince.

'Is – is this for you?' I whispered, reaching for Max's hand, no longer caring who saw.

I awaited a response as I watched all those soldiers kneeling on the ground in respect.

'No, Charlie. It's for you.'

THE QUEEN

She stood at the window watching her men – guards and soldiers alike – bow low before the girl. Baxter had done well delivering her message throughout the ranks, making sure that the new queen was welcomed properly.

This was the girl she'd been searching for. *This* was the heir she'd hoped to discover.

She would have to tread carefully to ensure the girl's cooperation, and to be certain she made no mistakes. If she played things right, this girl could buy her another lifetime as ruler. A new beginning.

If she was wrong, if what she'd discovered about the girl was untrue, then it was over. All of it.

Alexander materialized then from the vehicle and she stiffened, her heart momentarily stuttering as she was transported back in time to the days when he had her favor, the only boy child who ever had. He was the firstborn of her son's offspring, a mischievous child with an eye toward righteousness, even then. He'd always been immune to her impervious facade and icy stares. When he'd smiled and climbed onto her lap, something no other child had ever dared, her frosty heart had warmed. She'd offered him sweet treats and gifts. She had allowed him unparalleled access to her inner sanctum, and he was schooled and housed within the walls of her wing of the palace. She'd kept him close.

She'd loved him.

And he'd turned his back on her.

And now here he was, an enemy to her throne, standing at the girl's side. The sight of her once beloved grandson made her heart freeze in place.

She was suddenly eager to see his expression when she shared the *surprise* she had in store for him.

And then there was Maxmillian – just another of her grandsons, no more unique than the rest. He, too, stood beside this new royal heir. But he wasn't the reason her resolve slipped. It was his loyal protectors, flanking the girl, who concerned her. Their devotion would always be to Max, the child they were born to protect, and if his allegiance had already been decided, if he'd been swayed by a pretty face, then so had theirs.

And the royal guards were not a force to overlook.

Fortunately, the queen had her own agenda. A plan already set into motion that would rock them all.

XXI

My ears were still ringing with the echoes of Max's shouts as he was dragged away by Her Majesty's guards. None of us had anticipated that we'd be separated upon our arrival. And while not one of the armed guards who'd surrounded us had dared to touch either Claude or Zafir, it was clear that they, too, were included in the forced detention that had taken place . . . they were simply allowed to go quietly.

I wondered how many bones would have been broken had it gone down differently.

It had taken me far too long to adjust to our changed circumstances. I hadn't expected Queen Sabara to hold us captive in this way.

It was supposed to be a meeting, I argued silently in my head. All I wanted was my opportunity to reason with the queen.

But what surprised me most of all was that Zafir had refused to go with Max, the prince he had vowed his life to protect, and instead had insisted on remaining with me. I didn't understand clearly, and he refused to explain his reasons to me, but no one questioned the giant when he grabbed hold of my arm, refusing to leave my side. Apparently I had Zafir's protection, whether I'd asked for it or not.

I paced to the window, wearing a path in the thick rug beneath my feet. 'How much longer does she plan to keep us in here like this?'

Zafir didn't respond. He'd stopped answering my questions when I'd begun repeating the same ones again and again.

I stared out onto the grounds that we'd passed on our way to the palace. The same ones I'd at first thought were idyllic now felt isolating. One more barrier between us and the city we'd left behind.

Tears welled in my eyes, but I forced them back. Had there really been a meeting planned at all, or was this whole thing just a trap? And, if so, who had she meant to capture? Me or Xander?

I felt guilty for agreeing to let Xander come at all. He had responsibilities to those who supported and counted on him. I had no business allowing him to escort me to the palace. I should have forbidden it.

I ran my hand along the sill of the window, marveling at the artistry that had been put into even the most insignificant details of the room. The carvings appeared handcrafted and expertly done. In the hours we'd been held here so far, I'd memorized nearly every opulent detail of the bedchamber in which I was being held.

It was the most luxuriously furnished room I'd ever laid eyes on, or even imagined. Every fabric, right down to the linens on the bed, was finely woven and hand-stitched. Every piece of furniture was meticulously constructed. Every metal was of the purest form, expensive and polished to a blinding shine.

It was a well-appointed prison.

'Do you think Max is nearby?' I turned to face Zafir, unable to ask about my parents just yet, worried my voice would break under the strain.

Zafir stood in the exact spot he had since we'd arrived, just inside the door, never moving, barely blinking. His gaze fell on me, and I wondered if he felt pity for me when, at last, he answered, 'His chambers are on the next floor. I'm sure that's where he's been taken.'

'He has his own room?'

'He's a prince. This is his home.'

I took a step backward, grasping the back of a tall chair. *Home.* How had that thought never occurred to me? I felt as if the wind had just been knocked out of me. This didn't feel like anyone's home.

'What about his parents?' I asked, knowing I was prying but unable to stop myself.

Zafir didn't seem to mind revealing Max's history. 'His father – the queen's son – died in a hunting accident shortly after Max's birth. When the queen realized that Max's mother could no longer bear royal heirs, that a princess was no longer a possibility, she was paid off and sent away. She hasn't been heard from since.'

I tried to imagine what that must have been like for Max, and for Xander. To grow up without their father, knowing that their mother had abandoned them for a price. To live in this palace without their parents.

I looked up again, and this time I could feel the tears threatening to spill. My voice shook. 'What of *my* parents, Zafir? What about Aron? Where do you think they are right now?'

'They're here,' he stated flatly.

The scraping noise that came from the other side of the enormous carved canopy bed sounded like one heavy boulder sliding over the top of another. It wasn't until Zafir left his post at the door and grabbed my arm, dragging me close, that I could see the opening in the wall itself. A hidden doorway.

I peered inside the hole and saw Xander's wide smile. Claude stood by his side, no smile. And then I saw Max pushing past them both. He reached for me, hauling me close and kissing my hair, my cheeks, my lips.

'You're safe?' he breathed against my forehead, and I nodded, self-conscious to have so many eyes on us.

I could scarcely believe he'd come for me.

'Hurry,' Xander urged. 'I don't know how much time we have before they realize we're missing.'

'What is this place?' I asked, looking around at the narrow opening – a hidden hallway behind the walls of the castle – as Max was already pulling me along. Behind me, I heard that shrill grating sound once more as Zafir resealed the cavity.

'We used to play in these passageways when we were boys,' Max explained, and as the flame from Xander's lamp flickered over their faces, I could see the grins that he and Max exchanged. 'They run throughout the palace, connecting almost all of the rooms and running below ground. Xander and I would sneak into the cellars and hunt for treasure. There's an entire chamber filled with artifacts dating back to your family's reign.' More quietly, he added, 'It's where I found the locket.'

Xander led the way. His steps were sure, as if he could

have negotiated his way without any light at all. Mine were less so, and I clung to Max, following his physical cues. When he moved, I moved. When he halted, I did as well.

Zafir remained at the rear, guarding our backs. And ahead of Max and me, Claude looked ready for attack.

'Where are we going?' I asked.

It was Xander who answered, as we turned and turned again, traversing a twisting maze of tunnels. 'I was afraid Sabara might pull something like this, so I had Brooklynn gather some men to follow us. Of course, they didn't have the luxury of a royal transport, but they should be here soon.'

'And then what?'

Max squeezed my hand. 'Then we get your parents and your friend, and we get the hell out of here.'

Everything changed the moment we emerged from the narrow passages into a dungeonlike cellar. Oil-filled sconces lined the hallways, making everything just a little too clear as we found ourselves face-to-face with an armed contingent of at least twenty men, all dressed in bloodred – the color of the queen's guard.

Xander reacted first, moving slowly as he placed his lamp at his feet. Max gradually drew me behind him, away from the others, until our backs were braced against the wall.

One of the queen's men stepped forward from the rest. His uniform was decorated with the glittering gold stars and tassels of a commanding officer. His expression was formidable. 'Stop where you are,' he ordered. 'I want to see your hands.' And then he leveled his gaze on me. 'All of you.'

I obeyed, lifting my hands in front of me, but Max pushed them back down again, refusing to surrender. 'We've done nothing wrong,' he stated, his voice unwavering as he positioned himself to stand in front of me. 'Back down now and no one will get hurt.' A meaningful glance was exchanged among all four of the men I traveled with. I seemed to be the only one who thought we were outnumbered.

There was a charged silence, a moment when twenty men in red stood like an impassive, unbreachable wall staring back at Max and Xander and Claude and Zafir. We had size on our side. They had sheer numbers.

'Xander! Watch out!' It was Max's hoarse bellow that drew my attention as one of the queen's guards broke away from the ranks and was advancing on his brother.

Xander moved like a blur, reaching for his ankle and whipping back up again with a knife that had been hidden in the side of his boot. He slashed a wide arc through the air, quickly and efficiently, and the guard fell to the ground, thrashing violently while his fingers tried in vain to seal the open wound at his throat.

Claude and Zafir were in the fray before my heart could beat again.

Max pressed me farther back, refusing to leave me even though I knew he longed to join them.

Three men assailed Claude at once, and just when I thought he'd drop beneath their weight, Claude's fist crashed upward, striking one man's jaw with a sickening crack. A second man dropped to his knees when Claude snapped his arm like it was no more substantial than a child's. The third screamed when his nose was shattered.

Xander's blade easily cut down two more guards, blood staining the floor all around them.

Zafir fought like nothing I'd ever seen before, using his feet just as agilely as he used his hands, lashing out in powerful, sweeping chest kicks. He incapacitated several men before they learned to watch out for the rib-crushing maneuver.

'Help them,' I whispered, but Max just turned to look at me over his shoulder, his brows raised.

'I won't leave you again,' he vowed. 'Besides, they're doing just fine on their own.'

A guard holding a sword to Claude's throat was disarmed effortlessly when Zafir lunged behind him and wrapped a thick arm around his neck. After about twenty seconds, the man dropped to the ground like a sack of flour.

It was then that I saw Xander. He was assaulted by

two men at once, caught offguard when one of the men pulled a dagger from his belt and sliced Xander's arm. Blood oozed from the wound, and Xander dropped his blade, instinctively closing his fingers around the injury. The guard with the knife sneered, positioning his weapon at Xander's neck.

I saw the muscles in Max's jaw clench.

'Go!' I urged in a rough whisper, and that was all it took.

Max sprang forward, crashing into the armed guard and knocking him to the ground. The sound of the man's skull hitting the solid floor rippled through the air, echoing off the walls. His eyes rolled backward in his head.

Before Max was all the way to his feet again, his elbow was already smashing into the face of the other man, the second attacker who threatened his brother. The man tried to remain upright, but he wobbled, and then crumpled, his legs failing him.

'Enough!' The commander's voice bellowed against my ear, as he grabbed me from behind, and I wondered where he'd come from, how he'd managed to sneak up on me. But before I could react – move or even breathe – the steel of his blade found the hammering pulse hidden within my throat.

Xander was the first to turn, followed quickly by Zafir and Claude, and then Max, who looked so furious – his entire body quivering with rage – that I worried for the commander myself.

'Now, we're all going to move calmly and orderly,' the man stated, wrapping his arm tightly around my chest as he prompted me to take a step forward. 'The queen is waiting for us.'

XXII

There were now at least thirty of the queen's guards in all, although only one of them was armed with a combat rifle like those carried by the soldiers and guards who were stationed throughout the Capitol. Even the resistance fighters favored guns over blades. Yet here, in the queen's palace, I saw mostly hand-to-hand weapons, like knives, daggers, bows, and double-edged broadswords; it was an antiquated way to fight.

I glanced around at all four of the men who'd come to escort me. They were covered in blood – although mostly it wasn't their own. All were being held at knifepoint.

The steel edge pressed deeper into my flesh. 'Eyes ahead,' the commander hissed.

I wanted to tell him to go to hell, but mine wasn't the only neck on the line.

My heart leaped into my throat as we approached the huge gilded doors in a hallway that was wider than any room I'd ever been in, and taller than my entire home.

I was finally going to meet the queen.

The doors were opened by footmen who bent low at the waist as we passed. And despite the blood rushing noisily through my ears, my eyes swept the enormous room, taking in the high ceilings, the rich tapestries, and an ornate fireplace that took up nearly an entire wall. Royalty, it seemed, spared itself no luxury.

Even though summer approached, a fire blazed in a massive hearth that was framed by an enormous carved mantelpiece.

But my heart plummeted once more as my eyes fell upon the throne, and I wondered if this was yet another distraction, a new place to keep us captive. There was no one awaiting us inside.

I couldn't stop myself from wondering where my parents were at this moment, how close they were to the place in which I now stood. I clung to the hope that their prison was as lavish as mine had been, but I worried that the fate they'd suffered had been less than extravagant.

The thought that they'd been used, pawns in the queen's game, made my stomach ache and made me all the more apprehensive about meeting her.

But we didn't have to wait long, and Her Majesty's arrival came with all the fanfare I would have expected of a queen. However, if I'd expected a regal woman who could storm the room and exert dominance by her very presence, I'd been sorely mistaken. The queen could no more storm the room than she could walk into it of her own accord.

I certainly hadn't expected to see an old woman being wheeled to her place at the throne.

She looked shriveled and frail, this woman who commanded a queendom, the body she wore betraying her, withering around her.

At her arrival, all the guards restraining us took a step back, yet not one of us moved. I was astonished, then, when everyone in the room, including Xander – leader of the revolutionaries, grandson to the queen – and Max bowed down in her presence, despite the fact that she'd just taken them both as prisoners. I followed suit, and remained there until I was told otherwise.

Xander had warned me not to be fooled by her outward appearance, but it was difficult not to overlook her weakness. The queen was an elderly woman who could no longer carry her own weight from one place to another. It was nearly impossible to believe that she was as merciless as I had been led to believe.

Until the sound of her voice cut through the room, and

the crystal clarity of it belied her delicate physical state. 'Rise,' she commanded, not a quiver to be heard. Her opaque eyes fixed on me as I lifted my head. I counted silently as I drew in air, exhaling to quell my trembling nerves. 'Come closer, Charlaina Di Heyse.'

The surname she spoke meant nothing to me, just a name from a history book. It felt strange to hear it leaving her lips and finding its place beside the name my parents had given me.

I stood, my legs quivering beneath me.

I thought Max would remain where he was, rooted to his spot until he was ordered to do otherwise. There were still rules to obey, despite the unusual circumstances surrounding our meeting, and as far as I knew, he was still a prisoner. We all were.

But instead he moved to stand beside me, a prince at home in a castle. He laced his fingers through mine.

I have a purpose, I reminded myself once again. *My family is counting on me.*

The air around me smelled of a fire's smoke and a queen's power as her lips drew back from her teeth in a startling attempt to smile. I couldn't tell if it was meant to depict good humor or if she was mocking me, and her voice didn't make my assessment any clearer. 'So you are the girl who has turned my country upside down.' Her pale eyes looked dead already but felt as if they were boring right through me. She ignored Max's presence at my side.

I flinched from her statement. 'No, Your Majesty.' I wondered what sort of answer she'd expected. But from the tightening of her lips, I recognized immediately that I had misspoken. 'I – I certainly didn't mean to.'

'*Of course you didn't, my dear. But you have.*' Her use of the Royal tongue was deliberate, and I realized that she knew I understood her.

Max squeezed my hand, a gesture of encouragement as he tried to intervene. 'You can't do this,' he stated to his grandmother, his voice low and steady. 'You can't hold her hostage. She's not property to be bargained with. She can't be forced to take the throne.'

I waited for the queen to answer him, but instead she stared blankly at my face, memorizing me as if she'd never heard Max speaking at all. I felt myself wanting to recoil from her chalky gaze. '*I've searched for so long . . .*' Her voice faded, drifting off, before finding its way once more. '*You'll make a good queen. So strong. So lovely.*'

'But what if I don't want to be queen?'

I thought she'd raise her voice, berate me in anger. I didn't expect her to smile. 'It's not up to you, child. It never has been.'

Xander stepped forward then. He'd torn one of his sleeves from his shirt and tied it around his wounded arm. Blood still soaked through. He moved to stand in front of both me and Max, as if he'd listened to enough.

Hostility split the air as the two of them stared at each other, and I wondered how long it had been since they'd been face-to-face like this. The silence between them was palpable, and in that moment, I felt that Xander was in more danger than the rest of us.

It was the queen who spoke first, her voice low and menacing. '*How dare you show your face in my home? What right do you have to stand before me?*'

Xander's voice belied the bitterness that was etched across his scarred face. 'Grandmother,' he bowed comically– mockingly. He spoke in Englaise, an obvious jab at his royal heritage. 'Always a pleasure.'

'*Don't "grandmother" me, you insolent brat. I'm your queen, and you'll show me the respect I deserve while you stand within these walls.*' Her eyes grew glassy. '*There was a time I would have done anything for you,*' she said in a tone that neared affection. The way she spoke to him, the way her voice dropped, made me think she'd forgotten that it wasn't just the two of them, that she wasn't having a private conversation with her grandson, but rather a public discussion with the man hell-bent on destroying her. '*My sweet Alexander, you were the only boy I've ever truly cared about.*' She closed her eyes, permitting herself a moment with her memories. And again, I saw a weakened woman before me.

Xander grinned. 'You won't be my queen for long. Charlie will never agree to your terms. She won't accept your Essence.'

She opened her eyes just a sliver, and then she cackled, a sound eerily similar to laughter escaping her thin lips. *'We'll see about that, won't we?'*

At last, a grim smile settled over her face. She spoke not to Xander, or to me, but to the guard at her side. *'Bring in the prisoners.'*

XXIII

I saw my father first. His hands were bound behind his back and his mouth was gagged. The cuts and bruises I could see were a thousand times worse than I ever could have imagined. My mother stumbled in behind him, and when one of the guards shoved her from behind, she nearly tripped over the shackles that weighed down her ankles.

I belatedly realized that the gasp I heard was my own as I watched Aron being dragged in. Dragged, because he was incapable of walking on his own, as his feet dangled limply behind him and his head lolled forward, sagging uselessly against his chest. Even from where I stood, I could hear his jagged breaths; they were difficult to listen to.

He was dumped on the floor like refuse, as if his very presence was distasteful.

I didn't wait for a signal that it was okay for me to move. There wasn't enough willpower in the world to stop me from running to my parents. I couldn't reach them fast enough and didn't care who might try to stop me. They were barely through the doorway when I was hugging each one of them in turn. I was careful not to squeeze too tight, since I didn't know how badly they were injured.

It pained me not to go to Aron, but I knew he wasn't even aware of his surroundings. He was brought only as a message to me: The queen had shown restraint with my parents.

'*Are you okay?*' I whispered in Parshon, slipping the filthy cloth from my mother's cracked and bleeding lips. Her breath smelled sour, a combination of hunger and bile; I could no longer find the sweet scent of warm bread coming from her skin.

She nodded, her eyes filled with remorse. '*What are you doing here, Charlaina? We told you to stay away, to keep your sister safe at all costs.*'

I glanced back to the queen, grateful that I'd left Angelina behind. '*She's safe,*' I assured my mother softly. Speaking to the guards, I ordered, 'Untie them.' I unbound my father's mouth and used the dirty rag to blot fresh blood that oozed from a wound at his scalp.

I wondered how recently he'd been abused, and the thought made my stomach clench.

Neither of the guards moved, so I turned to the old woman in the throne. 'Please, they're not going anywhere. What harm could it do?'

The queen lifted an eyebrow and nodded, a silent consent to my request, and my parents were freed.

My father wasn't as gentle as I'd been. His arms reached around me, crushing me against him. '*I'm so sorry we didn't tell you, Charlaina, about who you were. We worried for your safety.*' He pulled back to gaze at me, and I could see the sorrow in his swollen, bloodshot eyes. '*We couldn't risk that she find out you existed.*' He squeezed me once more, and this time his words came out on the quietest breath, meant only for my ears. '*Don't do anything she wishes. Do whatever it takes to get out of here alive, Charlaina. Leave us behind if you must.*' His grip tightened, ensuring that I understood the significance of what he'd just asked of me.

But before I could formulate a denial of my own, the queen's voice struck like a flash of lightning, causing goose bumps to ripple over my skin and the hair at the back of my neck to bristle. 'She will do no such thing! If she does, she'll have no parents to return to.'

My mother reached for my hand, clutching it so hard that I could feel the tears she was unwilling to

shed. *'Don't listen to her, Charlie. You need to stay alive.*
Angelina needs you to stay alive.'

And then the world around me exploded as my
father's entire body convulsed, seizing as he fell to his
knees, his eyes widening with panic, his fingers clutching
at his throat.

From behind me, Max's voice rang out in fury. 'Stop
it! Release him!' I turned to see him hurtling toward
the throne, toward his own grandmother – the queen –
where she stood, her balled fist lifted, pointing directly
at my father. Xander intercepted one of the royal guards
who moved to stop his brother, and his fist crashed into
the man's nose. The crushing sound was revolting, and
the guard dropped forward, cupping his bloodied face
in his hands.

But Max never made it to the throne.

It was the rifle's blast that stilled everything. My blood
stopped pumping as ceiling plaster clattered in chunks
over the polished marble floor at our feet, a consequence
of the warning shot. But we all watched in horror as
the guard holding the firearm dropped the nose of his
weapon and directed it at Max.

No one moved. No one blinked.

Yet it was my father for whom I feared most.

He couldn't breathe. Somehow the queen was
blocking his airway as he writhed on the floor, struggling
against her spell.

I stood frozen, watching it all, yet unable to move from my spot on the floor. I turned to the old woman who was showing me just how ruthless she could be. 'Please, don't do this! Don't hurt him!' I implored.

The queen, indifferent to the weapon aimed at her grandson, quivered as she stared down at me, her fist still extended in front of her. '*You can stop it, Charlaina. All you have to do is offer yourself in their place.*' She pursed her already thinned lips.

I turned to look at my father. Blood began to drip from his nose and seep from his ears. My mother saw too, but her words were determined. '*Don't do it, Charlie. No matter what. Do you hear me? Never. Never!*'

Then she, too, fell to her knees, gasping at first . . . and then desperately silent as she, also, fought for air.

My entire body shook as I turned back to Sabara, seeing her for what she truly was . . . the quintessence of evil. It was the hardest decision I'd ever had to make. She was asking me for my life. Or to forfeit my parents.

I thought of Angelina, of what my decision would mean for her.

Scalding tears burned my cheeks as I searched for my voice. At last I closed my eyes and answered, 'I won't do it.'

The silence of a queen is deafening and can stretch into eternity and back. Standing before her, I understood the meaning of forever as I waited for her response.

'I was hoping we could do this the easy way, Charlaina,' she finally stated, demanding everyone's attention as she made a show of slowly, deliberately, opening her fist and then dropping her hand to her side.

The gasps for air that came from behind me were enough to let me know that she'd just released my parents from her grip, but I was afraid to take my eyes away from the queen.

'Take them away,' she said, ordering their removal. They were nothing more than trash to her.

As if on cue, the huge gilded doors opened from the outside, and she added, 'I can see you've opted to make things difficult.'

As my parents and Aron were being dragged away, a woman I almost didn't recognize through the bloodied bruises that mangled her face was carried inside by two guards and dropped onto the marble floor in front of me. Her lower lip was torn, the flesh hanging limply, ineffectively from her mouth, baring her teeth in an eternal sneer. Had it not been for the spikes of blue hair visible through the blood-soaked scalp, I would never have realized that it was Eden I was staring at.

At least not until Angelina was escorted inside.

XXIV

The look on Angelina's face terrified me almost as much as her presence in this room. She was far too calm for what she must have witnessed.

Xander's screams were primal as he clawed his way to Eden's discarded body. There were several guards around him, yet no one moved to stop him. The sob that escaped his lips, as he lifted Eden's head, was heartbreaking, and I was unable to look away, even when Angelina silently found her way to my side, her hand clasping mine.

I searched the room, feeling the air for something – that tangible charge that Eden always carried with her, the energy that would tell me she was still with us. But the space around me was empty, devoid of any indication that Eden was alive. It was a terrifying sensation.

Xander clutched Eden to his chest and shrieked at the elderly woman atop the throne. 'How could you? *Why would you do this to her?*'

She looked at no one in particular when she said, 'You think you're the only one with spies, Alexander? Did you think I wouldn't find your underground hideaway eventually? You can't defeat a queen.' Her voice was so majestic, so filled with self-assurance, that it was hard to imagine anyone else ever taking her place on the throne. And then her gaze fell to Xander as she ordered, 'Get him away from her.'

It took five of her guards to separate him from Eden, and he was spared no brutality as he fought to stay by her side. He was struck in the ribs, the stomach, the face, the back, yet he still struggled when the queen's men dragged him away.

And Max shouted after them. 'Get your hands off of him! Leave him be!' His voice was chilling, filled with menace and the guarantee of retribution. I feared for those he'd set his sights on.

From somewhere outside, on the vast lawns of the palace, there was the distant sounds of popping. *Gunfire*, I thought, although I barely had time to consider it, to wonder what was happening outside these walls. Not when there was a war waging within this very room.

But the queen heard it too, and her head snapped up as she gestured – an unspoken command – to the stout man at her side. He rushed out of the room, eager to do her bidding.

Yet it was Angelina who drew my attention as she knelt down to the woman at my feet. I worried that someone else might see her, might notice what she was doing as she brushed her small hand, ever so lightly, across Eden's bloodied forehead. Just the whisper of a touch, and over so quickly that I doubted anyone else had even seen it.

I waited, my eyes wide, for something to happen.

And then I heard it. Just the barest rattle of breath escaping Eden's mouth, the sole indicator that she wasn't yet dead. It was quite possibly the sweetest sound imaginable. I wished with all my heart that Xander could have heard it too.

'Well, well, well.' The cutting voice of the queen interrupted my moment of satisfaction. 'It seems we have not one princess . . . but two.' Her milky eyes looked from me to Angelina, who moved back to my side. 'And I certainly don't have need for the both of you.'

I would have expected Angelina to cower in the presence of the powerful woman, but she remained where she was, watching the queen through untroubled, crystalline eyes.

But *I* was worried. And I would never take a chance that any harm would come to my little sister. Not ever. I couldn't risk the queen taking possession of Angelina.

'You win,' I breathed at last, stepping into the path of her gaze and forcing her to take her eyes away from my sister. 'Take me instead.'

THE QUEEN

Anticipation coursed through Sabara, invigorating her with renewed energy, making her feel more alive than she had in years. Possibly decades.

Everything she wanted was within her grasp.

She had found the girl's weakness when she'd discovered the child. Charlaina would do anything to protect her sister. And without even realizing it, she'd spoken the words. She'd inadvertently started the process.

She could hear Maxmillian yelling at the girl to change her mind as he struggled to be released, but his words were in vain. Still, he'd overstepped his bounds, and family or not, he would have to die for his transgressions.

Not now, of course. She would bide her time, find a way to make his death appear accidental.

For now she had other matters to attend to.

Sabara concentrated on shutting out the sounds around her as she moved deeper into herself, calling forth her life force – her Essence – in preparation to make the transfer.

Soon she would have a new body. A beautiful, young body.

XXV

'No, Charlie! No!' I heard Max shouting over and over again. His voice was loud and clear and inescapable.

But already my skin tingled with an energy that wasn't my own. The pattern of my breathing felt off, and the rhythm of my heartbeat no longer belonged to me.

I glanced down at Angelina, relieved that she would be spared in all of this. She was the reason I'd made this unholy pact, and she would remain untouched by the darkness that I could already feel spilling into my veins.

In her blue eyes I could read her unspoken plea as she begged me not to do this. I had always understood my little sister's silent language.

I turned away, unable to bear the pain I was about to cause her.

My head began to swell with memories that were not my own. There were lovers and battles and births and deaths. Faces, names, and places, none of which I recognized. Everything inside of me faded to black, as joy and love were conquered, and hate and sin burgeoned anew. Malevolence became my very nature.

When it all became too much, I opened my mouth to take it back, to undo what I'd started, but all that emerged were silent screams, unheard cries for help. I could feel the queen's Essence smothering me, as her thoughts – not just her memories – began to take root and spread. It was she who stopped me from calling an end to this madness.

From outside, the sounds of gunfire, bombs, and the shouts of men grew louder. Closer. A full-scale battle was now underway. For what, I did not know.

I tried to concentrate, but the queen's memories lingered amid my own, taking them over, making it difficult to distinguish reality from illusion.

There were other things I sensed now too. Things the queen could no longer hide from me. She was older than any of us could have imagined. Her spirit was ancient, having survived centuries and spanning the ages. Now that she was within me, she was unable to mask her secrets, even behind languages that were long since dead and forgotten.

I heard them.

And in those silent whispers, she unwittingly revealed the key to my survival.

Time. I had only to endure the transfer. I must resist the overpowering desire to surrender to her, to let go.

It was harder than it seemed. My grip grew weaker and my resolve faded.

A detonation shook the walls, and the ground beneath us quaked. I fell to my knees, and a chandelier exploded as it struck the polished floor, sending pieces of crystal rocketing all around me.

A second blast, coming immediately after the first, shattered a huge window, and shards of glass blew inward. Instinctively I reached for Angelina, wrapping myself around her as splinters of pain prickled everywhere over my exposed skin.

I felt the queen's grip on my mind falter. But only for a moment.

And then she was back, black shadows moving around my soul, engulfing it like smoke, suffocating it until I felt myself – *my true self* – deteriorating.

Dying.

Max's shouts grew more distant. I didn't know how much longer I had, but I suspected there wasn't much of me remaining.

This wasn't a battle I could win, the one waging inside my own body. I knew, now that she was within me, that she was so much stronger than I was. I collapsed, feeling myself slipping away just as Angelina gripped my hands in hers.

At first my fingers tingled where Angelina touched them, and then they burned. And when I glanced up, I thought my eyesight must be failing me. Angelina's skin glowed, softly at first, like a delicate, ethereal apparition. Then more intensely, like an inferno, raging and bright. Everywhere I looked – her skin, her hair, her blue eyes – smoldered.

And then I felt what she was doing. It was as if she was healing me, as if she was lending me her power – fusing it with mine and willing me to fight. And suddenly I knew what I wanted. It was all so clear.

I wanted the queen to die. I wanted to live.

In the hallways outside the throne room, there were more shouts, more rounds of gunfire. I could hear Brooklynn's voice above all the others, and I knew that Xander's forces were here at last.

Behind Angelina, Sabara rose from her throne, and I knew she was abandoning her body now, completing the transformation to inhabit mine.

Angelina squeezed my fingers as if she would never release me, and my entire body burned as if it had just been set ablaze. And then she spoke to me, her voice soft and childlike, just as I'd always imagined she would sound. 'Don't go, Charlie. I need you.'

I'd never heard anything more beautiful in all my life, and my heart soared as hot, wet tears dropped onto my cheeks. I didn't know if they were hers or mine.

Across from me, I watched as the queen fell to the ground . . .

. . . and everything inside of me went black.

MAX

Max hardly noticed that Charlie's skin was flickering where Angelina touched her. Tears streaked down the little girl's cheeks as she clutched her sister's hand, her eyes never leaving Charlie's face, as if begging her to breathe, begging her to wake.

Everyone – guards and prisoners alike – stood motionless now, waiting to see which of the two women would die first. Max closed the distance in three long strides and knelt by Angelina's side as he took Charlie's other hand in his, pressing her icy fingers to his lips. His lungs ached, and his throat was tight.

Beside them all, at the foot of the dais, the queen lay equally still, with no one at her side beseeching her to live.

The gilded doors exploded open then, crashing so hard that they rattled the walls. Brook stormed in, followed by a coterie of soldiers whose weapons were as mismatched as their uniforms. Her face was lit by a triumphant grin.

She pointed the muzzle of her gun at the guards in the throne room. 'Seize their weapons.' Her voice boomed as if she'd been born to lead. Then her eyes fell to Charlie, and the victorious look crumpled. She rushed to her friend's side, her eyes searching Max's face. 'Is she . . . ?'

Max shook his head, refusing to even consider the possibility. He bent closer to the lifeless girl before him as he released a ragged breath against her cool skin. 'Charlie,' he whispered, begging her not to leave them . . . to leave him.

Tears scalded his eyes and his vision blurred; he couldn't lose her. But the ache was already spreading like a disease through his body, ravaging him, deadening him.

He almost didn't notice the tremor in her fingertips, but there was no mistaking the sudden, choking gasp that filled the space, echoing loudly throughout the room and filling his heart.

Charlie's eyelids fluttered, then opened. She searched past Max, past Angelina and Brook, focusing solely on the unconscious woman lying on the floor beneath the throne as she lifted her head. 'I win,' she rasped at last. And then she closed her eyes and collapsed again.

Behind him, Max could hear his grandmother's strangled wheeze, and he knew without a doubt that it was her final breath. He didn't even have to turn to know that she was gone; he could see it in Charlie, as her breathing became calm and even, as the glow from Angelina's touch spread over her skin like a lightning storm.

Ludania had a new queen.

XXVI

Fingers touched my face, moving lightly over my cheeks and my lips. My skin itself felt strange, foreign, as if it no longer fit me. As if it were no longer my own.

I turned my head away from the irritating sensation and felt a breathy chuckle against my ear. I was annoyed by the sound, and recognized why immediately. I hated to be laughed at.

I struggled to open my eyes, but even that was harder than it should have been; they felt heavy, weighted down. And when I finally pried them apart, I had to squint against the light. Wherever I was, it was far too bright, and it took several tries for my eyes to fully adjust. But when they did, I found myself staring into familiar gray eyes that I'd have known anywhere.

I was relieved to see someone I recognized when everything about me felt so unfamiliar. Still, I frowned, and a ghost of a smile curved his lips.

'Where am I?' I tried to ask, but my voice was lost in an arid whisper.

'Don't try to talk yet,' Max instructed, reaching for the glass of water beside the bed.

I was in a bed, I noted. But where? How?

And more importantly, *why*?

He lifted my head and brought the water to my lips. All I could manage was a sip, because again, I was besieged by the sensation that something was off, like I was a stranger inside my own body. Everything felt different and new.

'Better?'

I tried to smile but couldn't. 'Where am I?' I asked again, trying to register my surroundings. Rich tapestries, fine art, delicate linens.

'We're in the palace, Charlie. Don't you remember?'

And, like that, I did. I remembered everything. All at once it came crashing in on me, the queen, the pact, dying . . .

. . . and Angelina.

My skin tingled still.

I drew my hand out from beneath the silk coverlet and stared at it, turning it over and pulling back my sleeve, my eyes widening.

'Am I like this everywhere?'

Max nodded, watching me closely, and I wondered what I must look like from where he sat.

White light flickered from beneath my skin, all over, lighting my entire body. The smoldering glow radiated outward, making even my own eyes ache. It was the same radiant light I'd seen coming from Angelina.

'Your sister, it seems, has discovered her gift,' Max explained.

I didn't tell him that it wasn't new to her, the healing. Or that it wasn't her only power. There were still so many things I didn't understand about what had happened, about what Angelina had done to save me.

Instead I asked, 'Where is she? Where are my parents?' I sat up, suddenly needing to know that my family was safe.

'They aren't far, trust me. They've barely left your side. I'm sure they'll be back soon to check on you. They'll be glad you're awake.' His lazy grin made my heart stutter. 'Sydney's with them you know?'

I could hardly believe what I was hearing. 'Sydney? What's she doing here?'

'Once the news got out, it was impossible to keep her away. She's very determined when she sets her mind to something. Reminds me a little of Brooklynn.'

'You didn't tell Brook that, did you?'

His smile widened. 'She didn't really care for the

comparison,' he explained in mock innocence.

I slumped back against my pillows, amazed that so much had changed in so little time; I would never have imagined Sydney voluntarily under the same roof as my parents and Brook. But then I remembered the rest of what had happened. My throat was closing even as I dared to ask the question. 'What about . . . Aron . . . ?' I couldn't finish, he'd been too close to death the last time I'd seen him.

Max's brows lifted. 'Angelina. She's managed to heal Xander, Aron, your parents, and Eden. In fact, I'm not sure even Xander believed Eden would survive. If your sister weren't already a princess, Xander would treat her as one anyway. I think he plans to build statues in her honor.'

It was all the explanation I needed. Of course Angelina had helped them – she no longer had to hide what she could do. I looked at my hand again. 'Is she still . . .' I raised my eyes, hoping Max understood what I was asking.

He laughed again, but this time I didn't mind. 'Glowing?'

I nodded.

'No. She stopped the moment she released you. You're the only one. Angelina says she doesn't know why it happened. No one does.'

Tears burned my eyes as Max reminded me that

Angelina had spoken. I remembered the sound of her voice as if I'd only just heard it, and I was relieved that I hadn't been dreaming.

But I thought about what Max had said. 'Do you think I'll stop too?'

He reached over and ran a finger across my arm. 'I hope not.' He grinned, watching the sparks that followed in the trail of his touch, flickering brilliantly beneath my skin.

I released an awed breath, but the sensation itself was sinful. I wasn't certain I was ready to admit what that simple touch had just done to me.

It took several long moments until I felt composed enough to ask the question I'd been afraid to broach. It would have been impossible for him not to hear the tremble in my voice. 'What about the queen?' I bit my lip, an anxious knot forming in the pit of my stomach.

Max raised an eyebrow. 'The *queen* is safe.'

They were the last words I'd expected to hear, and I jerked upward, shoving Max away from me. 'Where is she now? We have to get out of here! You don't know what I know, Max. I've seen what she's done, what she's capable of.'

But Max put his hands on my shoulders and eased me back down. 'Relax, Charlie. *You're* the queen now. At least you will be once you're officially crowned.' His eyes remained locked with mine. 'My grandmother is dead.'

It took a moment for his words to sink in, but I still didn't understand. 'How could you be so sure that she was the one who'd died?' I asked. 'How did you know the transfer didn't work, that she wasn't' – I glanced down at myself, my voice dropping dangerously low – 'in here? In *my* body?'

Max took my hand, his fingers lacing through mine. Hot embers ignited within me, and my hand sparked with light. 'You really don't remember, do you?' He frowned, looking worried.

I met his gaze. 'I really don't.'

'She didn't die right away, my grandmother. She lived for several moments after you blacked out, not fully conscious but breathing nonetheless.' His grip tightened. 'Seconds before she took her last breath, you spoke.'

'What did I say?'

Max's face broke into an easy grin, and once again, I found myself craving his warmth, straining to be near him. 'You said . . . "I win."'

I wondered how I could possibly forget something like that, something so . . . *momentous*. Queen Sabara was dead. She really was dead this time.

The memory of so many funerals flashed through my mind. How many bodies had she buried? How many souls had she taken?

'Besides,' Max said, his gray eyes sparkling. 'Angelina

374

assured us it was you. Apparently she has a knack for these things.'

I smiled back at him, biting my lip. He knew about Angelina's other ability. It felt good to not have to hide what we could do.

'What if I don't want to be queen?' I finally asked.

Max sighed. 'It's too late for that. We need you, Charlie. The country needs a queen, and we no longer have one.'

'What about a king?' But I already knew the answer. He was right – of course, we needed a queen. Ludania couldn't afford to be cut off from the world again; we needed to maintain a balance with the monarchies around us. None of the other ruling queens would ever respect a king born without a power.

'You know it wouldn't work. You're *the One*, it's always been you. Just because your family was removed from the throne doesn't make you any less suited to rule. You're the eldest female heir. Besides, look at you. How much more special do you have to be before you believe it for yourself?' His fingertip brushed the back of my hand, and my cheeks burned. I hoped they weren't glowing as hot as they felt.

The door to the bedroom opened without warning, and I pulled the blankets up to cover my hands, knowing I could do nothing about my face.

Brooklynn came in, with Angelina trailing right

behind her. It hadn't been a hallucination after all; I *had* heard Brooklynn in the hallways.

Angelina was dressed in a pretty pink gown, and an attempt had been made to braid her flyaway blond hair. If it weren't for the dirt smudged on her chin, she would look exactly like a princess.

'I just checked on Eden,' Brook said to Max, not yet realizing that I was awake. 'She's ready to get out of bed. She's tired of being told to rest.'

Even though I knew what Angelina was capable of, the last time I'd seen Eden she was barely clinging to her last breath. It was hard to believe that anything – or anyone – could have brought her back from that.

But it was Aron who drew my attention as he sauntered through the door behind my sister and Brooklynn. His bruises and cuts were all but healed, his skin virtually unmarred. He was walking on his own now, without so much as a limp.

My heart skipped as I shifted in bed so I was fully upright. 'I told you I'd never leave you behind,' I told him boastfully.

Aron beamed at me, such a familiar look, so Aron-like that I grinned back. 'If I remember right, I think you said you'd leave me in a heartbeat.' His smile widened. 'I'm glad you changed your mind.'

Angelina's face lit up when she heard my voice, and she jumped onto the bed, wrapping her arms around me.

'I missed you,' she declared against my ear, squeezing me with all her might, and I wondered if I'd ever get used to the sound of her voice.

Silver wisps of her hair tickled my nose and my cheeks, and I breathed them in, hugging her back, tears stinging my eyes. 'I've missed you, too.'

When at last I released her I saw Xander, lingering in the doorway, watching us all with a crooked smile playing over his lips. This was the outcome he'd spent most of his life fighting for. This was the reason he'd turned his back on his family, on his country, on his queen.

The citizens of Ludania would finally be free, no longer forced into a class system that determined what language they could speak, what jobs they could do, or who they could be.

Everything Xander had ever hoped for had come true at last.

He stood straight then, moving to stand directly in front of me as he dropped low and bowed dramatically. 'Your Majesty.'

EPILOGUE

I lay there listening to the sounds of sleep beside me, the even breathing, the soft rustling of linens. If only my sleep could be so peaceful.

The nights were the worst, when I closed my eyes and let my guard down, surrendering to the will of my dreams.

She was with me still, I knew that now.

I moved with care, untangling my legs and easing my way from beneath the heavy blankets. There was no need to disturb someone else with my burdens.

The darkness parted around me, cleaved by my very presence as I padded to the window on bare feet and glanced out at the lawns below. The moon blazing brightly in the still night sky nearly matched the intensity of my skin. My own glow had faded over time, but only slightly.

Settling in with my country had not been difficult; I abolished laws, not languages, allowing people to make their own choices, to forge their own place in the world. Of course, not everyone agreed. There were always the voices of dissention – those who opposed change, even when it was for the best – and I worried that those voices might grow, gain a life of their own, much like the voice within me.

Even now, I could feel the veiled shadows straining to reach the surface.

At first I'd believed it was only in my imaginings, that side of me that whispered malice and dreamed dark deeds. A result of my new responsibilities on the throne. I'd hoped it would go away with time, much like the light living beneath my skin.

But now, as the months stretched on, and my country and I settled into a delicate accord, I knew it was something more. Something infinitely more sinister.

She was there – the ancient queen – wraithlike and vengeful, hoping to take her place once more.

I couldn't allow it, of course, and she understood that. For now, at least, I was stronger than she was. I was able to keep her at bay. So her only recourse was to find my weak spots, chinks in my defenses, places where she could inject her evils and try to infect me with fear and suspicion. And that was usually at night, while I slept.

Strong arms reached around me from behind, and a stubbled cheek nuzzled my shoulder.

'I didn't mean to wake you,' I breathed softly.

'I wasn't complaining.' Max's lips found their way to my neck, and in the darkness, sparks shimmered brilliantly, showering us both with a display of what his touch could do to me. 'Come back to bed,' he coaxed, and again, light flickered and danced around us.

I smiled, letting him lead me away from the window, knowing that, for the time being, everything was as it should be.

It didn't matter that later, when I closed my eyes, she would be there, making ugly promises and sinister threats.

For now, I had Max in my bed.

And a queendom to rule.

ACKNOWLEDGMENTS

Each book has its own cast of 'characters' who deserve special thanks. For this book, I have to start off by thanking one particular woman who, when I met her, shared heart-wrenching stories of her early childhood years in WWII Germany. Marie Lucas, somewhere in your reminiscing you sparked the very beginnings of what would eventually become *The Pledge*. Thank you for telling me stories about a frightened little girl who was awakened in the night by air-raid sirens and was then thrown over the fences by her older sisters so they could hide in the mineshafts outside of town until the fighting had passed. And thank you, too, for telling me about the battered little rag doll you treasured. You are the original Angelina.

As always, I have to thank my fearless and tireless agent, Laura Rennert. Thank you for being on *my* side.

And to my incredible editor, Gretchen Hirsch, for believing in me not once, but twice, and for being intuitive and patient and brilliant. I truly love working with you.

To the Smart Chicks, for letting me sit with the cool kids. To Jenny Jeffries and Shelli Johannes-Wells: thanks for staying up late to read for me. To Erin Gross and Heidi Bennett: thank you for being such great cheerleaders. To everyone at the Debs and the Tenners: thank you for making me feel sane in this crazy publishing world! And to my wonderful friends Jacqueline Sander, Tamara McDonald, and Carol Hildebrand, for helping me plan such fabulous launch parties for my books. (Seriously, I think the three of you should open your own business . . . or at least charge me for your services.)

To my husband, Josh, for being my first beta-reader, my patient advisor, and a sympathetic shoulder all rolled up in one. To my children, for being willing to eat fast food again and again and again. To my mom, for constantly telling me I could do anything . . . and genuinely meaning it. And to my dad, for always making me laugh when I need it most.

And a special thank-you to my brother, Scot, who I've both loved and hated over the years (as most sisters do), but who has taught me the incredible value of having siblings. There's no one I would rather have shared my childhood with . . . *I love you!*